D1046251

DIY High

Also by Amanda L. Webster

Valley of the Bees

F-ing Freddy Fisher

Coming soon by Amanda L. Webster

Demons of the Night

DIY HIGH

Amanda L. Webster

Published 2019
By Elderfly Press
Printed in the United States of America
ISBN-13: 9781093976335

Cover design by Blue Canary Books
Interior design by Amanda L. Webster

For information, address:
Amanda L. Webster
PO Box 135
McLean, Illinois 61754

Elderfly Press is a DBA of Amanda L. Webster.

DEDICATION

This book is for you:

Don't do what
"they say"
is the practical
thing to do.

What's practical
for them
may not be
practical for you.

CHAPTER ONE

Gabby rested her forehead against the cool school bus window and stared out at the crisp, browning corn stalks flashing by outside in long, endless rows as the school bus bumped along the narrow country road. The window glass was grimy with harvest dust that added a soft edge to the sharp outlines of early fall. As the glass warmed from the heat of Gabby's skin, she turned her forehead into a cooler spot. Somehow, the cool glass, combined with the bus's vibrations, calmed the persistent tension headache that was starting to become a part of her daily life. Gabby sighed. At least she didn't have to work that evening. Maybe she would take one of her mom's pain pills and sink into oblivion for the night like her mom did sometimes when her fibromyalgia got too bad. She shook away the thought. The headache probably wasn't bad enough to warrant that. But still. Gabby could use a break from helping her mom parent her younger siblings.

The bus hit a pot hole, bouncing Gabby's head against the window. Ouch. The kids at the back of the bus shrieked with glee as they were flung into the air and then back onto the hard bus seats. Gabby used to be one of those kids until her brother, Owen, started middle school and turned her daily commute into a babysitting job. If he got into trouble one more time, he was going to be expelled from the bus.

Owen sat across the aisle from Gabby, chattering away about some video game with one of his friends. Gabby glanced toward the front of the bus just in time to catch Jamie Norton turning in his seat to glare at Owen. The two of them were mortal enemies this school year, and someone had gotten the bright idea to make them both sit toward the front of the bus so the bus driver could keep a closer eye on them. But old Harry had a hard enough time just keeping his eyes on the road. What they really needed was another adult on the bus. One whose sole job was to keep an eye on the kids so the bus driver could focus on driving. Jamie's lips parted. It was obvious he was about to say something rude to Owen.

Gabby slid across her seat to the aisle and leaned toward Jamie. "Don't," she said.

Jamie clamped his lips together and scowled at her. Then, he parted his lips again as if he might have something to say to Gabby. She cocked her head to the side and raised an eyebrow, daring him to smart off to her. She wouldn't do anything to him on the bus, but there was no one to stop her from pounding the little brat once the bus dropped them off at their stop. Jamie whipped his head around to the front of the bus and crossed his arms in front of him.

Gabby smiled. Let the little brat pout. Her mom would be screwed if she had to start going into work late every morning to drive Owen to school. None of them could afford for him to get kicked off the bus right now.

Soon, the bus passed her town's population sign at the edge of town. Eight hundred and fifty people. Her boss at the truckstop diner had told her just the other day that the truck stop got more customers than that each day during the busy summer months. Gabby often wondered what the travelers who stopped in off the interstate thought of her tiny town—if they even thought about it at all. Most of them probably never looked past the truck stop and the McDonald's that sat at the foot of the interstate exit. They sure didn't see her while she was waiting on them. Well, except for the occasional dirty old man.

When the bus finally pulled up to their stop, Jamie was the first to clamber down the stairs to the sidewalk. He stumbled a few steps, then glanced over his shoulder looking for Owen. Gabby had jumped into the aisle as soon as the bus stopped so she could escort her brother from his seat. She hooked her fingers through the loop at the top of his backpack and clenched it in her fist as they climbed down from the bus.

Jamie grinned at them as soon as the bus doors folded shut. "Lick my butt, you big butt licker!" he yelled.

Gabby rolled her eyes. Middle schoolers were so eloquent when they trash-talked each other. Jamie took off down the street knowing full well that he was no match for an angry Owen. Or for Owen's older sisters.

Owen's feet were scrambling toward Jamie, but Gabby jerked him backward by his backpack strap.

"Let me go!" he said. He swung his fists in the air, but Gabby had become a master at holding on to him when he had one of his meltdowns without getting herself hurt. He gave up fighting against his sister, but she couldn't control his mouth. "You better run, Jamie!" He said.

Gabby turned Owen the opposite direction and headed him down the sidewalk toward their apartment building. "Meg!" She called over her shoulder to her younger sister.

Meg was busy giggling with a bunch of her little girlfriends and pretending not to notice what was going on with Owen. She was perpetually mortified by their brother since he had joined her at the middle school earlier that year. If they didn't live in such a small town, she would probably pretend they weren't related. She tore herself away from her friends and followed several feet behind Gabby and Owen toward their apartment building a few blocks away.

"I hate that Jamie," Owen grumbled. "Why is he such a jerk?"

"I don't know," Gabby said. "Some people just are. You have to learn to ignore him. Just pretend like he doesn't exist, and he'll get bored and move on to a different target."

"How am I supposed to do that when he follows me around everywhere I go?"

"I don't know," Gabby said. "Have you told the teachers that he's following you around?"

"Yeah, but they won't do anything about it. They want us to 'just get along.'" Owen did a pretty good imitation of most of the middle school teachers on the phrase, "just get along." He pitched his voice up to that sing-song tone a lot of the teachers used to tell you that they weren't really listening to a word you were saying and wished you'd just leave them alone with your middle school nonsense. "How am I supposed to just get along with someone who is literally stalking me all day long? Jamie should be in jail. They should send him to juvie."

"Yeah, but they're not going to." Meg had caught up to them despite her best effort to remain aloof. "I bet you they don't do anything about him until he actually hurts someone. Then they'll act all shocked and pretend like they didn't have a clue what was happening. That's what they did last year with Evan Burbank. He terrorized the whole seventh grade, and when we tried to tell the principal, she just laughed at us and said we were being overly dramatic."

"Did you ever hear what happened with that?" Gabby asked.

"He's finally in juvie, and Andy will be drinking his meat through a straw for the rest of his life." Meg tossed her hair over her shoulder.

A car horn honked at them as they rounded the corner onto their street. The three of them waved at the local library director as she passed. Seeing Miss Lynn reminded Gabby that she needed to return a library book. She should probably also check to see if her brothers had any books or DVDs that needed to be returned so her mom wouldn't get charged for them.

"Looks like Mom's home early," Meg said.

The family's dirty white van was parked half in the ditch in front of their apartment building. Owen took off at a run so he could be the first to talk to their mom. He was one of those kids who needed to fill his mother in on every detail of his life that she had missed since he saw her last. When he reached the front porch where their youngest brother sat drawing on the concrete with chalk, he stopped to say a couple of words to him before heading inside the apartment.

Gabby and Meg shared a glance. Their mom had been missing a lot of work lately. It started out small, when she was first diagnosed with fibromyalgia, but the problem quickly escalated. She always assured them it would be okay. She was taking family medical leave time when she hurt too bad to make it in to work, so her job was safe. Gabby wasn't exactly sure what FMLA was or how it worked, but her mother never seemed to worry about it, so she didn't either.

"It's your turn to cook," Gabby told Meg.

Together, the two of them stepped onto the long porch that ran the length of their eight-family townhouse apartment building. Their youngest brother, Ben sat among his colorful sidewalk chalks working on what he called his "infinite artwork." It had started that summer with a chalk picture their mother had drawn of Ben holding a cake with ten candles for his birthday. Ben had started at one side of the picture, chalking up that end of their shared front porch until he had run out of concrete to draw on. Then, he started at the opposite end of the porch and colored with his chalk until he reached his cake picture in front of their doorstep. By then, the chalk had been smudged up by the family's feet as they came and went through their front door. He then drew a new picture in the remains of his birthday cake and continued on to the opposite end of the porch, only to circle back around once he'd run out of space again. Ben was now so deep into his artwork, he barely seemed to register his sisters' presence as they argued over whose turn it was to make dinner.

"Nope," Meg said. "I made pizza two nights ago. Mom cooked last night. It's your turn."

"Frozen pizzas don't count. All you did was throw them in the oven and then slice them after you took them out of the oven. You didn't even make any vegetables to go with them."

Meg shrugged. "Mom said it did count. It's not my fault you always pick something complicated to make when it's your turn." She opened the front door and disappeared inside.

Gabby sighed. She hated to cook, but she also hated to eat frozen pizzas or ramen noodles or grilled cheese sandwiches and canned soup every day. She missed the days when her mother felt up to cooking a real dinner every night.

"How's the infinite artwork coming along, Ben?"

Ben shrugged. "Is it coming, or is it going?" he asked. He liked to answer questions with additional questions.

"It looks to me like it's going on forever."

"That's kind of the definition of 'infinite,' isn't it?"

"You are a strange one," Gabby said.

Ben shrugged. He set aside the color he'd been working with and reached for a different piece of chalk.

Gabby went inside and left Ben to his art. She dragged her heavy backpack up the stairs and dropped it in the bedroom she shared with Meg before going to check on their mom. Her mother's bedroom was surprisingly silent, aside from the whirring of the fan that always ran when she slept. The lights were off, and Owen lay next to their mother and patted her arm.

"Mom?"

Kim rolled over and muttered something that sounded like, "Leave me alone," but Gabby wasn't quite sure.

"Is she okay?" Gabby asked.

"Shh——" Owen sat up and swung his legs over the edge of the bed. "Let her sleep," he whispered. He approached Gabby on soft footsteps and edged her out into the hallway before closing the door behind him.

"What's wrong?" Gabby asked.

"Mom got fired."

"Wh—what?"

"She got fired," Owen said.

"Did you just say Mom got fired?" Meg poked her head out of the girls' bedroom. Her eyes were wide with worry.

"Are you sure?" Gabby asked. She wrung her hands. What would they do? Money was tight enough as it was. Their father hadn't paid his child support in years except a couple of dollars here and there. When the child support did occasionally show up, it was usually not enough to feed all of them for even one day.

Owen shrugged. "That's what Ben said."

"So, you didn't hear it for yourself?" Gabby asked. "What did mom say to you?"

"I'm not sure. She must have taken a muscle relaxer or something when she got home because she's pretty out of it. But I asked her about it, and it sounded like she said that's what happened."

"It must be true," Meg said. "Why would Ben lie?"

"Ben doesn't lie," Gabby said. "He may be a genius, but he's still only ten. Sometimes he doesn't always hear things right."

"This isn't the kind of thing that you would mishear," Owen said. "Besides, she's acting to me like someone who just lost her job."

"I'm never going to get a cellphone now, am I?" Meg said.

Gabby and Owen both glared at her.

"Selfish much?" Gabby asked.

"Screw you," Meg said. She stomped into the girls' bedroom and slammed the door behind her.

"She is such a bitch sometimes," Owen said.

Gabby frowned at her brother. She should correct his language, but she didn't feel like it. She didn't have to babysit when their mom was home, did she?

"It's your turn to cook dinner, you know," Owen said. "What are we having? I'm starving."

Gabby groaned and headed down the stairs with Owen clattering after her.

"Can we have tacos?" he asked. "It is Tuesday. You're supposed to have tacos on Tuesdays."

"Let me see if Mom left any meat out to thaw," Gabby said.

Ben was in the kitchen now, methodically washing chalk dust out of each of his fingernails at the sink.

"Ben," Gabby said. "What did Mom tell you about why she's home early?"

Ben turned the water off. He began to dry his hands on a kitchen towel, one finger at a time. "Why?" he asked. "What did she tell you?"

"Not much," Gabby said. "She's too high on pain meds to make any sense. Was she already in bed when you got home?"

"No," Ben said. He froze in place with the towel gripped between his fingers. "She came in right after I got home from school. She was crying, and she told me she got fired. Then, she went to bed."

"So, she did say she got fired? She used those exact words?"

Ben nodded his head.

"Did she say why? I don't understand."

Ben thought for a moment before answering. "She said, 'Effing FMLA.' Only she said the actual F-word. And, she said the A-word, too."

It sure sounded like their mom had been fired. But Gabby wanted to hear the words from her mother's mouth before she could believe it herself. That wouldn't be possible until her mom had slept off whatever pills she had taken before she went to bed. In the meantime, there wasn't much to do but wait. She would do her homework and make sure everyone ate dinner, as she always did when their mom was hurting too much to take care of it.

Gabby opened the refrigerator door. A pound of thawed ground turkey sat on a plate on the top shelf. "You're in luck, Owen," she said. "Taco Tuesday it is."

It was almost eleven by the time Kim finally stumbled out of her bedroom and down the hallway to the bathroom. The boys had been asleep in their bunk beds for at least an hour. Meg was busy scribbling in her journal with her head under her blanket in the girls' room, even though Gabby had told her to go to sleep as well. Gabby was tired herself, but she couldn't fall asleep without talking to her mom and finding out what was going on. She huddled at the top of the stairs and waited for Kim to come out of the bathroom.

The bathroom was silent for a while, and soon Gabby began to wonder if she should go in and check on her mom. But then, she heard the muffled sound of Kim gargling and knew she was okay. A few seconds later, the door opened, and Kim startled when she noticed Gabby sitting at the top of the stairs.

"What are you doing up?" Kim asked. Her voice was slow and tired. "You have school tomorrow. You should be in bed."

"I'm waiting for you," Gabby said.

Kim braced herself against the wall and slid down to sit next to her. "Why are you waiting for me?"

"Did you get fired?"

Gabby's mom slumped over with her head in her hands. She sighed. "Yes," she said. She drew a deep breath as though she were trying not to cry.

Gabby patted her mom's arm. "What happened?" What were they going to do now?

Kim turned her eyes toward the ceiling and wiped the tears from her face with both hands. She sniffled, then took a deep breath before speaking. "I—I was hurting really bad this morning. I should have just come home, but I've been missing so much work. I'm completely out of sick time, so I would have had to take the time off unpaid. I thought I'd just take a pill and relax in the car over my lunch hour, and then I'd be able to make it through the afternoon. But then, I fell asleep."

"You fell asleep?"

Kim nodded. Tears streamed down her cheeks. "It—I'm so stupid. If I had just come home, I could have put it down as FMLA sick time, and I would have been protected. But, I fell asleep for like two whole hours, and when I got back to the office, they had someone from HR waiting for me. It was like they were just waiting for me to slip up so they could get rid of me."

Gabby's breath caught in her throat. She forced back a sob. How were they going to live now? They already had a hard enough time keeping food in the house. She'd been buying all her own clothes and toiletries since she got her part-time job at the diner. Meg and Ben's clothes were all hand-me-downs, but there would be no clothes to hand down to Ben if their mom couldn't afford to buy clothes for Owen.

"Hey." Kim put her arms around Gabby and pulled her in for a tight hug. "This isn't your problem to figure out. I'm the mom. I'll figure it out. I'll apply for unemployment tomorrow, and we'll find a way to manage until I can get a new job."

Gabby nodded, her forehead brushing her mother's chin. But, her mom's words weren't very reassuring. There was a time when Gabby could go through life without a care, knowing her mom would take care of everything. Even through everything that had happened with her dad, her mom had always known what to do. Her dad had almost left them homeless and destitute, but her mom was resourceful. There was a time when Gabby's mother's embrace could wipe away all her fears and leave her feeling safe in the knowledge that she would find a way. They may not have everything they wanted, but Gabby's mom had made sure they always had what they needed.

But now, Gabby wasn't so sure. Her mother had changed. Where her embrace used to remind her of cookies baking and pot roast cooking, she now just smelled like stale sweat and sticky morning breath. Her once strong body now trembled with an obvious fear that infected Gabby. Kim might tell her not to worry, but there was no way she could obey her this time.

Gabby pulled away from her mom and got to her feet. "I have school tomorrow," she said. "I guess I'll go to bed." Her mom seemed so small, huddled on the steps at her feet.

"I meant what I said, Gabby." Kim stood up and leaned against the wall for support. "Don't you dare lay awake all night worrying. I got this."

"I know, Mom." Gabby gave Kim a half smile, then headed down the hall to her bedroom. She wished she could believe her mom did have things under control. The truth was, she didn't know. She wasn't sure she could count on her mom anymore. That thought alone was enough to keep her awake until the early morning hours.

CHAPTER TWO

Kim was sprawled out in a battered lounge chair, fast asleep on the front porch, when Gabby and her siblings got home from school the next day. Her purse was wedged in her armpit, and she clutched her keys in her hand. A line of drool crept across her cheek. The front door hung open. It was a wonder Kim could sleep through the noise of Ben's afternoon cartoons blaring from the living room.

Meg tapped their mom's shoulder. "Mom," she said.

Kim moaned. Her eyes fluttered, then closed again.

"Mom, wake up!" Owen yelled. He bounced on the foot of the lounge chair and almost rocketed Kim from her seat.

She jerked awake, her arms flailing. "What?" Her eyes flitted back and forth in search of danger. Then, she relaxed. "You're home."

"Mom, what are you doing out here?" Gabby asked.

Kim sat up and felt for her purse. "Waiting for you," she said. "I need you to run to town with me to—um—get some groceries."

Owen jumped up and down. "I want to go!"

Kim shook her head. "No, you're going to stay here and get your homework done. Meg, you're in charge until we get back."

"Mo-om." Meg scowled. "I told Lily I'd go over to her house as soon as I checked in with you. To do homework."

"She can come over here this time. I need you to watch the boys."

"I don't need watched," Owen said. "Neither does Ben. We know how to be good."

"They really do," Meg said. "Even if I'm here, I'll just be in my room with the door closed. I won't even talk to them the whole time you're gone."

Kim got up and handed her keys to Gabby. "You drive," she said. "You need to get your permit hours in so you can get your license as soon as you turn sixteen."

Gabby wasn't going to argue with that. She couldn't wait to get her license and was already saving up her waitressing money to buy her own car. She headed through the house toward the back door to get to the small parking lot out back where her mom's van was parked. Meg and Owen continued to argue with their mother as they followed her through the house.

A few minutes later, Gabby's mom joined her in the van. Gabby backed out of the parking lot as soon as Kim was settled into her seat with her seatbelt latched.

"You know, I was about Owen's age when you first started leaving me home alone," Gabby said. "And I had much younger siblings to watch." She pointed the van in the direction of the interstate that would take them "into town" where the grocery stores were. The only groceries available in her hometown were the high-priced snack foods at the truck stop and the gas station attached to the McDonald's.

Kim reclined in her seat and closed her eyes. "That was different," she said. "You were much more responsible than either of the boys are—well, more than Owen is, at least. Plus, I didn't have much choice. I didn't have the money for daycare, but I made too much to qualify for enough assistance to cover it. Sometimes, you do what you have to, even when you know it's maybe not the best idea."

A few minutes later, Gabby had to poke her mom to wake her up again so she could ask her which grocery store she wanted to go to.

Kim sat her seat back up with a groan. "We're not going to the grocery store," she said.

"But you said we were getting groceries."

"Yeah, getting. Not buying. I just got fired. I don't have any money, and it looks like it's going to take some time for me to start getting my unemployment checks."

"So, where are we getting groceries, then?"

Kim bit her lip and looked out her window. She seemed embarrassed to answer. Then, she said. "There's this food pantry at a church out by the airport. The lady I talked to at the unemployment agency this morning told me about it."

Gabby gripped the steering wheel so hard, her knuckles started to turn white. She gulped down the lump that had started to form in her throat. A food pantry? They'd been through some hard times, but as far as she knew, they had never had to resort to using a food pantry. The family usually ate a lot of ramen noodles, cheap frozen pizzas, potatoes, and whatever else they could find on sale. A while back, the price of eggs had dropped to twenty cents a dozen at Aldi, and they had eaten eggs at every meal for several weeks in a row. But, a food pantry?

"You know how to get to the airport?" Kim asked.

"I think so."

"Well, just head that way, and I'll tell you where to go once we get to Airport Road."

Gabby nodded. She kept her eyes on the highway and her hands at ten and two on the steering wheel. Her cheeks burned with shame. The food pantry. Hopefully she wouldn't run into anyone she knew there.

When they got to Airport Road, Kim gave Gabby directions from a slip of paper she had scribbled on. She counted the street numbers until the residential area they were driving through gave way to corn fields.

"According to the directions that lady gave me, it should be right up ahead."

"Maybe it's on the other side of this building up here. What is that, a hospital or something?" At the next corner stood a large block of buildings that looked like a small hospital or a large medical clinic. As they drew closer, Gabby read the huge welcome sign that stood in front of the complex at the corner. "Eastline Church," she read aloud.

"That's it," Kim said.

"That's a church? Are you kidding me?"

Kim shrugged. "It must be one of those mega churches you hear about on TV."

Gabby pressed her foot to the brake and pulled the van to a stop at the corner. "Which way do we go in?" The church appeared to have several entrances from two different streets. How would they even find the food pantry?

A car beeped its horn behind them. Gabby released the brake and crept forward through the intersection.

"Just turn into this next driveway, and then we'll figure it out."

Gabby turned toward the church and followed the long, curvy drive toward the first of several parking lots. At the lot's entrance stood a sign just like the ones at the hospital, with arrows directing visitors to the various entrances. Instead of listing an emergency room, prompt care, and various specialty offices, this sign gave directions to a gym, worship center, daycare center, café, bookstore, and yes—food pantry. Gabby turned into the gigantic lot that sat in front of the main entrance. She parked as close as she could to the front doors, but it was still going to be a bit of a hike for them.

The main building's brick façade was broken up by several tall slabs of gleaming glass that rose at least two stories high. Just inside the entrance, a fountain sparkled in the fading sunlight. Gabby followed her mom through one set of several banks of double doors and into the atrium beyond the fountain. A brick walkway led them through groups of round tables with chairs that reminded her of the food court at the mall. The walkway forked at a large snack bar that sat outside the church's bookstore.

"Are you sure this is a church and not a mall?" Gabby whispered. A small group of ladies sat around a table near the snack bar with Bibles unfolded in front of them. Their eyes followed Gabby and her mom like the dead stares of a figure in a creepy old portrait.

Kim shrugged and followed the walkway off to the right, away from the staring church ladies. She pointed to a sign that listed the various destinations they were heading toward. According to the sign, the food pantry was straight ahead.

They continued down the walkway, passing a small waiting room, until they reached an open door with a shiny, chrome "Food Pantry" sign above it. The sign matched the one that hung over the bookstore. It really did feel like they were at a shopping mall. Shopping carts were lined up across the small foyer in front of the food pantry. Inside its sliding glass doors was a long row of coolers on one side of an aisle with shelving opposite. It looked like a regular grocery store. Maybe this wouldn't be so bad.

Gabby followed her mom to a folding table that was staffed by a couple of older ladies. One of them seemed to be training the other on the iPad that they held out in front of them. A couple of rows of clipboards, each bearing a pen and a slip of bright orange paper, lined the table in front of them.

Kim glanced at her watch. "We're a little early," she said.

The ladies turned their attention to Gabby and her mom. "That's okay," one of them said. "Is this your first time here?" She grabbed a clipboard and handed it to Kim without waiting for her to answer.

Kim nodded and took the clipboard.

"Fill out this sheet," the lady told her. "Sign in here, and then you can have a seat in the waiting room until we call your name. At that time, we'll need to see a photo ID and proof of residence. A utility bill, for example. You have both of those items with you, correct?"

Kim nodded her head again. She signed in below two other names on the sheet the lady had shoved across the table to her. Good, they weren't the only ones to show up early. Then, she led Gabby into the waiting room across the hall.

The two of them took seats on hard chairs at the front of the room, and Kim began to fill out the orange sheet on her clipboard. Gabby tried to ignore the noisy toddler who was stamping around the room as if it was a playground. He grabbed a tall stack of paper coffee cups from the beverage cart by the door and started to scatter the cups all over the room.

"Put those back." His mother hissed at him without looking up from her cell phone screen. The boy continued to do what he was doing as though his mother hadn't noticed him at all. Another woman, who Gabby guessed to be the toddler's aunt, sat next to a tattooed young man. They both stared at their cell phone screens as well.

The toddler climbed onto a chair and wobbled on its edge. He slurped up a glob of snot that was dangling from his nose, and then wiped his nose on the back of his hand. The chair started to tip, but then righted itself. Gabby cringed. Should she try to grab him or mind her own business? She didn't want to see him get hurt, but would his mom get upset if she interfered?

The little boy's aunt suddenly jumped up and snatched him out of the chair. She gave his behind a swat and then set him back on the floor. "Pick up those cups and put them back," she said. She sat back in her seat and stared at her phone again. Her nephew laughed and then went on about his business, placing a cup on each empty chair in the room.

Meanwhile, just outside the waiting room door, a boy about Owen's age, dressed in basketball gear and carrying a gym bag, walked through the hall on his way to the gym. He stared inside the waiting room. Gabby looked away from his curious eyes.

That kid was soon followed by others, many of them with their parents. While many of the kids would glance inside the food pantry waiting room as they passed, several of their parents stared, as if they wanted to see if anyone they knew had been reduced to accepting handouts from the church. Gabby slid down in her seat and covered her face in her hands in case someone she knew should pass by. As all this took place, more food pantry patrons wandered in and took up the empty seats in the waiting room.

One of the food pantry workers finally stepped into the waiting room and called out a name.

"I'm right here," the toddler's mother said. She finally stuck her phone in her pocket and then began to gather up the cups that her son had distributed throughout the room. She took her sweet time, stacking them up neatly and then putting the stack next to the coffee urn on the cart. As if anyone would want to use those cups after her son had rubbed his snotty little hands all over them. Then, she dragged her son over to her sister and handed him over. "Keep an eye on him," she said. The boy's mother followed the food pantry worker through a side door and disappeared.

A few minutes later, another food pantry worker came for the little boy's aunt. She set the boy on the seat next to her boyfriend so hard, the seat clunked against its legs, echoing through the room. "Stay there," she said. She followed her food pantry worker through the same door her sister had disappeared through.

The little boy slid from his seat and started to run circles around the room. A couple of the other patrons glared at him, and then at the man who was supposed to be watching him. The young man didn't look up from his phone once.

Gabby grabbed her mom's wrist to look at her watch. The food pantry had been open a full fifteen minutes now, but the workers had yet to distribute any food. At this rate, they weren't going to get home until bedtime. And they were only third in line! She should have brought her homework along. She was going to probably be up all night working algebra equations now.

"This is ridiculous," Kim whispered.

Gabby glanced at the orange sheet on her mom's clipboard. Next to the question, "Do you have a church home?" Kim had marked the "Yes" box. Gabby poked the sheet with her finger and raised an eyebrow at her mom. Kim wasn't normally one to lie.

She shrugged. "If I tell them I don't have a church, they'll be trying to recruit me to theirs," Kim said. "I came here to get groceries, not religion."

The little boy's mom stormed through the waiting room's front entrance. She grabbed her son by the arm and dragged him across the room to the tattooed man and shoved the boy into his lap. "The whole reason we brought you along was so you could keep an eye on him," she yelled.

The man rolled his eyes at her. He stuck his phone in his pocket and moved the boy to the chair next to him. "Sit there and be still," he said.

The boy's mother headed to the food pantry finally and followed an older man who pushed a shopping cart inside for her. The boy slid out of his seat and tried to chase after his mom, but his aunt came around the corner just in time and snatched him up. He began to wail and kick. She took him back to his seat and glared at her boyfriend. "You're supposed to be watching him," she said.

"What do you want me to do?" He threw his hands up in the air. "He don't listen to no one."

The boy's aunt sat in the chair on his other side and pulled her phone out. Her boyfriend pulled his phone out. Soon, the boy was running wild again.

"Kim?" A young man in a neatly ironed, button-down dress shirt stood in the doorway with a clipboard in hand. "Kim Gimble?"

Gabby blushed. Did he have to say her mom's full name so everyone would know exactly who they were?

Kim stood up. "That's me," she said.

The young man shook her hand. "Jeff," he said. "Follow me this way, and we'll just go in the next room and sit down to talk for a few minutes."

Gabby followed her mom and Jeff. He led them into the atrium and settled them at one of the many food court-style tables nearby. The table even had a napkin holder with an advertisement stuck in its clear side compartment, just like the ones at the mall's food court.

Jeff went down the list on his check sheet as if this was his first time counseling a food pantry patron. "Let's see here," he said. "So, this says you already have a church? What church do you go to?"

"Well—um—" Kim's cheeks turned red. She was such a terrible liar. "You see, we don't live here in town. We come from a small town on the county border. We go to a church there. It's such a long drive for us to come here."

Jeff nodded his head. "Uh-huh—okay. Well, what can we help you with today?"

Gabby's mom caught her eye. Gabby shrugged at her. She thought it was pretty obvious that they were there for groceries.

Jeff seemed to sense their confusion. "What I mean is, what's your situation? Is there anything we can pray for today?"

Kim pinched Gabby's leg under the table. Gabby stifled a laugh. They were going to pray? What?

Kim pursed her lips and wrinkled her brow in a serious expression that Gabby recognized as her attempt to keep from bursting out laughing. Gabby's reaction wasn't far behind. It had never occurred to her that a food pantry visit might include forced prayer. Would Jeff refuse to feed their family if they refused to let him pray for them? The thought of going home empty handed after all they'd been through already was enough to sober Gabby up.

Her mom collected herself as well. She sighed as though she was carrying the entire weight of the world's worries all on her own. "Well," she said. "I did just lose my job. So, I guess you could pray on that."

Jeff bent over his clipboard and made a note on the back of the bright orange form that Kim had filled out earlier. Then he looked up again. "What else?"

"Hmmm— I have fibromyalgia. It would be great if you could pray that away."

"Mmm-hmm—" Jeff noted that down next. "Anything else?"

Did he have some sort of quota to meet? Gabby wondered if they were going to end up on the church's prayer list. Hopefully no one at her school went to church here!

"Nope, I think that does it," Kim said.

"What about you, young lady?"

Gabby sat up straight. "Me?" Her cheeks burned. "I'm good," she said.

"Oh, come on. Surely you can think of one thing for us to pray for."

The only thought to cross Gabby's mind was a prayer that Jeff would hurry the hell up and let them get their groceries.

"She's saving up to buy a car when she gets her driver's license," Kim said. She patted Gabby's arm and grinned as if she were happy to have Jeff's attention diverted.

"Oh, you have a job?" Jeff asked.

"Umm-yeah—" Did he have to say it as if the last thing he expected was to hear that a food pantry patron actually had a job?

"Good for you," Jeff said. "A good work ethic is an important thing to have." He shot an accusing glance at Gabby's mom.

"That it is," Kim said. She looked like she might punch this guy in the throat if he kept it up.

"Well, then. Shall we pray?" Jeff held a hand out to each of them.

Gabby stared at his outstretched hand. Kim took his other hand in hers and then reached for Gabby's closest hand. Gabby had no choice but to take one of Jeff's, completing the circle. He had already bent his head and was praying out loud for them. He went down the list he had made and prayed for each of the areas they had discussed.

"And finally, we ask you, Oh Lord, to please help Little Miss Gabby maintain her strong work ethic so she can buy her very own car and be a productive and useful member of society as she becomes a woman."

Gabby snatched her hand away from Jeff's and stuck it under her armpit where he couldn't touch it again. He said a few more words to Kim and then finally led them back to the waiting room where he told them to have a seat until someone was ready to walk them through the food pantry.

Their previous seats had been taken by an ancient woman and a young woman with Down's syndrome. The old woman now held the toddler who had been terrorizing the waiting room earlier. She pulled an old story book from her giant handbag and began to read to him.

The younger woman leaned in to listen to the story. She grinned at the little boy, and he smiled back. "What a good little boy you are," she said. He beamed at her like a little angel. Someone must have wiped his nose since Gabby saw him last. He was actually kind of cute when he wasn't being a hoodlum. The tattooed guy who was supposed to be watching the little boy was too focused on his phone to notice that a stranger had taken over his babysitting duties. Maybe he just didn't care.

"Kim Gimble?" Another older lady dressed in pressed slacks and a blouse that probably cost more than Gabby's entire wardrobe stood in the door now, looking for Gabby's mom.

Again, with the full name! Gabby followed her mom into the passageway between the waiting room and the food pantry.

The rich lady frowned at Gabby. "I'm sorry, but we don't allow more than one person in the food pantry at a time."

What, did she think Gabby was going to try to steal some free food while she was in there? Whatever. Gabby shrugged and started to turn away, but her mom stopped her.

Kim clutched at her belly. "Actually, Gabby—I'm not feeling very well all of a sudden. Can you take care of this while I run to the restroom?" She ran off before Gabby could protest.

"I guess we're doing this," Gabby said. She started to grab the shopping cart that the woman had waiting for her, but the woman got to it first.

"I push the cart," the woman said.

"Oh—kay—" Gabby followed her personal shopper into the food pantry. They started at the cooler on the left-hand side of the first aisle.

"You can have one item from each of the shelves in this cooler," the woman said.

Gabby eyed the tubs of butter, yogurt, and cottage cheese. She opened the door and grabbed one of each.

When she turned around, the woman was waiting with an open grocery bag, of the plastic variety. Gabby dropped the items inside. The woman put the bag into the cart and then tied its handles together to close it. She sure didn't want Gabby shoving anything extra in the bag when her back was turned, did she? Then, she gestured across the aisle at the wall of shelving that was packed with boxes of cereal, oatmeal, pancake mixes, and Pop-tarts.

"You can have two breakfast items from this section," the woman told her.

So this was how it was going to be. Gabby selected a couple of items that the woman then placed into the paper grocery bag that she had opened up in the cart. They went on down the aisle, with the woman telling Gabby how many items she could take from each section of canned fruits, plain veggies, and "fancy veggies" like sloppy joe sauce. It was a relief that Gabby was able to take two rolls of toilet paper, but she didn't know if they needed any of the cleaning supplies. The old lady seemed irritated that Gabby was taking so long to decide, so she hurried to grab a few items and moved on. At the end of the aisle, she took a couple of boxes of instant potatoes.

"You're almost to the top of your paper bag," the lady said for the third or fourth time. "We still have a whole other section on the other side here."

Gabby shrugged. Apparently, the woman enjoyed stating the obvious. Or maybe she just couldn't think of anything else to say to span the awkward silences between choosing items. They turned the corner into a second aisle. Sugar. Gabby knew they needed that. And cooking oil. She practically ran for the items and brought them back to the cart. The paper shopping bag was pretty full, so she set the bag of sugar and the cooking oil in the cart next to them.

The lady snatched them back up. "They have to fit in your bag," she said. "You can put something back if you need these."

Was she serious? Gabby pulled out a couple of cans of ravioli that she doubted anyone at her house would want to eat anyway.

The woman stuck the cooking oil down the side of the shopping bag and then laid the sugar on its side on top. She waved a hand across the top of the other items in the bag and frowned because the sugar stuck up over the top of the bag. "You're really not supposed to fill the bag above the top," she said.

If the woman had informed Gabby of this to begin with, she might not have taken so many cleaning supplies. Gabby was too embarrassed to take them back, though. She stared down the aisle at the piles of bakery bread on shelves at the end. Surely this wasn't all the food she was going to be allowed to take. She and her mom had wasted an awful lot of time there – not to mention being forced to hold hands and pray with some weirdo – for this to be all the food they could get.

Gabby's personal shopper led her down the long aisle past all the rest of the items she no longer had room for in her bag. There were several things she would have rather had than the cleaning supplies she had taken. She didn't speak up, though. This was all so embarrassing, and she didn't want to seem greedy. At the end of the aisle, they stopped in front of the bread.

"You can take as much as you want from these shelves," the worker said. "The bread doesn't have to fit in your bag. You can also grab a sweet bakery item from this section."

Gabby took a loaf of white bread and a loaf of wheat. Then, she took a container of cinnamon rolls that had been donated by one of the expensive grocery stores that no one in her family would ever be able to afford to set foot in.

"Are you sure that's all the bread you want? You can have as much as you want."

Why was she being so generous with the bread? Gabby didn't want to take too much and have it go bad before they could eat it all. She grabbed a bag of dinner rolls and some hot dog buns. Then, she followed the woman to a rack of meat. Frozen packages of beef, chicken, turkey, and fish were divided into several large plastic bins that set on the rolling shelf unit.

"You can take a total of six pounds of meat."

Gabby started to look through the packages. Her stomach roiled at the sight of the gray packages of hamburger and steaks. Red meat wasn't supposed to be gray, was it? She knew it wasn't. She'd seen the cooks at the diner throw out redder meat than this because it was too old to serve. Gabby gave up on the red meat and took some chicken. Hopefully it would be safer than the rotting beef.

Then, she spotted a half-thawed package of brats that looked okay. The label said they had veggies in them. And a lone package of bacon. She grabbed both and was led next to a bin of rotting fruit and vegetables. Fruit flies flittered around the apples and onions. The potatoes had loose skins. Gabby didn't want to touch anything in the bins for fear that the items would squish into mush when she picked them up. The rotting odor was starting to make her feel sick, and she wished her mom had felt up to doing this.

Gabby shook her head. The canned beans and the veggies in the brats would have to do. She pursed her lips tight and hurried out of the food pantry.

Kim was waiting for her in the hallway. Her skin held a gray pallor, and she was sweating, as though she'd just ran a couple of miles. "Ready?" she asked.

"Yup."

The two of them pushed the cart to the parking lot and emptied the groceries into their van. Gabby ran the cart back inside and then returned to the van. They were silent as they pulled out of the parking lot and headed toward home.

Once they were on the interstate, Gabby finally spoke. "FYI, Mom. I am never doing that again."

"FYI, Gabby. I'm never going to make you do that again. That was one of the most demeaning experiences I have ever been through in my entire life."

"You? You didn't have to go food pantry shopping with your own personal poverty tour guide."

Kim laughed. "Technically, you're the poor person. You weren't on the tour. You were the tour."

Since the brats were thawed out by the time they got home, Kim decided they should eat them for dinner. She directed Meg to heat the cast iron skillet on the stove top and get the brats cooking while she and Gabby put the groceries away.

"These smell funky." Meg wrinkled her nose at the brats while she dropped them into the sizzling hot skillet.

"It's probably the veggies and spices in them," Gabby said.

"Well, I'm not eating any. What else did you get?"

Gabby tossed a box of au gratin potatoes on the counter. "These sound good."

"Yummy, we haven't had au gratin potatoes in forever," Meg said.

"They're too expensive," Kim said. "It's a lot cheaper to just buy a bag of potatoes, especially with four kids to feed. You'd better make two boxes. Open this can of green beans, too."

"But there are vegetables in the brats."

"Cook them," Kim said. "I need to go lay down for a bit."

Meg rolled her eyes but did as she was told. She got the potatoes and green beans going without further complaint.

Gabby was just putting the rest of the non-perishable goods in the pantry when she was overcome by a putrid odor. It reminded her of the time they'd found a dead mouse decaying behind the bookcase in the living room. It had taken them over a week to figure out where the smell was coming from, and even longer to get rid of it once the mouse was removed. "Yuck, what is that?"

Meg was pinching her nostrils closed with one hand as she turned the brats with the other. "It's these brats," she said. "They smell awful. Are you sure they're not rotten?"

Gabby stuck her nose over the pan of frying meat, then jerked away at the smell. "Those are totally rotten," she said. "We can't eat that. Throw them out."

"I told you so." Meg opened the garbage can and started to dump the brats into it.

"Wait!" Gabby said. "Take them outside. They're already stinking the house up."

Meg did as she was told, and Gabby took over cooking the side dishes. What were they going to have with their vegetables, now? How could they even eat the chicken they'd brought home? How did they know it wouldn't be rotten, too?

"What's that smell?" Owen barged into the kitchen and slid across the linoleum in his socks. "Pew, that's awful!"

"It's rotten meat," Gabby said. "Meg just took it outside to dump it."

"Why'd you buy rotten meat?"

Gabby was about to tell Owen they hadn't bought it, but then she thought better of it. All she needed was for Owen to go to school the next day and tell everyone that his mom had brought rotten meat home from the food pantry. He didn't understand the concept of keeping family business private.

Instead, she shrugged. "Just bad luck, I guess." How many other food pantry patrons were taking rotten meat home with them that evening? Was it legal to give people rotten meat, even if it was free? Just because they were poor, that didn't mean they wanted to eat bad meat, any more than the rich lady who had led her through the food pantry would. What was wrong with people, anyway?

Owen went to the refrigerator and pulled out a giant carton of vanilla yogurt that had also come from the food pantry. "This looks good," he said.

"I guess you may as well have some since we don't have any other protein thawed out to eat with our dinner."

Owen tore into the container and pulled the shiny seal off. "Yuck," he said. "The yogurt is rotten, too!" He ran out of the room to save his notoriously sensitive nose.

"Are you kidding me?" Gabby went to the table where Owen had left the container of yogurt. Sure enough, it was no good. She clamped the lid on it to seal in the odor, then checked the expiration date.

Meg came inside and dropped the cast iron skillet into the kitchen sink. "What's wrong?"

"This yogurt expired a month ago."

"What? Where did you go shopping, anyway? Out of the back of someone's van?"

"We may as well have," Gabby said. "But, no. We went to a food pantry. Come on, we have to check the expiration dates on everything we brought home today."

"Are you kidding me? You do that. I'll finish cooking dinner. I'm not touching that garbage."

By the time Gabby was done, she had piled a paper grocery bag – the same one the poverty tour guide had insisted she not overfill – with outdated food. Some of the foods would still be okay even though they were expired, but there were other items she wasn't about to take a chance on. She headed for the back door with the heavy bag to take it to the dumpster.

"You're throwing all that out?" Meg asked.

"Yup."

"This sucks," Meg said. The metal spoon she was using to stir the potatoes clanked against the side of the pan. "I hate being poor."

CHAPTER THREE

Saturday mornings always started early for Gabby. She liked to work the early shift at the restaurant inside the truck stop whenever she could. Her eight-hour shift would fly by in the busy rush of breakfast followed by travelers wandering in from the interstate all through the morning and then the lunch rush. She woke up to a quiet house and showered for as long as she wanted. She rolled her damp hair into a tight bun and then headed to her room to put on her uniform.

Meg curled tighter into her blankets and squeezed her eyes shut against the light of their bedside lamp. Gabby hadn't woke her sister up on purpose, but the sun was already rising later each morning, and she needed the light so she could see to get dressed.

"Why is it so cold in here?" Meg asked.

"It must be cold outside," Gabby said. She hurried into her clothes with chattering teeth. She would be glad when their mom agreed to turn the heat on. It was already cold for October, and everyone in the family had taken to wearing extra layers and walking around the house with blankets wrapped around them to keep warm. She grabbed her fleece blanket and threw it over her shoulders before she sat on the edge of her bed to put her shoes on.

"I hate winter," Meg said. "When I grow up, I'm going to live someplace that's warm all year round."

Once Gabby had finished tying her shoes, she pulled the blankets off her bed and draped them over Meg. "Go back to sleep," she said.

Meg pulled the extra blankets around herself and burrowed in deeper. "Have fun at work."

Gabby flipped the light off and closed the door as she left the bedroom. Downstairs, Owen and Ben were already camped out on the living room floor watching TV. Their small play tent held their body heat inside, and they had filled it with all their blankets and pillows. They crunched on bowls of dry cereal and peered at the television through a small gap they had left in the tent's door panel. Their mom had turned off their internet service and cancelled their Netflix subscription since she'd lost her job but luckily, they could still watch PBS Kids through the television antenna. The boys only acknowledged Gabby's presence long enough to tell her to get out of the way when she crossed the living room between them and the TV.

In the kitchen, she picked up the cereal box the boys had left open on the table. Empty. She tossed it in the garbage. Their mom rarely bought sugary cereal, so when they'd brought some home from the food pantry, it had gone fast. When Gabby opened the refrigerator, she was struck by the odor of rotting food. The perishables that they had been able to keep were going bad fast, but no one had wanted to be the one to throw any of it away. It seemed such a waste. Gabby sighed and started sniffing containers to determine what could still be saved.

Before she knew it, she had run out of time to eat and needed to head out the door to work. Gabby bundled up in her coat and put on her scarf, hat, and gloves for the cold walk across town to the truck stop. At least it would be warm at work.

When she arrived, Gabby threw on her apron and headed for her table section to start taking orders. She threw on her waitress mask and started hustling for tips, flirting with the customers where appropriate and dodging groping hands when necessary.

Before she knew it, her first break time had come around, and her boss, Steve was whipping up an omelet for her in the kitchen.

"You girls don't eat enough," Steve said. He flipped the omelet on the griddle as Gabby looked on. "I could tell you were hungry when you walked in this morning. Why don't you eat before you come to work?"

"I tried to," Gabby said. "I couldn't find anything to eat, and then I got distracted with cleaning the refrigerator out."

Steve grunted. He didn't have to work the griddle, but sometimes he liked to step in when they were busy and help out. He seemed to especially enjoy feeding his employees. Steve slid Gabby's omelet onto a steaming plate and handed it to her. "Eat," he said. "You can't wait tables with hunger in your eyes. You're making the customers feel bad."

"Maybe they'll tip me better if they think I'm starving," Gabby said. The hot plate warmed her chilled fingers. She forked up a mound of omelet and stuck it into her mouth. It warmed her insides as it made its way down her throat to her hollow stomach.

"Go sit somewhere," Steve said. "You're in the way."

Jodie, the other morning waitress that day, rapped on the counter between the kitchen and the dining area. "Table nine is still waiting for hash browns!" she said. Jodie was all business and hated it when the kitchen held up her orders. No one else in the restaurant ever hustled as hard for tips as she did. Unfortunately, the friendly tone her voice took on with her customers never carried over to her conversations with her coworkers.

"Almost ready," Mac the cook said. "Don't take off yet, Gabby. Some of these hash browns are for you."

"Gabby, have you started looking at colleges yet?" Steve asked. He was always asking Gabby about school and pushing her to start making plans.

Gabby shrugged. "I still have another year before I need to worry about that."

Steve clucked at her as he broke a few more eggs over the hot griddle. "It's never too early to plan ahead. Your college applications will go much faster next year if you've already picked your top schools and researched their requirements. You could be writing application essays already, you know."

Gabby eyed her hash browns on the griddle as Mac added a sprinkling of shredded cheddar cheese on top, just the way she liked them. He slid two helpings of plain hash browns onto the plates that were on their way to table nine and then tossed them up on the counter for Jodie. Then, he flipped Gabby's cheesy hash browns onto her plate.

Jodie rolled her eyes at Gabby. "Eating on the job again?" she asked. She pulled her plates of hash browns off the counter and turned away before Gabby could answer.

"I'm on break," Gabby said. She headed to a table in the back corner of the restaurant that was reserved for employee breaks. Why did Jodie have to be so mean? What business was it of hers if Gabby ate at work if it was okay with their boss?

Later, during the lunch rush, Jodie shoved past Gabby to get to her orders on the counter.

"What the hell?" Gabby said. "I was here first."

Jodie grabbed several plates from the counter and lined them up on her arm. She might be a bitch, but no one else in the restaurant could carry as many plates at one time as she did. "Stay out of my way, college girl," she said. "Some of us are stuck here for life, and I have kids to feed. I can't afford for you to slow down my tables or my tips."

Once again, Jodie zipped off before Gabby could respond. It was a good thing Jodie worked mostly weekdays while Gabby was at school so she didn't have to put up with her abuse during every shift. She did her best to avoid Jodie for the rest of the day.

Gabby huddled into her threadbare coat as she hurried home after work. The wind had picked up since that morning, and the temperature seemed to have plunged another ten degrees, at least. She hoped to find that her mother had broken down and turned the heat on when she got home, but when she stepped inside, she found that the living room was almost as cold as it was out on the porch. She didn't take her coat off before heading upstairs to her room.

Music came from inside her mother's bedroom, so she poked her head inside. The boys were huddled in bed with their mom, watching a DVD on her TV.

"Come get in bed with us," Ben said. "Mom's heating pad is keeping the whole bed warm."

"Yeah, come feel this," Owen said. He lifted the blankets just enough for Gabby to slip a hand underneath.

The heat under the blankets eased the pain in Gabby's aching finger bones. She wanted to slide right into the bed with her mom and brothers, but she knew she stank of the restaurant. She needed a shower before she could get into the clean fuzzy pajamas that she planned to wear for the rest of the weekend.

"Where's Meg?" Gabby asked.

"She's at Lily's house," Kim said. "I told her she could spend the night there and borrow their heat."

"Still no check today?" Gabby asked.

Her mom shook her head. "I don't know what is taking them so long. I was hoping the cold would hold off until I had some money again."

"Can't we go ahead and turn the heat on now anyway?" Gabby asked. "It's not like you have to pay the bill today. Surely you'll be getting your unemployment checks by the time you get the next heat bill."

Gabby's mom shifted in the bed and adjusted the heat pad lower on her back. "I don't want to risk it," she said. "I want to know exactly how much money we'll have coming in so I can budget for the heat and decide how warm we can afford to keep the house."

Gabby sighed. "I guess I'm going to go take an ice-cold shower," she said.

"The shower won't be cold," Ben said. "It's when you get out of the shower that you're going to freeze to death."

"You should bring us some hot chocolate when you're done," Owen said. "That will warm you up."

Gabby smirked at her brothers. "Or, you could have some waiting for me when I get out of the shower," she said.

"Good luck with that," their mom said. "These two spent the morning at the library until it closed, and they've been in my bed since they got home. I think I'm stuck with them for the long haul."

"Please?" Owen said.

"Please, can you bring us some hot chocolate?" Ben said.

Gabby laughed. "We'll see," she said. She headed toward the bedroom door, cringing all the way at the dread of taking a shower in this cold house.

"Close the door on your way out," her mom said. "We're trying to keep our body heat in here."

Gabby tried to warm the bathroom up by turning the hot water on and closing the door while she got her clean clothes together in her bedroom. By the time she returned to the bathroom, the steam from the shower had only warmed the room slightly more than it had been before. Once inside the shower, she huddled under the hot water as much as possible. The parts of her body that stuck out from the shower stream were chilled, regardless of the heat that was generated by the hot water. She washed her hair and jumped out of the shower in record time, hardly bothering to towel off before she threw her pajamas on. Gabby wrapped her long hair in a towel and wound the towel on top of her head to keep her damp tresses off her back. Then, she ran straight for her mom's bedroom.

"Where's our hot chocolate?" Owen asked.

Gabby threw the covers back and started to climb into the bed on top of her brothers. "Scoot over," she said. "I'm freezing." Her teeth chattered as she wiggled into the small space her brothers made for her.

"Here, take the heat pad," her mom said. "Just don't get your wet hair on it and electrocute yourself."

Gabby pulled the heat pad to her chest and curled around it, soaking its warmth into her body. Her teeth slowly stopped their chattering as her body core came back to its normal temperature.

"What about our hot chocolate?" Owen asked.

Gabby's mom threw the blankets back on her side of the bed and hefted her legs over the edge. "I'll go make us all some hot chocolate," she said. She groaned with the pain of stepping out of the bed.

Gabby knew her mom was in pain, but the knowledge wasn't enough for her to tear herself out of the bed when she was just finally getting warm. Why should she have to do everything for everyone after she'd been working all day? There was a great deal more room in the bed with her mom gone, and Gabby snuggled in and immediately began to drift off to sleep.

When she was awakened some time later, she was surprised to find her mom spreading a picnic blanket over the middle of the bed. A tray sat on the nightstand with plates of food and steaming cups of hot chocolate. "You know I don't allow food in my bed," Kim said. "So, you little monkeys better keep your food on this picnic blanket."

Gabby sat up next to her brothers and pulled the picnic blanket higher on their laps. Their mom handed them plates piled high with triangles of grilled tuna melt sandwiches. Thank goodness for canned tuna and the infinite shelf life of processed cheese! The plates warmed their laps through the blankets. It had been several days since Gabby's mom had cooked dinner. It was nice to be able to sit in the bed and let someone else take care of her after a hard day at work.

As they finished their meal with minimal spillage, Gabby's mom popped a couple of pain pills, and Gabby knew that was the last they would hear out of her for the rest of the night. She was getting used to seeing only glimpses of the awesome mom she had grown up with as this tired, hibernating stranger took over her mother's body.

Gabby's real mom always made sure there was a hot meal on the table every single night, even if it was occasionally grilled cheese sandwiches, ramen noodles, or frozen pizza. They used to always sit at the kitchen table to eat dinner together every night, except the occasional Friday when they watched a movie together on the couch and ate cheap but delicious Little Caesars pizzas.

Gabby's real mom checked the younger kids' school folders every day. She helped them with homework, signed school paperwork, and always made sure they got to buy book club books and class t-shirts and donate change to the penny drives, even if doing so usually meant that she went without something she needed.

Gabby's real mom couldn't stand for dirty dishes to be left in the kitchen sink overnight. She made sure everyone in the household did their assigned chores every week. The house was never spotless, and there was usually at least one basket of clean laundry waiting to be folded and put away. But, Gabby's real mom made sure the entire family worked as a team to keep the home running as smoothly as possible, even when she worked a full-time job and sometimes picked up odd jobs on the side whenever she could get them, just to make ends meet.

But this new mom – this stranger who was taking over her mother's body – was different. Kim was sullen and tired. She had trouble getting out of bed and couldn't always be bothered to shower. She kept her pills within arm's reach at all times, and she seemed to rely on them more with each passing day.

Gabby's real mom could have probably found a new job by now, but this woman—well, Gabby was beginning to wonder if she would ever return to work at all. And what would they do if she didn't? Gabby shoved the thought away and refused to look at it again. If her real mom was there, she would tell her that they would find a way. One way or another, Gabby's old mom always found a way.

CHAPTER FOUR

B en burst through the front door of their apartment as Gabby, Owen, and Meg arrived home from school several days later. "Get in the van!" he said. "We're going grocery shopping!"

Gabby raised an eyebrow at him. Their mother never took them grocery shopping with her. She always complained that she ended up spending too much money on stuff they didn't really need when they went shopping with her. But sure enough, Kim was coming out the back door with her purse slung over her shoulder. She took slow steps down the back steps and then made her way across the yard toward them.

"What's going on?" Meg asked. "I told Lily I would meet her at the square later."

Their mom grinned at them. "Guess what," she said.

"What?" Meg and Owen asked.

Kim glanced around as if she didn't want anyone else to hear what she was about to tell them. Grouchy Mr. Dodd who lived in the end unit was busy picking the last rotting tomatoes from his upside down hanging baskets that hung above the porch.

"Get in the van," she said. "Then I'll tell you. Gabby, you drive, okay? I'm so tired, I don't know if I could keep the van on the road."

Everyone got in the vehicle, and Gabby started the van up. "What's going on?" she asked.

Kim turned in her seat so she could talk across the van at everyone. "I called Human Services today to talk to them about my job situation. I wanted to know if there was any way I could get a little more in food stamps this month so we can still eat even if I pay all of our bills for the month when I get my unemployment check."

Gabby backed the van out of the driveway and headed toward the interstate. Apparently, they were going grocery shopping. But, she didn't understand why the entire family needed to go. Her mom usually only got about eleven dollars a month on her SNAP card because she made too much money to get any real money out of it. Not that she made enough money to feed them without it. The only reason she continued to apply was for the free school lunches that came with being a food stamp recipient. The free lunches – and recently breakfasts, too – were the only thing that stood between her kids and starvation some months.

"Anyway, I just happened to get ahold of the right person this time," Gabby's mom said. "After I explained our situation, she talked to a manager and got him to approve an emergency payment. They loaded my SNAP card, and you wouldn't believe how much money they gave me."

"How much?" Owen asked.

"Seven hundred dollars!"

Gabby glanced in the rearview at her siblings and laughed. Their jaws had all dropped, and their tongues practically rolled out of their mouths. She couldn't believe she had heard her mother right. Seven hundred dollars? Just to spend on food? She wasn't sure how much groceries usually cost, but she was pretty sure they'd never had that much money for food all at once.

"How much money do we usually spend on groceries?" Ben asked.

Kim laughed. Gabby couldn't remember the last time she'd seen her mom grin like this. "Most of the time, I feel lucky if I can scrounge up two hundred dollars to keep us all fed for the month," she said. "That's why I always tell you to fill up at school!"

"Are we going to get this much every month, now?" Meg asked. Even she was getting excited over the prospect of a real grocery shopping trip.

"Probably not," Kim said. "This is the amount we get with no income. Once my unemployment checks start coming in, the amount will be reduced, I'm sure."

"We should stock up then," Gabby said.

Several minutes later, Gabby took the Market Street exit and headed toward Aldi. She pulled the van into the right turn lane and flipped on the turn signal.

Kim put her hand out and pointed back to the lane next to them. "Nope," she said. "We're going to Wal-mart."

Wal-mart? Really? Kim hadn't bought groceries at Wal-mart in forever. It was just too expensive. Gabby signaled and veered back into the next lane to continue on to the next traffic light.

"Drop me at the door so I don't have to walk so far," Kim said.

Gabby pulled up in front of the sliding glass doors and let everyone out. Then, she went to park the van. Once she had caught up to her family inside the store, she was dismayed to find her mother sitting in one of the motorized shopping cart scooters that typically carted people who Gabby thought were just too lazy to walk. It was embarrassing that people might think that of her mother now. Gabby's mom didn't look like she had anything wrong with her. People would think she was just being lazy. For the first time, it occurred to Gabby that maybe some of the people she had judged for the same thing in the past really did need the motorized scooters to get around after all. She couldn't imagine her mom holding up long enough to get through an entire shopping trip in this gigantic store if she had to be on her feet the whole time.

The entire family was so bubbly with excitement, one might think they had won a shopping spree at a toy store rather than a grocery shopping spree at Wal-Mart. Even Meg, who had reached that age where she was usually too cool to get excited about anything other than boys and makeup, practically skipped after her mother as she led the way in the motorized scooter toward the back of the grocery section. Gabby followed along with a shopping cart and tried not to pretend she wasn't with them.

They started in the cereal aisle, where their mother told them they could each pick out their own box of cereal. "Family-sized, if you want," she said. She was like some sort of cereal-giving Oprah, waving her hand at her minions as they scuffled for their favorite name brand cereals like they were full of gold. You get a box of cereal! You get a box of cereal! Everybody gets a box of cereal!

They went on to the snack cake aisle, where they picked up more sweet cakes and chocolate rolls than the entire family typically saw in a year's time. The rest of the shopping trip went on in much the same way. For once, Gabby's mom didn't say no to anything. She hardly ever bought potato chips or fruit snacks or any other unnecessary extras, but on this day, they got it all. It wasn't long before she was sending Meg for a second shopping cart.

By the meat coolers, they completely bypassed the giant packages of cheap chicken that the family typically ate and picked up steaks, a giant beef roast, and even a couple of packages of expensive brat burgers that none of them had ever had before.

Kim sent Meg back to the bread aisle to grab some buns for the brat burgers and then rolled into the sea food section. She stopped her scooter and stared. "Gabby, you've never had lobster before, have you?"

Gabby shoved her overloaded shopping cart up next to her mom and stopped. "I don't think so," she said. "It looks pretty expensive."

Her mom reached into the cooler and pulled out several packages of frozen lobster tails. She grinned at Gabby as she dropped them into the basket on her scooter. "Just this once," she said. "We deserve to live a little every now and then, don't you think?" She zoomed toward the bakery and rolled right up to the cake counter. She eyed the selection for several seconds before settling on a giant sheet cake that was covered with fluffy frosting in dazzling colors.

Gabby stopped her shopping cart next to her mom and glanced at the cake that was now inside the scooter's basket with the lobster tails. "Thirty dollars!" she said. "Thirty dollars for a cake? Mom, seriously. This is nuts. We don't need this."

Kim scowled at her. "It's just this once," she said. "Don't be a party pooper." She zipped over to the produce to pick up some asparagus while the other kids all grabbed for apples, oranges, grapes, and berries.

They picked up what would normally be a year's worth of produce for their family. Gabby's mom usually bought canned veggies because they were cheaper than fresh vegetables. She usually bought one or two fresh fruits on each shopping trip, depending on what was on sale. But it wasn't something they normally kept on hand. It was going to be so strange to see their cupboards and refrigerator laden with food, and good food at that!

By the time they made it to the checkout, the long afternoon of activity was obviously taking a toll on Kim. She pulled her scooter up to the register and waited while the children unloaded the shopping carts onto the conveyer belt. They had to work around her to grab the bags from the turnstile as the cashier filled them. It seemed to take all of her remaining energy to swipe her SNAP card and punched in her pin number. She perked up when she checked her SNAP balance on her receipt. "We still have $400 left," she said.

"We're eating good this month," Owen said. He practically danced around the shopping carts as Gabby and Meg pushed them toward the exit. Ben didn't say much as he had already ripped open the candy bar that he'd gotten as they checked out. His mouth was too full of chocolaty caramel for him to speak.

Kim fell asleep in the passenger seat as they drove home. The van filled with the sounds of her snores and the chomping of everyone else's teeth as they each dug into their own favorite treat. When they got home, Kim went inside and went straight to bed while Gabby directed the unloading of the van.

They had a hard time finding a place to put all the items they had bought, and each of the kids ended up stashing some of their favorite snack foods in their bedrooms. Gabby put the lobster tails in the freezer since her mom probably wouldn't be up to cooking them that night. It took some maneuvering to get the freezer door shut with all the stuff they had packed inside. Gabby finally decided to cook an entire super-sized bag of pizza rolls for dinner since they wouldn't fit in the freezer. If nothing else, at least they wouldn't have to worry about food again for a while.

Gabby's alarm clock wouldn't stop nagging her to get up. It seemed like she had only just fallen asleep when it began to bleat incessantly. Across the sunlit room, Meg's messy bed had long been empty. She liked to get up early to shower and fix her hair and makeup before everyone else got up and entered the morning battle for the sole bathroom in the house.

Gabby finally slapped the button on her clock to turn off the alarm. She threw her blankets off as she sat up. She dangled her legs over the edge of the bed and stretched her arms toward the ceiling. She pulled her top blanket over her shoulders to stay warm and wrinkled her nose. What was that smell? She got up and stumbled over Meg's discarded pajamas on her way to the bedroom door. She stuck her head into the hallway and sniffed the air. Bacon. Someone was cooking bacon.

Bacon was expensive, so it was a rare treat in their house. Bacon on a weekday morning was unheard of. Who had time to cook before work and school with five people fighting over one bathroom and stumbling over one another in their small place as they prepared to go their separate ways for the day? But meals at the Gimble house had changed for the better since her mom's food stamp card was loaded.

Gabby scrambled down the stairs to find out what was going on. The bacon smell grew stronger as she neared the kitchen and was soon accompanied by the smell of toasting bread. In the kitchen, Kim stood at the stove. She was lifting cooked strips of bacon from the giant cast iron skillet with a fork and laying them out on a paper towel. She smiled at Gabby when she came into the room.

"It's about time you got up," Kim said. "Breakfast is as good as done." She reached into a bag of shredded cheddar cheese on the counter and pulled out of handful to sprinkle over the scrambled eggs in the pan next to the bacon.

Meg carried a stack of buttered toast to the table and glared at Gabby. "No thanks to you," she said. "I got jerked out of the bathroom to help with breakfast before I was done with my face while you got to sleep half the morning."

"You had been in there long enough," Kim said. "The boys needed to use the bathroom, too."

Ben pulled a stack of plates from the cabinet and brought them over to the table. Gabby went to pour herself a glass of milk.

Owen dashed into the room with one shoe on, its laces flopping around untied. "I can't find my other shoe," he said.

"Did you look under the couch?" Kim asked. She carried the plate of bacon and the pan of scrambled eggs to the table. She set the bacon down and handed the pan to Gabby. "Here, portion out the eggs. Make sure everyone gets the same amount."

"Yes, of course, I did," Owen said. He rolled his eyes and flipped his overgrown hair out of his eyes.

Kim headed for the living room. "Boy, if I find your shoe under the couch—"

Owen shoved past her. "I looked! Really, I did!"

Gabby rolled her eyes as she slid a serving of scrambled eggs onto Meg's outstretched plate. Owen's shoes were a daily mystery that everyone but he had grown tired of. Meg grabbed several slices of bacon and a piece of toast and tore into her food. Ben took the next plate from the stack and held it out so Gabby could drop a mound of scrambled eggs on it. He slid the plate across the table to Owen's spot and then took up the next plate.

"Thanks," Gabby said. She finished doling out the eggs, then took the pan to the sink and ran water in it to soak.

Meg was already dropping her empty plate into the sink by the time Gabby had finished filling the pan with water.

"Hungry?" Gabby asked.

"Not anymore," Meg said. "I got to finish my makeup while the bathroom is empty." She ran out the kitchen door as Kim and Owen entered.

"So much for everyone eating a nice, leisurely breakfast together," Kim said. She dropped into her chair with Owen's newly discovered shoe in her lap and began to work at the tangled mess he had left of its laces.

Gabby sat down to eat her own breakfast. She glanced at the clock on the microwave. She needed a shower, but she wasn't sure it was worth dragging Meg out of the bathroom in the short time they had left.

"Mom, can I have ten dollars for a t-shirt?" Owen asked. Anyway, that's what it sounded like he had said. He had practically buried his face in his plate and was shoveling his eggs in his mouth as he spoke.

"Don't talk with your mouth full," Kim said.

Owen swallowed a mouthful. "Please?" he said. "It's to feed hungry kids."

Gabby laughed. "She's already feeding four hungry kids this morning."

"No, these kids are really hungry. They live where the hurricanes were, and they don't have any food at all. They're even poorer than we are."

Kim sighed. "Go get my purse," she said. She stood up to clear the empty dishes that had been left on the table.

Ben took his own plate to the sink and went to finish getting ready for school.

"Mom," Gabby said. "Owen doesn't need another t-shirt. Besides, I thought you didn't have any money."

"It's for hurricane victims."

"What about the fibromyalgia victims here in our own house?" Gabby asked. "Who's going to buy t-shirts to feed us?"

Kim dropped the dishes into the sink with a clatter. She spun around and pointed her finger at Gabby. "I told you this is not for you worry about," she said. "I'll figure something out. Don't I always?"

Gabby's cheeks burned. It was true. Her mother had always figured things out for them in the past. But, her mother's health had never been this bad in the past. Her mother had never been fired before. This was very different from all those other times after Gabby's father had ruined them financially and left her mom to pick up the pieces. Her mom was the problem now. How could she also be the solution?

"You need to go get ready for school," Kim said. "I'm going to wash these dishes and then get myself cleaned up and dressed as soon as all of you are out the door. Then, I'm going down to the unemployment office to find out what's taking them so long to process my claim. I'll spend the rest of the day applying for jobs. Something will come along. It always does."

Gabby nodded. She slipped out of the room as fast as she could. It was a horrible feeling, wondering if she could have faith in her mom. But maybe she should just have faith in the universe the way her mom did. Her mom always said there was no point losing sleep over money. She always told Gabby that every time she thought they were going to run out of money, something unexpected would happen, and everything would turn out fine. Gabby's mom liked to joke that the universe always gave her exactly what she needed, but not a penny more. Gabby just wasn't sure she could believe in the universe the way her mom did.

CHAPTER FIVE

I t only took Gabby a few days to get used to waffles or fried eggs or homemade ham, egg, and cheese sandwiches for breakfast every morning before school instead of cold cereal or plain toast. Kim seemed to be at her best first thing in the morning, and she also seemed to enjoy being able to finally feed her kids so well. It was beginning to feel like real breakfasts were Gabby's new reality, so it was a rude awakening a couple of weeks later when she awoke to a silent house ten minutes before she was due to get on the bus to go to school.

"The alarm!" Gabby yelled as she threw herself out of bed. "I forgot to set the alarm last night!"

"Huh?" Meg poked her head out from under her blanket and squinted at the alarm clock that sat on the nightstand between their beds. Her eyes widened when she saw what time it was. "Oh, crap!" She rolled out of bed and ran for the bathroom.

Gabby ran to the boys' room and threw the door open, but the bunk beds were empty. She went to her mom's room next, flipping the light on when she walked in the door. Gabby's mom pulled her blanket over her head and groaned. "What's wrong?" Her voice was muffled through her old quilt.

"We overslept!" Gabby said.

Kim lifted the blanket just enough to look at her alarm clock, then she covered her head back up. "So, go get dressed, then. You still have time to get to the bus. You can get breakfast at school."

"The bus is going to be here in like five minutes, and it's going to take longer than that to drag Meg out of the bathroom."

Gabby's mom groaned. "I am really not in the mood for this today," she said. She sounded like she was already falling back to asleep again.

Gabby went to her mom and shook her. "Mom, seriously! Wake up!"

Kim groaned again. "Just take the van," she said. "I don't need it for anything today."

"What? You want me to drive everyone to school? I don't have my driver's license yet!" Gabby's mom had never let her take her van alone yet, not even to run a quick errand for her. She always said they would be screwed if something happened to their sole source of transportation. There was no public transportation Kim could take to get into town to get to her job. She didn't want to have to be mad at Gabby if something happened to the van. There was always the chance that Kim could wreck the van herself, but then she could only be mad at herself and not at Gabby.

"Yes, Gabby. There's no sense in my driving the van all over the countryside wasting gas when you can just make one trip and be done with it. Besides, I just took a pill an hour or so ago, so I probably shouldn't be driving anyway."

Gabby took a deep breath. She wasn't afraid to drive. She was just afraid to be the one to blame if something happened to their van.

"You'll be okay," Kim said. "I was driving my dad's pickup all over the country by the time I was twelve. It's not like you have to drive into town. Just drive the speed limit and keep your eyes on the road."

Gabby let out the long breath she had been holding. "Okay, then," she said. She turned the bedroom light off so her mom could go back to sleep. She was about to close the door when she thought of something else. "One more thing. Ben's bus was here forty minutes ago, so he's probably already late for school."

"Just take him into the office and sign him in. It will be okay."

Gabby closed the bedroom door. Then she ran to the bathroom door and pounded on it. "Hurry up!" she said. "I'm going to drive us all to school, but Ben's already late. We need to get out of here."

"I have to get the shampoo out of my hair!" Meg said.

Gabby groaned and then scrambled down the stairs. Why did Meg think she even had time for a shower when she needed to be at the bus stop in just a few minutes? "Ben! Owen!" she called. "Where are you?"

Gabby ran into the kitchen and found Owen sitting at the table eating a bowl of cereal. He was fully dressed aside from one untied shoe and a second shoe that was − of course − altogether missing. He swung his feet under the table and hummed to himself as he ate.

"Where's Ben?" Gabby asked.

Owen gave her a puzzled look. For once, he swallowed his food before he spoke. "It's almost eight o'clock," he said. "Ben got on the bus like forty-five minutes ago."

"And it didn't occur to either of you to wake the rest of us up?"

Owen shrugged. "It was kind of nice to have the place to myself for a while." He returned to his bowl of cereal.

Gabby sank into a chair at the table and breathed a sigh of relief. Now that she didn't need to get Ben to school or catch her own bus, they actually had time to get to school. Though it took the bus almost an hour to get to their high school/middle school, due to the winding route it had to take through the countryside to pick up the farm kids this side of the small town where the school was located, it was only about a ten-minute drive when you could go straight there. There might even be time for Gabby to have a shower, too.

"Owen," she said. "If this happens again—if Meg and I oversleep and Mom doesn't get us up, I need you to wake us up so we can all get to school on time."

Owen turned to look at the clock on the microwave. He frowned. "I think we already missed the bus," he said. "I lost track of the time."

"I'm going to drive us today," Gabby said. "But I doubt Mom is going to let me take the van every day. So, I need you to do your part and help make sure everyone gets up on time since you usually wake up early anyway."

"I can do that," Owen said. He picked up his cereal bowl and slurped at the milk that remained in the bottom.

"Thank you. I'm going to go drag Meg out of the shower now so I can get ready for school. You go find your other shoe."

Owen set his bowl down with a clatter. "I can't," he said. "I looked everywhere, and it's nowhere to be found."

Gabby got up and headed into the living room. She glanced around at all the usual places. She bent over to look under the couch. Finally, she opened the front door. There it was. Owen's missing shoe must have gotten closed up between the main door and the screen door as Ben left for school. It was no surprise, considering this wasn't the first time it had happened. Gabby took the shoe to the kitchen and held it up to show it to Owen.

Owen dropped his cereal bowl into the kitchen sink and then turned to Gabby. "Where did you find it?" He went to Gabby to take the shoe from her. "I swear, I looked everywhere."

Gabby handed the shoe to him. "We're leaving in twenty-five minutes. Make sure you're ready to go." She turned away and then headed upstairs to kick Meg out of the shower.

Meg poked her head out the bathroom door almost immediately after Gabby knocked. She had one towel wrapped around her body and another one wrapped around her hair. She must have showered in record time. "I know! I'm trying to hurry," she said. "What time is it? We haven't missed the bus yet, have we?"

"I'm sure the bus has already come and gone by now," Gabby said. "But, it's okay. Ben made it to his bus, and Owen's almost ready. I'm going to drive us to school."

"Really?" Meg said. "No school bus today? Awesome!"

"Can I get in the shower now?" Gabby asked.

Meg stepped into the hallway. "I'm not done in there," she said. "Yell when you're in the shower so I can come in and fix my hair and makeup."

Twenty minutes later, the laces on both of Owen's shoes were still flopping about untied as they climbed into the van.

"Owen, your shoes!" Gabby said.

Owen plopped onto his seat in the middle of the van and stuck his feet up on the center console next to Gabby. "Can you help me?" he said. "I can't get them tight like Mom does."

Gabby groaned, but she knew there was no use arguing with Owen when they were running late. He would only bull up and make them even later. She grabbed one of Owen's feet and pulled his shoelaces as tight as she could.

"Tighter," Owen said. "Otherwise, they'll fall off."

"Your shoes are not going to fall off," Gabby said. "They are seriously way too tight for that." She pulled the laces tighter anyway and knotted them off. It was a wonder the kid didn't cut off his circulation wearing his shoes so tight. He was constantly obsessing over how his shoes and clothes fit.

"You don't know," Owen said. "They might."

Gabby tied the other shoe and then turned back to the front to start the van. She glanced at the clock on the dashboard as she pulled out of the driveway. Tying Owen's shoes had set them back a bit, but if she drove just a little over the speed limit, they might still make it on time.

After school, Gabby got the van from the parking lot on the high school side of the campus and then drove around to the middle school side to pick up Meg and Owen. Meg slid the van's rear door open as soon as Gabby put the van in park.

"I told Lily she could ride home with us. That's okay, right?" Meg climbed into the back of the van. Her friend Lily, who lived a few blocks from them, climbed in after her. They moved to the back row of seats and soon filled the back of the van with their whispered gossip and high-pitched giggles.

Gabby edged the van forward as the vehicles in front of her picked up their passengers and left. Kids streamed out the front doors for a while, but then the crowd dispersed as the students were picked up. Soon, Gabby's was the only vehicle in the drive. She turned the van off to save gas while they waited for Owen to appear. What could be taking him so long?

"Gah, where is he?" Meg said. "At this rate, the bus will beat us home."

"If I don't get home by my usual time, my mom will find out I didn't ride the bus, and then I'll be in trouble," Lily said.

Gabby eyed her in the rear-view mirror. Maybe Lily should have ridden the bus home then if she wasn't allowed to ride home with a friend. That wasn't Gabby's fault.

A teacher headed toward the van. "Who are you waiting for?" he asked.

"Owen Gimble," Gabby said. "Have you seen him?"

"Owen? I'm pretty sure he got on his regular bus."

"Are you freaking kidding me?" Meg said.

"What a moron," Lily said.

The teacher pulled a walkie-talkie from his belt. He pressed a button on the side and talked into it. "Hey, Helen," he said. "Can you call Owen Gimble's bus and find out if he's on it? His ride is out here in the parking lot waiting to pick him up."

There was a second of static over the walkie-talkie. "Will do," Helen said.

The teacher smiled at Gabby. "We'll find out if Owen's on the bus. If he's not, then we'll call for him over the intercom in the school and see if we can find him."

"Thanks," Gabby said.

"Are you Gabby?" the teacher asked.

Gabby blushed. How did this teacher know her name? She didn't recognize him. He must be new since she left middle school. "Yup, that's me," she said.

"I'm Mr. Stein. I have Owen for science and social studies," the teacher. "He really looks up to you, you know?"

"I guess so," Gabby said. "If he's talking to his teachers about me." She'd heard plenty about Mr. Stein from Owen, but it had never occurred to her that he talked to his teachers about her as much as he talked to her about them.

"Mr. Stein?" Helen called back over the walkie-talkie.

"Yup?"

"Owen's on his bus," she said. "It sounds like he's been into it with Jamie again."

Gabby groaned. What now? Why couldn't those two just stay away from each other?

Mr. Stein raised an eyebrow at Gabby, and she shrugged.

"Thanks, Helen," he said. "I think Owen's sister is on her way to get him."

Gabby nodded.

"Ten-four," Helen said.

Mr. Stein hooked the walkie-talkie back onto his belt. "Owen's a good kid," he said. He put his hands on his hips and studied her.

"I know he is," Gabby said. She turned the key in the ignition. She didn't need anyone to tell her anything about Owen. She was about to shift the van into drive when Mr. Stein stepped closer and leaned against the door.

"I mean it," he said. "Owen is a good kid, and really smart, too. He does talk a bit too much in class sometimes, but that's okay. He has a lot to say and needs to be listened to. I want you to know I'm looking out for him."

"Um—okay," Gabby said. How was she supposed to respond? She'd heard Owen talk about Mr. Stein enough to know that he was a favored teacher, but that was all she really knew about the guy. Owen talked so much, it was hard to pay attention to everything he said.

Mr. Stein took a step back. "Take it easy on the kid, okay?" he said. "And don't be too hard on Jamie either, if you see him. Those two have a lot more in common than either of them would care to admit."

"Okay," Gabby said. She put the van in gear and started to pull away. "Thanks for your help."

"Any time." Mr. Stein turned and headed back into the school as Gabby drove away.

Meg and Lily broke out into a fit of giggles.

"I think he likes you, Gabby," Lily said.

"OMG, he is so cute!" Meg said. "I wish he could have been my teacher in sixth grade."

"Whatever," Gabby said. Even if a teacher would be interested in her, that would be creepy.

"He's not that old," Meg said. "This is his first year teaching. I bet he's not even ten years older than you."

"Okay, that's enough," Gabby said. She turned the van out of the school parking lot and onto the country road that would take them toward home.

Meg and Lily turned their attention to each other and continued to giggle for the rest of the drive home. Most of the corn had been taken out of the fields now, and Gabby could see for miles around. Gabby knew a lot of her classmates complained about the long drive to their school, which had been built in the middle of a cornfield that happened to be at the center of their school district. For her, the drive was calming, as long as she could ignore the babbling eighth graders in the back of the van.

Hopefully Owen's most recent dust-up with Jamie wouldn't get him kicked off the bus. If only he had remembered that Gabby was supposed to drive him home today. She couldn't totally blame him, though. She was the one who had forgotten to set her alarm. If she had gotten out of bed on time, everyone would have made it to the bus stop that morning. But then again, her mom could have just as easily gotten herself out of bed and made sure everyone got out the door on time. They were her children, after all. Anyway, who was going to look after Owen on the bus after Gabby graduated from high school next year?

Gabby caught up to the school bus as it turned into town. The bus slowed to a stop in front of the rec center, and Gabby stopped behind it. The bus's stop arm swung outward, and its door folded open. Kids streamed out onto the sidewalk and headed their separate ways. The bus door closed, and the bus moved forward. Gabby followed it when it turned at the next corner and headed to her usual bus stop.

When the van pulled up behind the bus this time, Lily hopped out of her seat. "I'm getting out here," she said. She slid the van door open and hopped down. Then, she poked her head back inside. "I'll be at the square as soon as I get my homework done."

"I'll meet you there," Meg said.

Gabby watched for Owen and Jamie as the kids streamed off the bus at her regular stop. Owen was the last one off the bus before it rolled away. Jamie was nowhere in sight.

"Owen!" Gabby leaned out the window to holler at him. He hadn't even glanced her way and didn't notice she was waiting for him.

Owen spun around. His face lit up when he saw his sisters waiting for him, and he ran toward the van. He jumped into the door that Lily had left open and then slid it shut. "Guess what!" he said.

"What?" Gabby pulled away from the grassy shoulder and pointed the van toward home.

"I'm pretty sure Jamie just got kicked off the bus for good."

"But not you?" Gabby asked.

"Nah, I didn't do anything wrong," Owen said. "He punched me, and the bus driver actually saw what happened for once. He's driving Jamie straight to his door after he drops everyone else off. The school called Jamie's dad, and Jamie is going to get it when he gets home."

Gabby sighed. It certainly sounded like Owen was safe this time, but you never could tell. He had gotten detentions in the past for fighting back when Jamie hit him. What did the school expect Owen to do, roll over and let the other kid beat the crap out of him?

Owen chattered on about the argument that had led up to Jamie's assault. He had "burned" Jamie really good. It was beginning to sound to Gabby like Owen might have instigated the argument to begin with. She sighed as she pulled the van into the parking lot behind their apartment. Well, at least Owen hadn't gotten kicked off the bus this time. Whatever might happen to Jamie at this point wasn't her concern.

CHAPTER SIX

Halloween hadn't quite arrived in central Illinois when Gabby came home from school one day to find that her mother had finally turned the heat on. The warmth inside the house embraced her like a giant hug as she followed her siblings indoors. They all glanced at each other in surprise and began throwing off their coats, hats, and gloves. Owen tossed his gloves into the air like confetti at a birthday party and whooped.

"What's going on?" Gabby asked. "It's not November yet." Kim had been telling them for a week that she would turn the heat on November first whether her checks had started to come or not.

Kim came out of the kitchen, smiling as she stirred chocolate batter in a glass mixing bowl. "I got my check today," she said.

"Thank. God," Meg said. "I am totally out of mascara. Can we have our allowance from the past few weeks?" She hung her coat from the hook behind the front door and then shoved her gloves into her coat pockets.

Gabby's mom's face fell. She sighed. "Sorry," she said. My check didn't quite cover all the bills that are stacking up already. You're going to probably have to give up on allowances until I can find another job." She turned back into the kitchen and went to the counter where she had the brownie pan all greased up and ready to go.

"Oh, come on." Meg followed her mom into the kitchen. "This is so unfair. Why should I get less money when I've been doing more and more work?"

Gabby went to the sink to pour herself a glass of water. She wondered what bills her mom hadn't been able to pay and what they would do if she couldn't pay them at all. "Maybe you should get a job, Meg," she said. "Why should mom buy mascara for an eighth grader? She's never bought me makeup."

Meg rolled her eyes like only a thirteen-year-old could. "That's because you don't wear makeup, dingo," she said. "It's not my fault you have no interest in boys."

"Gabby likes girls!" Owen danced around the kitchen and stuck his tongue out at his sisters.

Kim poured the brownie batter into the pan and scraped at the edges of the bowl. "That's enough, Owen," she said. "Gabby can like whoever she wants. It's none of your business."

"But I don't like girls," Gabby said. It wasn't that she didn't like boys either. She just preferred books to most of the humans she went to school with. "Why are we talking about my love life again?" She grabbed the batter-covered spatula from her mom's hand before she could drop it into the sink and began to lick the batter from it.

"Hey, why does she get to lick the spatula?" Owen said.

"Because she's being picked on, and I am all about the underdog." Kim opened the oven and stuck the brownie pan inside to bake. Then, she leaned against the counter next to the stove. "Ben, come in here!" She paused while they waited for Ben to join them in the kitchen. Once she had the whole family together, she studied them for a moment. Then she said, "Money's going to be tight around here for a while."

"Money is always tight around here," Meg said. She crossed her arms and scowled.

"Money is going to be tighter than usual," Kim said. "I got my first unemployment check, but it wasn't as much as my paychecks were. Almost all the money I have coming in right now is going to have to go to bills. The only spending money I'm holding back from my checks now will be for necessities like toilet paper and soap. I'm sorry Meg, but mascara is not a necessity."

Meg groaned, but to her credit, she kept her mouth shut.

"The heat is on," their mom said. "But we're not turning it up past 68 degrees. The gas company can't shut our heat off through the winter months for not paying the bill, but I don't want to have a huge bill racked up come spring if I haven't found a job by then."

"It's okay, Mom," Ben said. "We'll be okay." He went to their mom and wrapped his arms around her middle. She hugged him back with a tear in her eye.

"So, who wants to try lobster for dinner tonight?" Kim asked.

"Me!" Owen said.

"Sure," Gabby said. "That's sounds good. I was going to try to cook it myself, but I was afraid I'd ruin it."

"It's easy," Kim. "Come on, I'll show you."

The two of them made dinner together that night, and they all sat at the kitchen table for dinner for the first time in weeks. Gabby's mom was grimacing in pain by the time they got to the warm brownies and ice cream she had planned for dessert. She could barely squeeze the handle on the ice cream scoop to serve the ice cream.

"Meg, can you do this for me while I get the chocolate syrup?" she asked.

Meg took over the ice cream scoop.

"Are your hands bothering you?" Gabby asked her mom.

Kim nodded. "My hands and my knees today. I took some ibuprofen so I could focus to pay the bills and then decided to hold off on taking my prescription until after dinner since I was doing so well this afternoon without the pills." Her hands shook as she drizzled chocolate over the top of each scoop of ice cream.

As much as she hated to see her mom turn into a zombie, Gabby hated even more to see her in such pain. It shouldn't be this difficult for a person to throw together some brownie sundaes. Gabby took the chocolate syrup from her mom's hands. "Go take your meds," she said. "I got this."

Gabby's mom sighed. How much effort had it taken her to stay off her pills that afternoon and into the evening? How could she ever work a full-time job again in this state? "I'm going up to my room," she said. "I don't want to have to drag myself upstairs once I'm flying high on my pain meds."

"I'll bring your ice cream," Ben said. He took two bowls and followed their mother from the kitchen. Owen grabbed a bowl for himself and followed them.

"Jeez," Meg said. "Our mother has turned into a freaking drug addict." She sat at the table and dug into her sundae.

"Don't say that," Gabby said. "It's not her fault she got fibromyalgia." She took the ice cream and put it in the freezer.

"Maybe not," Meg said. "But she's still starting to remind me of Dad."

Gabby slammed the freezer door and spun on her sister. "Mom is nothing like that—that—sperm donor," she said. "Mom would never hurt us."

"Probably not, but she's not really taking care of us either, is she?" Meg raised an eyebrow at Gabby. Then, she took a bite of her ice cream as if she hadn't just said the most hateful thing in the world about their mother.

Gabby grabbed her ice cream and headed for the door. "You don't have to be a bitch just because you're not getting your makeup," she said.

Meg's spoon clattered in her bowl. "Screw you!" she said.

Gabby ignored her sister and went up to their bedroom. Once inside, she slammed the door shut. She silently dared Meg to try to come into their shared bedroom right now. She wished she had slapped her face in the kitchen instead of walking away.

But, Meg didn't come upstairs until later, long after Gabby's anger had fizzled. They didn't speak to each other as they got ready for bed.

CHAPTER SEVEN

Halloween came and went. It wasn't much different from previous years. Store-bought costumes had never been in their price range in the past, so this year's lack of money had little effect on their costume choices. Gabby and her siblings dug through the costume box that was filled with bits and pieces they had collected over the years and cobbled together what they could. Gabby took the kids trick-or-treating, which gave her the excuse to dress up with them. She even let Meg put a little bit of makeup on her and bought her a tube of mascara in return. They didn't talk about their mom's prescription drug habit anymore, but it still hung in the air between them whenever they were together.

Soon, it was almost Thanksgiving. Gabby wondered if she was going to have to figure out how to cook a turkey by herself. The idea terrified her. Gabby hated to cook, and Thanksgiving dinner was a big deal. She was relieved when her mom asked her to drive her to the grocery store the Saturday before Thanksgiving to buy supplies for their holiday dinner.

"Don't worry," Gabby's mom said. "I'm going to do the cooking Thursday no matter what. You've been a huge help the past few months, and you deserve a break."

They decided to go all out on Thanksgiving that year since they had plenty of money left on their SNAP card. They would never have been able to afford it otherwise. They got the biggest turkey they could find, along with the ingredients for all their favorite side dishes. Kim even picked up a few pre-made pies so no one would have to bake. No child would be disappointed in Thanksgiving that year. Not if Gabby's mom could help it.

Gabby had just put the last of the canned goods away in the kitchen cupboards when there was a knock at the front door. "Meg, can you get that?" she asked. Meg was the only person in the family who regularly had friends knock at their door, so it was probably for her anyway.

Meg dragged herself out of the kitchen like it was the hardest thing she had ever accomplished in her whole life. When she opened the door, the wind whooshed into the living room, bringing a cold gust all the way into the kitchen.

"Oh. My. Gosh," Meg said. "You have got to be kidding me." She burst into laughter.

"Who's there?" Gabby asked. She stepped into the living room as her mom came down the stairs.

"Close the door, Meg," Kim said. "You're letting all the heat out."

"Mom, look," Meg said. She stepped outside and bent to pick up a grocery bag from the concrete. There were several other grocery bags placed around it, but no one in sight.

"What is it?" Gabby asked. She ran out to help Meg bring the bags into the living room so they could close the door. Once she had carried all the bags in, the family gathered around them to look inside. Gabby cracked up when she saw a turkey in the bag, even bigger than the one they had just purchased. The other bags held all the fixings for a complete Thanksgiving dinner.

"You have got to be kidding me," Kim said. She shook her head. "Who would do such a thing?"

"Someone who wanted to help, I guess," Gabby said.

Her mom sighed. "Their heart was in the right place, I guess," she said. "But where are we going to put all this food? We just packed the refrigerator full."

Meg gasped. Her hand flew to her mouth, and tears glittered in her eyes.

"What's wrong?" Kim asked.

Meg shook her head. "I cannot believe this is happening to me," she said.

"What?" Gabby asked. She couldn't see that anything had happened to Meg that wasn't happening to all of them.

"This is so embarrassing," Meg said. "The whole town knows how poor we are now, don't they?"

"Oh Meg, don't be so dramatic," Kim said. "Someone was just being nice. One of the churches probably raised money to hand out Thanksgiving dinners to all the single moms in town, or maybe to all the families with lots of kids."

Meg shook her head. "No," she said. "Lily's mom did this. Her church group was looking for names of poor people in town they could help over the holidays. They didn't reach their fundraising goal, so they were only giving Thanksgiving dinners to the poorest people they could think of."

"I doubt we were among the poorest people they could think of," Kim said. "There are plenty of people who are worse off than we are."

"If Lily's mom thinks we're that poor, then everyone else in town probably does too," Gabby said. Lily's mom was one of the biggest gossips in town.

"We can't keep this," Meg said. "It's humiliating. I'm taking this turkey back to Lily's mom and throwing it right in her face."

"Now, now," Kim said. "We don't know for sure that Lily's mom had anything to do with this."

"Yes, we do," Meg said. "Who else could it be?" She kicked at a bag full of canned goods and then yelped and hopped on one foot.

Kim laughed. "There's no point hurting yourself over it," she said. "But, you're right. We can't keep all this food. We don't have a place to put it all. We should share it with someone who actually needs it."

"Like who?" Gabby asked. She tried to think of another poor family they could give the extra food to, but she was getting the idea that the other unemployed parents in town probably got plenty of money on their SNAP cards like they did.

"I don't know," Kim said. "Can you think of any single parents who work full-time and are supporting several kids by themselves? Or even married couples with kids living on just one income? Those are the people who really need help with food. I mean, unless they're high-powered executives. I bet there are lots of single-income families who make enough money to pay their bills but not enough to feed their family too. That was us before I lost my job."

For some reason, Jodie was the first person to pop into Gabby's head. She hated the idea of doing something nice for Jodie, but she also knew that her coworker fit the description her mother had just given. It would be sad if Jodie worked as hard as she did to feed other people's families at the restaurant without making enough money to feed her own family. Gabby had never considered that she and Jodie's families might have that much in common.

Gabby sighed. "I think I know someone," she said. "Let me call Steve and find out where she lives."

Steve refused to give up Jodie's address. "It wouldn't be professional," he said. "I can't just go around giving out my employees' addresses without their permission."

"But it's for a good cause," Gabby said.

"It sounds like it is," Steve said. "But I can't be held responsible if it were to turn out you had something evil in mind. You and Jodie don't exactly like each other, you know."

"Steve, really? You think I would go—I don't know—egg her house or something?"

"I doubt you would," Steve said. "But that's not the point."

"So, what is the point?"

"The point is, I can't give you her address," Steve said. "But I can do something else to help, if you'll let me. Why don't I run by your place to pick the stuff up, and then I'll get it to Jodie? She's not going to take too kindly to you showing up on her front porch with a charity dinner anyway, you know?"

Gabby hadn't thought of it that way, but Steve was probably right. Jodie would probably hate being treated like a charity case by a co-worker she didn't care for as much as Meg had hated being treated that way by her friend's gossipy mom. "What makes you think she'll be okay with a charity dinner from you?" Gabby asked.

"I'm her boss. I'll present it as a holiday bonus. It'll be cool."

Gabby nodded her head. Of course, Steve couldn't see her nodding through the phone. "That sounds okay then," she said.

"Great. I'll be over in a few minutes."

True to his word, Steve showed up at Gabby's front door just a few minutes later.

"Hey, Steve," Gabby's mom said. "Thanks for helping us out. There was no way we were going to fit a second turkey in our tiny fridge."

"It's no problem," Steve said. "Are you sure you don't want to keep any of the non-perishables? They might come in handy later."

"Nah," Gabby's mom said. "We have plenty of food. Jodie may as well have the full Thanksgiving meal if we're going to give her the turkey."

Gabby and Steve gathered up the bags of food that were still sitting on the living room floor.

Steve chuckled as he stood up with an armload of bags and shifted them around so he could carry them out to his car. "I wonder how many hands this stuff has passed through to get to Jodie," he said. "I bet most of the canned goods were donated by folks who were cleaning out all the almost-expired cans from their cupboards. My grandma used to get food deliveries from the church the last couple of years before she passed away, and half the time the canned goods were expired or about to expire by the time she got them."

"I guess that's all us poor people are worth," Meg said. She was still pouting over the whole town—or at least everyone at Lily's church—thinking of her as poor. "Why do people think we want their nasty old food from the backs of their pantries, anyway?"

"They mean well," Gabby's mom said. "But you know, if they really wanted to help, they could have paid our water bill or dropped off a bag of toiletries. Even a gas card would have been more helpful than a second turkey dinner."

Gabby opened the front door and stepped out onto the porch. Steve followed her outside and headed for his car.

"It's funny," Gabby's mom said. "Everyone thinks they know what's best for people in need, but no one ever bothers to ask them what they actually need. I wonder how much food and money goes to waste because of misplaced intentions?"

"I don't know," Meg said. "But I'm going to go call Lily and tell her that we donated the food they left us to an actual needy family since we didn't have room for more food in our refrigerator."

"I wouldn't," Kim said. "Don't draw any more attention to yourself, Meg. My mom always used to say, "Least said, fastest mended.""

"What's that supposed to mean?" Meg asked.

"It means," Gabby said. "The less you say about it, the sooner they'll forget it ever happened."

At work the next morning, Steve gathered his employees in the kitchen during a slow period. "Jodie," he said. "Can you do me a favor and look inside the freezer and tell us what you see?"

Jodie huffed as though she thought they were all about to get a lecture on proper freezer organization. She yanked the door open and stepped inside. "What the—what is this, Steve?"

Steve chuckled. "It's a holiday bonus," he said.

Jodie stepped out of the freezer with a frozen turkey dangling by its webbed plastic handle in each of her hands. She grinned at her co-workers for the first time Gabby could remember. "Would you look at this?" she said. "We're all going to eat well this Thanksgiving."

Where had the second turkey come from? Gabby's family had only provided Steve with one. The rest of her co-workers pushed past each other to look inside the freezer. They laughed and exclaimed over the bags of groceries that accompanied a stack of turkeys in the freezer. Steve winked at Gabby over the commotion. Her coworkers squeezed into the walk-in to see what else was inside.

"Look at all of this stuff." Jodie dug through a paper grocery sack with her name written on the side. "Potatoes, stuffing, green beans—hey, there's everything you need to make green bean casserole." She glanced up at Steve in wonder. "Did you do all this, Steve?"

Steve shrugged. "It's a write-off," he said.

"Yeah, sure." Jodie grinned. She returned her groceries to the freezer to take home with her after her shift. As she stepped back out of the freezer, she bumped a playful shoulder against Steve's and headed back to the dining room with a smile plastered on her face.

"Hey, Steve." Dana the hostess called out from inside the freezer. "I don't see Gabby's name on any of these bags. You didn't forget her, did you?"

Steve snapped his fingers. "That reminds me," he said. He shook an accusing finger in Gabby's direction. "It's a good thing you mentioned your mom already bought her turkey the other day, or your family would have ended up with two of them." He reached into his shirt pocket and pulled out a folded card. "Since your family is already covered for Thanksgiving, I just grabbed you a little something else. I hope that's okay."

Gabby took the card from Steve and opened it up. Inside was a gas card from the gas station that was attached to the restaurant. Her mouth dropped open when she saw the amount scrawled on the front. Fifty dollars would last them several weeks now that her mom wasn't driving to town every day for work. Tears filled Gabby's eyes. "Thanks, Steve," she said. She wanted to hug him. This was the last thing she had expected. Not only had Steve made it so Jodie would accept the turkey and fixings that Gabby's family had wanted to give her, but he had also paid the gift forward in a big way.

Steve took a step back as if he recognized that Gabby was about to hug him. He waved her off. "Don't worry about it," he said. "It's a write-off. Now, don't stand around here gawking all morning. Get back to work." His voice cracked on the last sentence. He spun around and headed into his office.

CHAPTER EIGHT

Mother Nature could be moody in Central Illinois, especially in December. The walk home from the bus stop a couple of weeks later was particularly cold, and none of Gabby's siblings seemed to be dressed for the weather. Gabby huddled into the lightweight jacket that had been too warm the afternoon before when she walked home in a fifty-degree heat wave. Ben was the only one who had paid attention to the weather report that morning on the news and wore his winter coat. It was just too bad his arms seemed to have grown three inches since the previous winter. His twig-like wrists poked out the end of his coat sleeves, and he had to tuck them under his armpits to protect the bare expanse of skin between the ends of his sleeves and the beginnings of his gloves.

The four of them practically ran down the street toward home. They stopped short, colliding with one another as they each realized that the woman getting out of their grouchy old neighbor's car in front of their apartment building was their mother.

Gabby's mom smiled at Mr. Dodd as he popped his trunk open. He reached inside and pulled out a giant package of toilet paper.

"Mother!" Meg's voice took an accusing tone. "What are you doing?" She stomped her feet toward their mother as though she might grab her by the ear and drag her into the house for a spanking.

Gabby's mom glanced up at her children. Her cheeks colored as if she had been caught in the act of some embarrassing wrong. "Oh good, you're here," she said. She took the package of toilet paper and held it out to Meg. "Take this inside, would you?" Then, she pointed at the boys. "You two help Mr. Dodd take his groceries inside his apartment."

Mr. Dodd frowned. "That won't be necessary," he said. "I don't want any kids in my house."

Gabby's mom shrugged. "Okay, then. Grab all the bags from this side of the trunk and take them inside our house."

Gabby's siblings glanced at one another in bewilderment, but they saved their questions until they'd carried the bags inside and closed the door on Mr. Dodd.

"Mom, what is this all about?" Meg asked. She hung her coat on its hook behind the door, and then turned to glare at Kim.

Gabby's mom plopped onto the couch and started to dig through the grocery bags they had piled up on the coffee table in front of her. She sorted out soap, shampoo, toothpaste, and all the other toiletries they had been running out of into a couple of bags together. Then she handed the bags to Meg. "Take these upstairs and put them away," she said.

"Mom!" Meg said. "Did Mr. Dodd buy all this stuff for you? Is he—are you dating him, now?"

Owen and Ben's heads whipped around so fast, Gabby thought their heads might fly off. Their eyes bulged in concern. Owen tripped over one of his shoelaces and almost toppled onto the coffee table.

Gabby burst out laughing. "Mom and Mr. Dodd?" she asked. "Really, Meg?"

Kim's smile told Gabby that she found the idea of her dating Mr. Dodd amusing as well. "No, I'm not dating Oscar," she said. "We were just helping each other out, that's all."

"Oscar?" Meg said. "You're calling him by his first name, now? Are you kidding me?"

Kim frowned. "That will be enough," she said. "Oscar is our neighbor, and he's a nice man. He doesn't like to be around other people very much, but that doesn't make him a bad person."

"So, he just bought us all this stuff to be nice?" Meg asked. "Really, mother? Are you that naïve?"

"Actually, no," Kim said. "He bought us all this stuff in exchange for me buying him groceries on my SNAP card at a discount." She rifled through another grocery bag and pulled out a thin, black plastic tube. Then, she held the tube out to Meg. "He bought you a new eyeliner just to be nice. I know yours ran out."

Meg's expression softened, and her eyes lit up at the sight of the eyeliner. But then, Kim closed her fist around it and pulled it back.

"I'm not so sure you deserve his kindness, though," Kim said. "You've been acting like a spoiled brat lately."

Meg stamped her foot like a toddler. Then, she seemed to think twice about what she was doing. "Fine," she said. "I'll just take these bags upstairs and put them away." She grabbed the bags her mom had set aside for her and took them up the stairs to put them away.

Kim set the eyeliner down on the table and turned to the other bags. She pulled out some paper towels and cleaning supplies and divvied them up among the rest of her children to be put away. Then, she settled back into the couch and put her feet up on the coffee table next to the last remaining shopping bag. After they had put everything away, Gabby and her siblings returned to the living room and hovered over their mom.

Kim sat with her head tilted against the back of the couch and her eyes closed. For a moment, Gabby thought she had fallen asleep. Trips to the grocery store did tend to wipe her out. Owen cleared his throat.

Kim opened her eyes. She eyed her children. "Yes?" she said.

"So, what's the deal with Mr. Dodd?" Owen asked.

Kim grinned. "Don't let your imaginations run away with you," she said. "It turns out that Mr. Dodd is a very nice old hermit, but neither of us have any interest in each other. At least not in the way you're thinking, Meg."

Meg's cheeks burned pink. She averted her eyes from her mother's, but her gaze quickly returned to the shiny eyeliner pen that lay in the middle of the coffee table. She tried to pretend like she didn't want that makeup more than anything else in the world in that moment, but she wasn't fooling anyone.

Kim groaned with the effort it took her to put her feet down and lean forward to take the grocery bag off the table. She also picked up the eyeliner and held it in her lap with the bag. "Sit down," she said. "You're making me nervous hovering over me like that."

Gabby and her siblings plopped onto the furniture around their mom and relaxed.

"I'm pretty sure Mr. Dodd is responsible for the turkey dinner that showed up on our front porch a while back," she said.

"Really?" Gabby asked. "It wasn't Lily's mom?"

Kim shook her head. "I don't think so. I ran into Oscar outside this afternoon, and he asked me how our turkey dinner was. He wouldn't admit that it was him, but he had this mischievous look in his eye."

"Mischievous?" Gabby said. "Mr. Dodd?"

Kim laughed. "I know he seems like a mean old crank, but he is actually pretty nice. When I told him we'd ended up with two turkey dinners, he seemed a little disappointed. But then he got to asking about our foodstamps—well, not asking, really— he seemed to know quite a bit about how it all works. Anyway, he said he figured if we had plenty of food, then we were probably hurting for toilet paper. The next thing I knew, he was offering to buy us some toilet paper and such in exchange for a discount on some groceries. Before I knew it, we were getting in his car and heading into town."

"That was nice of him," Gabby said. "I would have never pictured him buying us a turkey, though. He doesn't seem that friendly."

"I know, right?" Kim laughed. "Usually, when I say hi to him, he just grunts at me. But, he was in a talkative mood today. He told me he doesn't like a lot of noise and fuss, and he prefers to be left alone most of the time. Once in a while, he gets in a sociable mood, and I didn't seem too annoying, so he decided to spend his one sociable day of the year with me."

"Are you sure he wasn't hitting on you?" Meg asked.

Kim laughed again. "I'm sure," she said. "The man has zero interest in me in that way. He was adamant that I not take today's interaction as an invitation to try to converse with him every time I see him now. He likes to be left alone."

"Thank God," Meg said.

Gabby rolled her eyes. Sometimes she wished her mom would find a nice man to be with. Just not Mr. Dodd. "So, what's in the other bag?" she asked.

"Oh, that." Kim opened the bag and looked inside. Then, she glanced up at Gabby and winked. "These are early Christmas presents from Mr. Dodd."

"Presents?" Ben asked.

"It's not much," Kim said. "But, Mr. Dodd wanted to get you each a little something. The eyeliner is yours, Meg."

Meg snatched the eyeliner from the table before it could be yanked from her grasp again. Kim pulled several packs of Pokémon cards from the bag and handed them to the boys. They immediately tore into them and started comparing their cards. Kim handed Gabby a journal with a vintage map of the world on its cover. It had a matching pen attached by a gold cord.

"Wow, this is really nice," Gabby said. She flipped the journal open and fingered its gold-edged pages. "If I'd known what was going on, I would have thanked Mr. Dodd before he went in his house."

"Don't worry about it," Kim said. "He seemed embarrassed by my thank yous. In fact, he told me you kids better not come around trying to thank him either. He's serious about not wanting to be bothered. Today seemed to really wear him out."

"What a weirdo," Meg said.

"I don't know," Gabby said. "I think I understand how he feels. I like to be left alone sometimes, too. And being around other people wears me out sometimes." What she didn't say was that just because she liked to be alone most of the time, that didn't mean she didn't sometimes wish she had someone to hang out with in the rare times when she did feel like having company. Gabby wasn't totally friendless. She didn't eat her lunches alone. She had acquaintances at school that she chatted with. She just didn't feel the need to invite them into her personal space at home or spend every possible waking minute with them the way Meg did with her friends.

"It's not weird," Kim said. "It's just different. Some people like company more than others." She put her arm around Gabby as if she knew what she was thinking.

Gabby leaned into her mom's embrace. She was such a good mother when her illness and medications didn't get in the way.

The following weekend, Gabby came home from a long shift at the restaurant to find her mom with her head under the van's hood. An open toolbox sat on the ground next to her. This did not look good. Kim did most of their minor maintenance – windshield wiper fluid and air filters, that sort of thing – but she didn't know enough about car repairs to have any business doing anything under the hood that required more than a tool or two.

"What's wrong?" Gabby asked. She peered under the hood in an attempt to determine what her mom might be working on, but she really had no clue what she was looking at.

Kim threw a screwdriver into her toolbox with a clank. "I don't know," she said. "The damn thing won't start. I have no idea what I'm doing. I just kind of hoped I'd look under here and see something obvious. Maybe a loose hose or something that I could put back together." She pulled the prop rod from its hole in the hood before laying it back in its place and letting the hood drop with a bang.

This was bad. Really bad. Gabby was supposed to watch her siblings that evening so her mom could go get her Christmas shopping done and get some groceries in town. One of her mom's biggest fears had always been that something might happen to their van. There were no grocery stores in their small town and no public transportation that would take them into either of the two closest big towns fifteen miles down the interstate in either direction. A cab ride to town and back would probably cost near a hundred dollars. There was just no way to live in a small town like theirs without having your own vehicle.

"What are we going to do?" Gabby asked.

Kim picked up her scattered tools and tossed them back into the toolbox. She closed the lid and picked it up, shaking her head. "I don't know. I just don't know. I wish I knew someone who was good with cars that could come figure out what's wrong with it."

The two of them went inside, and Gabby started dinner while her mom sat at the kitchen table and flipped through the van's owner's manual in search of an easy answer to its problem.

Kim groaned and sighed the entire time before finally tossing the manual on the table. "I give up," she said. "I think I'm going to have to call a shop and probably have it towed."

"That sounds expensive," Gabby said. She poured the rice she'd just finished cooking into the pan of browned ground turkey next to it.

"It will be," Kim said. "It's going to probably eat up all the money I had stashed away for Christmas shopping."

Gabby frowned. Why couldn't the van have waited until after the holidays to break down?

Kim got up from the table and went to the refrigerator. She pulled out a package of chopped broccoli and cauliflower and a package of shredded cheddar. She tossed the veggies and cheese on the counter next to the stove and then dug through the cabinets for her microwave veggie steamer. Gabby opened the shredded cheese, sprinkled a handful on the ground turkey and rice, and followed it up with garlic salt and pepper. Then, she stirred the ingredients together.

"Is dinner ready yet?" Owen asked from the kitchen door.

"Almost," Kim said. "Come set the table, why don't you?"

Owen groaned but went to gather plates and silverware anyway.

"Meg! Ben!" Kim yelled.

Ben came into the kitchen by himself.

"Where's your sister?" Kim asked.

"Meg? She's in her room, I think."

"Go get her. Dinner's almost ready."

A few minutes later, Ben buttered slices of bread while Meg poured drinks for everyone. Once the kids had all filled their plates and settled around the table to eat, Kim took her plate and drink and headed out the kitchen door.

"Where are you going?" Gabby asked. It had been a while since their mom had sat down to eat dinner with them, and she had been looking forward to having a family dinner, despite worrying over the car.

"I'm going to go make some phone calls and see if I can find someone to look at the car before it gets any later," Kim said. "Make sure the kitchen gets cleaned up and the leftovers put away after dinner." She disappeared upstairs, and Gabby didn't see or hear from her for the rest of the night.

The van repairs did end up eating Kim's entire Christmas stash. And then some. The worst part was being without a vehicle for almost two whole weeks. The pantry and refrigerator emptied fast. Soon, the only food in the house was the expensive convenience items available at the truck stop and the other gas station across the street from the truck stop. There was a McDonald's and a Subway in town, in addition to the restaurant at the truck stop, but none of them took food stamps. For the first time in her life, Gabby was thankful for her free school lunches.

One morning, Gabby pretended to be sick and sent her siblings off to the bus stop without her. Once they were gone, she got dressed and went to the truck stop to pick up her paycheck. After a quick stop at the little bank downtown, she rode her bike to the next town south of them on Route 66. It was a long, cold ride, but there was a hot slice of Casey's pizza and a donut waiting for her at the end of it. After having her donut with a cappuccino to warm herself up, she hopped on her bike and headed across the highway to the Dollar General.

Gabby grabbed a bright yellow shopping cart and pushed it into the store. She walked up and down the aisles, looking for ideas. There were plenty of items they needed, which she would have gladly picked up, if she'd had a way to carry them home. If only she had one of those little carts that people often used to pull their toddlers around behind their bicycles. She could have stocked up on toilet paper and such. Instead, she grabbed a four-pack and then moved on to her real purpose in playing hooky to go shopping: Christmas gifts for her family.

She didn't want to spend a lot of money. She was, after all, still saving up for a car of her own. It would be nice to have a second vehicle to rely on when one broke down. But, she couldn't let her siblings wake up Christmas morning and find nothing under the tree. She was done having faith that something would just magically work out as her mom seemed to think it would.

Gabby picked out a couple of cheap toys for the boys and some makeup and a blouse for Meg. Then, she got her mom a scented candle and a bag of lavender-scented Epsom salts. The salts were heavy, but she knew they were good for her mom's aches and pains. She got a roll of tape but skipped the wrapping paper. There were free advertisers at the restaurant that she could wrap the presents in. Wrapping paper kind of seemed like a stupid waste of money at this point.

After she checked out, Gabby had to figure out the best way to carry her purchases home on her bike. She stuffed the empty backpack she'd brought along and put it on her back. Then, she hung the remaining shopping bags on her handlebars. When she pedaled her bike out onto Route 66, she realized she would be riding into the wind the entire way home. She tucked her chin into her chest to protect her face from the wind and steeled herself for the five-mile bike ride home.

CHAPTER NINE

B en and Owen shook Gabby and Meg awake early on Christmas morning. The floodlight that illuminated the parking lot behind their building still poked through the gap between their bedroom curtains. Gabby yawned and tried to roll away from Owen.

"It's four o'clock in the morning," Meg said. "Go away, morons."

"Santa came," Ben said. "Come on! You know we can't open our presents until everyone is up."

Gabby grinned, remembering how she had snuck downstairs the previous night after everyone had gone to bed to put her gifts under the tree. It was kind of fun playing Santa. She didn't even care if her brothers didn't realize the gifts were from her.

"Did Santa really come?" Meg asked. "Like, did you go downstairs and verify that there were actually presents under the tree?" She hadn't believed in Santa for several years, but she did still pretend for her little brothers.

"Yes, I did," Owen said. "Santa came, and there are presents under the tree to prove it."

"Of course Santa came," Ben said. "Why wouldn't he? We've all been good this year."

"I don't know," Meg said. "I've heard Santa doesn't like poor kids. I thought maybe he'd decide to skip over us this year."

"Meg!" Gabby sat up and swung her feet over the side of the bed. The floor was icy against her bare toes. She reached over to her nightstand and grabbed the threadbare socks she had taken off the night before. She couldn't stand to sleep with socks on. Once she had her socks on her feet, she got up. "Come on, Meg. Let's go see what Santa brought us."

The boys beamed at them and ran out the bedroom door.

"If 'Santa' actually came," Meg said, making air quotes with her fingers, "maybe he brought me a cell phone." Her eyes lit up at the idea of even that slim possibility, and she hopped out of her bed to follow her brothers downstairs.

Gabby met her mom outside the bathroom. Kim's skin was pale and ragged. She had dark circles under her eyes. "Morning," she mumbled. She grabbed the banister to steady herself.

"Are you okay?" Gabby asked.

Kim shook her head slowly. "I'm really hurting this morning," she said. She stared down the long flight of stairs. "Maybe we should have set the Christmas tree up in my room this year."

"We'll get you set up on the couch with your heat pad and some hot cocoa," Gabby said. "I'll bring you breakfast on the couch, and you won't have to move for the rest of the day."

Kim gave Gabby a wan smile. "Except to go to the bathroom," she said. "Someday, I want to have a house with my bedroom and a bathroom on the first floor so I don't have to manage stairs anymore."

"Come on, you guys!" Owen yelled up the stairs at them. "We want to open our presents!"

"I'll be right there," Gabby said. She needed to use the bathroom first. She ducked inside while her mom dragged herself downstairs, one painful step at a time.

When Gabby finally joined her family around their small, fake Christmas tree in the living room, she was surprised to find a few extra gifts underneath. When had her mom managed to go get presents? The holiday season had held up their van repairs, and they didn't expect to have their vehicle back until later that week.

"It's my turn to play Santa," Owen said. He had already picked through the gifts and arranged them into tiny piles, with two gifts in each pile. He checked each of the tags and handed a package to each person in the family. He started with the newspaper advertisers that Gabby had wrapped her gifts in.

Meg held up the blouse that Gabby had bought her. "Oh, this is cute," she said. Then she grabbed the tag that Gabby had forgotten to remove from the shirt's armpit. Meg wrinkled her nose in disgust. "Dollar General," she said.

"That's the only store I could get to." Gabby hissed at her.

Meg shrugged, balled the blouse up in her lap, and seemed to forget about it while she waited for her next gift.

"I could tell those were from you, Gabby," Owen said. "You're the only person who didn't get a present wrapped in newspaper."

Ben held up the toy handcuffs and sheriff's badge that he'd found inside his package. "Thanks, Gabby," he said. "I always wanted handcuffs."

"Yes, thank you," Kim said. "I can't wait to take a nice relaxing bath in these bath salts with my candle burning next to me."

Owen handed out the next round of presents. There was something for their mom in this round as well. "That's funny," Ben said. "Santa doesn't usually bring mom anything. I guess she's been extra good this year."

They all tore into their packages at once. Meg gasped as she unrolled the ugliest handmade scarf and lopsided gloves any of them had ever seen in their entire lives. "What the hell is this?" Meg asked.

"Meg, language," Kim said.

The boys cracked up laughing.

"Meg must have been extra bad this year," Owen said.

Gabby stared at the toy horse that she had opened. It was something she might have played with when she was Owen's age. Maybe. Was her mom losing her mind along with her body?

Meg threw the scarf down. "This is ridiculous," she said. "I want a cell phone."

Ben's package had a miniature remote-controlled drone inside, and Owen's had a warm new winter coat.

"Awesome!" Ben said.

"No fair," Owen said. "Why does Ben get a drone, and I just get a coat?"

Kim's face had grown even paler than before. Tears welled up in her eyes. "I—I—"

"It's okay, Mom," Gabby said. Her own throat was thick with the tears she refused to shed in front of her mom. She didn't want to make her feel even worse.

"No, it's not okay," Kim said. "I put our names on the list at one of the churches so we could be on their angel tree. It looks like some of the people who got our names thought we needed fun presents, and others thought we should have something practical."

"Apparently, they thought I was still ten," Gabby said. She tried to force a laugh so her mom would know she was trying to make light of the situation. But, she couldn't help feeling as though she had been punched in the stomach.

"So, Santa didn't come?" Owen asked.

"Why does Santa hate poor people?" Ben said. "It's not our fault. We didn't do anything wrong!" Tears began to stream down his face.

Kim leaned forward and grabbed her youngest son. He was small, but she still winced with the pain it caused her to drag his little body toward her to cuddle him into her lap. "I'm so sorry," she said. "I should have opened the presents and made sure everything was fair before I put them under the tree."

"This is stupid." Meg jumped to her feet, letting the presents in her lap tumble to the floor. She stomped upstairs. The whole house shook when she slammed her bedroom door.

Owen clenched his coat in his hands and stared at Ben's drone. "I don't know why you're crying," he said. "You got something you wanted for Christmas."

"So did you," Gabby said. "You've been wanting one of those foam dart guns forever." Besides, she had ridden her bike five miles each way in the freezing cold to get it for him.

"Gabby's right," Kim said. She patted Ben's leg. "It's not like we didn't get anything. Some people have even less than we do this morning. And I know Gabby worked hard to buy us all presents."

"I'll share my drone with you," Ben said.

"That's the spirit," Kim said. "And, Ben will end up with Owen's coat when he outgrows it anyway, so it will all be even in the end."

"You boys can have my horse, too," Gabby said. She handed her package to Owen and smiled.

Owen sniffled, but he smiled and took the horse. "I'm going to name him Cracker Jack," he said.

"We can take turns being sheriff," Ben said. "And, Cracker Jack can be our horse."

"Here, you be sheriff first," Owen said. He handed the horse to Ben. Then, he grabbed the drone. "You're going to have a hard time catching the bad guys on your horse when they try to escape in their drone!"

The boys were all smiles now as they laughed and tore the toys out of their packages. Soon, they were running around the house making up a whole game scenario as they went.

"Oh, the joys of having a rich imagination," Kim said. She struggled to pull herself up off the floor. Then, she moved to the couch and settled in at one end.

"Too bad Meg doesn't have any imagination left," Gabby said. She started to pick up the wrapping paper and toy packaging from the floor.

Kim laughed. "To be fair," she said. "It would take an awful lot of imagination to turn that ugly scarf and gloves into something worth having."

The two of them laughed. Meg's gift was atrocious. At least Gabby had gotten something the boys could enjoy. No one wanted what Meg got.

"You have to admit though," Gabby said. "Meg is kind of stuck up. I mean, she was fine with the blouse I got her until she saw where it came from."

"It's her age," Kim said.

Gabby rolled her eyes. She had been Meg's age not that long ago, and she didn't think she had ever acted that way.

"She probably spends a bit too much time with Lily and her mother, too," Kim said. "Lily's mom has always been one of the most stuck-up people I have ever known, and that sort of thing rubs off on impressionable children."

"But Lily's mom is such a 'good Christian woman,'" Gabby said, making air quotes with her fingers.

"Psht—whatever. That woman may do a lot of good in the community, but it has nothing to do with Christianity. She likes being in a position to lord over everyone else. She doesn't ever do anything nice for anyone without considering how it will make her look. She was like that even in middle school."

Gabby stepped into the kitchen and shoved the wrinkled wrapping paper into the recycling bin by the door. "So, why do you let Meg spend so much time over there, then?" she asked.

"Meg is entitled to choose her own friends. She needs to learn for herself what her friends are really like. And who knows? Maybe she's rubbing off on Lily as much as Lily is rubbing off on her."

"Gee, Mom. You sound like the good Christian woman in this situation, and you don't even go to church."

CHAPTER TEN

Winter seemed like it would never end that year. Gabby's mom kept inching the thermostat down, degree-by-degree, as the balance on her heat bill increased each month. By the end of March, it was freezing in their house all day every day. Kim seemed to spend every waking minute muttering over how she was going to get the bill paid before the winter energy moratorium was lifted. Come April first, their gas was going to be shut off if they didn't get that bill paid. When April came and went without the gas being shut off, it occurred to Gabby a few times to wonder how her mom had managed it. But then, she was so busy putting in extra hours at the diner and trying to keep up with her homework, the thought always slipped away from her before she got a chance to ask.

Things seemed to calm down a bit that summer as the family settled into their lowest austerity level yet. It was easy to forget about the things they had to do without as long as they continued to have so much food in the house. They had never eaten as well when their mom was working as they did now that she was receiving almost full food stamp benefits. Whenever the family went to Walmart together, they all got candy bars and sodas at the checkout. They'd never before had money for Kim to buy them treats of any kind, so they almost felt as though they were rich. Gabby was working full-time that summer, so she had extra money to buy the boys their game cards that they normally had to save up for with their own allowance and the occasional makeup for Meg. Even after paying for the gas that she kept in the van so they could get around when they needed to, she still had plenty left over to sock away toward her own car.

It all fell apart one blistering afternoon when Gabby came home from work to find a tow truck driver hitching the family van up to his truck. He stood by and watched as the lift dragged the front end of the vehicle up onto the back of his truck.

Gabby's hair had stuck to the sides of her face from the humid walk home. The thick air lifted her hair as she started to run toward her mom's van. "Wait!" she said. "What are you doing?"

The man sighed and averted his eyes in an obvious attempt to pretend like Gabby wasn't yelling at him. Gabby stopped a few feet from him and panted like a dog. A bead of sweat dripped down her cheek.

"Please," she said. "Don't take our van. It's the only way we have to get to the grocery store."

The tow truck driver shrugged. "Not my problem, kid," he said. The lift ground to a halt, and he walked around the truck to secure the van.

"Please!" Gabby was desperate. She had plans to go into town that afternoon to get groceries. "Why are you doing this?"

The man turned to face her and put his hands on his hips. "Look," he said. "You don't pay your car payments, you don't get to keep your car. It's as simple as that."

A movement at Gabby's mom's bedroom window caught her eye. Her mom was peeking outside, watching. She dropped the curtain closed when she realized Gabby had seen her. Good. Her mom would come out now and fix this. She had to. Gabby just needed to stall the guy a little while longer.

"There has to be something we can do," she said. "There has to be some misunderstanding. Let me get my mom so she can call and talk to the bank."

"Honey, I already talked to your mom," he said. "She came out to see what I was doing, and then she turned around and went back inside when I told her I was here to repo her van."

Gabby shook her head. She swallowed the words that were about to spill out of her mouth. Surely her mom was going to do something to stop this. Surely she wouldn't just allow this dirty truck guy to take away their only transportation, especially after she'd spent so much money to get it fixed just that winter.

"Loo—look," Gabby said. "You can't take our van. We need it. Surely there's some way you could give us a little more time."

The guy rolled his eyes and sighed.

"I don't do this for the fun of it, you know," he said. "You may find this hard to believe, but I have hungry kids at home too, and this is how I feed them. I don't pick out whose car to take. The banks send me their lists, and I go get the cars. That's how I get paid. That's how I make my car payments."

"Yeah, yeah, I get that," Gabby said. And she did, but it didn't really do much to help her family, did it? An image of the stack of twenty-dollar bills she had stashed in an old plastic container in the back of her closet popped into her head. "What if I could make a payment?" she asked. "I could go get you the money right now, and then you could come back next month if we don't have things settled by then."

"Honey, it doesn't work that way," the driver said. "You've got to work all that out with the bank. Once they tell me to get the car, the only way to stop it is on their say-so."

"But—but what would happen if the car wasn't here when you came to get it?" Gabby asked. "Please, I have the money. I can make the payment right now, and then my mom will get things caught up. I know she will. She just got a little behind paying off our winter heat bill."

The driver shook his head and stalked around to the driver's side of his truck. His hand was on the cab door handle. He was going to get in his truck and drag Gabby's family van away without a thought for what it would do to them.

"Please!" Gabby yelled. Tears flowed down her cheeks now, and she didn't try to stop them.

The tears seemed to help. The driver sighed. His shoulders drooped. He pulled his hand away from the door and headed back toward Gabby. "Look," he said. "For two hundred dollars, I can move your name to the bottom of the list and take my time getting back around here to you. That's the best I can do. If I give you any more time than that, I could lose my contract. But you'll have to talk to your bank and probably send them a bunch of money in the meantime. Are you going to be able to do that?"

Gabby nodded. She tried to look sure of herself, but she didn't know just how much money it would take to catch up the van payments. She'd been working full-time hours since school let out for summer, and she'd been saving most of her money toward her own car. Her stomach twisted at the thought of spending her own money to save her mom's van, but she didn't see that she had much choice.

"Are you sure about that?" the guy asked. "Because if you don't get your payments caught up, the bank is going to keep sending me out here until I take your van. There's no point to you giving me all your milk money now just so I can come back and take your van in a couple of weeks."

"I—I'm sure," Gabby said. "I have a job, and I've been saving my money."

"Uh-huh." The driver looked Gabby up and down with skepticism. "Well, go get your money," he said. "I ain't got all day."

Gabby breathed a sigh of relief. She dashed the tears from her eyes. "St—stay right here," she said. "Don't go anywhere. I'll be back, I promise."

"You got five minutes," he said. "And then I'm driving out of here with your van."

Gabby spun away from him and ran for the house. Once inside, her heart pounded along with her feet as she ran up the stairs. She peeked out the window at the top of the stairwell to make sure he hadn't taken the opportunity to drive away. He was still there, leaning against the shady side of his truck and picking at his fingernails. Gabby ran into her bedroom and went to her closet. It only took her a few seconds to grab the plastic container of money from the back. She didn't need to see it to feel exactly where it was.

"What are you doing?" Kim stood in the bedroom doorway. Dried tears had left paths down her cheeks, and her face was flushed.

"I'm paying the tow truck driver so we can keep our van." Gabby twisted the lid off the container and pulled out the roll of bills. She peeled off several twenties, counting them as she went.

"What? Why? That's not how it works. The bank said I would have to pay them directly over the phone to stop the repossession process."

Gabby recounted the money to make sure she had the right amount. The wheel of bills left inside the container seemed so thin now. She twisted the lid shut and stuck the container back in the closet. "This isn't going to stop the repossession process," she said. "I'm just paying the guy to hold off while we figure something out."

"Oh, Gabby. You're wasting your money. I've tried everything I can think of to come up with the money to catch the car payments up. It's a lost cause."

Gabby shook her head. "No," she said. "It can't be. How are you going to get to work when you find a new job without a car? It's not like there are any jobs out here in the middle of nowhere. You have to be able to drive into town."

"I'll find a way to work somehow," Kim said. "Things will work out somehow. They always do."

"Gah! Would you stop with that bullshit?" Gabby said. "These things aren't going to magically work themselves out just because you have faith in the universe. Sometimes, it takes money, too. If you're not going to do anything to fix this, then I will." She shoved past her mom and ran down the stairs. Hopefully the van would still be outside when she got there.

"Gabby, wait!" Her mom called after her one last time but didn't follow her outside.

Gabby breathed a sigh of relief when she found the tow truck driver still leaning against his truck. He was looking at his cell phone now, no doubt checking to see if her five minutes were almost up.

"Here it is," Gabby said. She shoved the roll of bills at him. "Two-hundred dollars, as promised. Now, can you please unhook our van?"

The man took the money from her and eyed it as if he thought she might be trying to pass off a roll of play money as the real thing. He flipped through the bills and counted them. Then, he held them to his nose and sniffed. He seemed satisfied the money was real and shoved the wad in his pocket. "You're not hiding all this money in your mattress, are you?"

Gabby shook her head. "No," she said. "I just got paid and haven't made it to the bank yet. That's all I got." It probably wasn't a good idea to let this stranger know she still had several hundred dollars more stashed around her bedroom.

"Uh-huh." The man narrowed his eyes at her. Then, he turned and began to pull the van down from the back of his tow truck. When he was done, he unhooked the chain and rolled it back onto his truck. Then he stepped back over to Gabby. "Get a bank account," he said. "You shouldn't be keeping all that money in the house. And, make sure you get that car loan caught up so I don't have to come back here again."

Gabby nodded her head. "I will," she said. "I promise. Thank you so much, sir."

The driver scowled. "Don't call me sir," he said. "I work for a living." Then, he stalked away and jumped up into his truck, slamming the door shut behind him.

Gabby held her breath until he disappeared around the corner. Then, she went to the van and touched her palm to the warm hood as if to reassure herself that the vehicle was still there. "Don't worry," she said. "I'll find a way to pay for you." She shoved away all thoughts of the car she had hoped to buy for herself. It was just going to have to wait.

CHAPTER ELEVEN

Gabby managed to save up quite a bit of money that summer, despite the huge bite the van loan had taken out of her savings. She probably had enough to go ahead and buy a car, but she wasn't sure she could afford the insurance yet. She worked as many hours as she could, and her mom was now keeping the van payments current since Gabby had gotten them caught up. They did without air conditioning that summer to keep their energy bills low, and the younger kids spent a lot of time at the library on the hottest days. At least they always had plenty of good food to eat.

School was only a few weeks in, and Gabby was starting to miss her big summer paychecks. She was still working as many hours as she could, but Steve had hired a new full-timer to take her day shifts since she was back in school. Gabby was also spending more money on gas than she wanted to, as Owen and his nemesis, Jamie, had gotten themselves suspended from the bus for two weeks. She was driving herself and her siblings to school until the suspension ended, and her mom never seemed to have any gas money to spare.

Gabby was calculating in her head the expenses she'd have to cover with her latest tiny paycheck one afternoon as she and her siblings arrived home from school. No matter how she ran the numbers, she kept coming up short. She was going to have to dip into her savings to pay Owen's wrestling fees. Her mom had told her that Owen would just have to sit out this year, but Gabby knew if he missed a year, he'd never get back into it. She herself had missed out on basketball in the sixth grade because of a money shortage and had never been able to make the team again after missing practices for an entire year. Meg had missed out on volleyball for similar reasons. It sucked that the poor kids seemed to her to need school sports the most, but they were the ones who were often left out when they couldn't come up with the resources to participate. Gabby was determined not to let that happen to Owen. He needed to be in sports more than any of them.

Ben, who had joined Owen at the middle school that year, was the first to get to the front door and see the notice flapping in the breeze. "Gabby!" he yelled. "Come here! Hurry!"

Gabby groaned. What now? She hitched her backpack onto her shoulder and quickened her steps. Her entire body went cold when she saw it. *Eviction,* stamped in red block letters across the top of a sheet of ordinary letter paper. She smacked her hand against the bottom of the flapping letter to hold it still so she could read it.

"Is that what I think it is?" Meg asked. She sniffled, her eyes welling with tears.

"What's eviction?" Owen asked.

"It means we have to move," Ben said. His voice was soft. He bit his lip and tried not to cry.

"Maybe not," Gabby said. "It says we have seven days to pay up or move out." Seven days. Two-thousand dollars. Her entire savings. Her breath caught in her chest. How could their mom let this happen? Gabby tore the notice off the door and glanced around. Hopefully none of their neighbors had seen it.

Meg burst into tears and shoved her way past the others to get inside. Gabby held the door for her brothers and then followed them in. She searched the house, but their mother was nowhere to be found. Where could she be? Had she overdosed on her meds and gone to the hospital? Maybe she had given up and abandoned them. Or, maybe she was at the truck stop knocking on sleeper doors, looking to make some money that way. Gabby had never wanted to believe that prostitution was something that could exist in her own small town, but she had seen too many made-up women disappear into the sleeper section of too many semi cabs to be able to ignore it. This was the first time it had ever occurred to her that such a thing might ever be an option for someone in her family. Her stomach roiled at the thought. No. Her mom would never do that. Would she?

Gabby sat at the kitchen table and stared out the window at their van where she had left it parked on the street. What if she had saved their vehicle just so they could live in it someday? She had enough savings to pay up the back rent, but her part-time paychecks weren't enough to pay future rent. She knew her mom's unemployment checks weren't going to last much longer.

The cordless phone, which sat on a stack of newspaper classified ads in front of Gabby rang. She started at the sound and grabbed for the handset. Maybe someone was calling her mom for a job interview. Several of the jobs ads in the newspaper were circled in red pen. At least her mom was trying.

"Hello?" Gabby said in her most adult voice.

The line was silent.

"Hello?"

An electronic voice came through the speaker. "This is Sally from your credit card company. Don't worry, there's not a problem with your card. We just—"

Gabby clicked the talk button to shut computerized Sally off. Sally was a regular caller. Gabby's mom always said she didn't have any credit cards, but if Sally were really from her credit card company, she would at least use the company's name when she called. They still got more phone calls from scammers than from debt collectors, and that was saying something at this point. Gabby stared at the phone in her hand. It was one of the bills that her mom had made sure she kept paying so she could get calls for job interviews. But those calls had been few and far between.

Gabby looked through the missed call list on the phone to see if there had been any legitimate phone calls. Maybe her mom had run out to a job interview and forgot to leave a note. But, there was nothing local. Just calls from states where they didn't know anyone. More scam phone calls. The scammers should be paying their phone bills since they called more than anyone else did.

An idea popped into Gabby's head just as she was about to drop the phone onto the table and go get ready for work. She turned the keypad toward her and stared at the numbers. Her heart fluttered in her chest, and her intestines clenched up. It was a bad idea. She knew it was. But what if it worked? She dialed the number before she could change her mind and held the phone to her ear. She tried to keep her breathing normal.

"Hello?" Her dad picked up on the first ring, as though he'd been sitting there all day just waiting for her to call. He sounded exactly the way she remembered. "Hello?" he said again.

"Daddy?" Gabby said. Her voice creaked out.

"Who's this?" he asked.

Gabby cleared her throat. "Dad, it's me," she said. "Gabby." Heat rushed to her cheeks. She hadn't talked to her dad in years.

There was a pause. "Gabby!" he said. "Hey, baby! You finally remembered you had a dad, huh?"

"Um—I guess so," she said. He seemed happy to hear from her. Maybe this wasn't such a bad idea after all.

"When are you going to come visit your old man, huh? I've missed you. You always were my favorite, you know?"

Gabby reminded herself that her father was full of it, even though it did feel good to hear him say she was his favorite. There wasn't any chance of her visiting him, and she knew for a fact that Meg had always been his number one. "Well," she said.

There was no point beating around the bush. Besides, she needed to hurry up so she wouldn't be late for work. Plus, she suddenly needed to use the restroom very, very bad. "The reason I'm calling is because we got an eviction notice today."

The line went silent, and Gabby thought for a moment that she'd lost the connection. But then, her father laughed.

"Oh, how the mighty have fallen," he said. "Your mom always did think she was better than me, but guess what? I'm not getting kicked out of my house right now, am I?" He laughed again as if he had forgotten that he was living rent-free in an apartment provided to him by the VA because of his fake disability.

Gabby's cheeks flushed. She was a traitor, telling her mom's business to the last person on earth she would want to know. But, she had to ask. "Dad, do you think you could help us get our rent paid up so we don't have to move?"

Gabby's dad laughed again. "Sorry, kid," he said. "I can't do that. But how about this? Why don't you just come live with me? I could use a little help around here."

Gabby could just imagine the kind of help her dad needed. She wasn't interested in moving in with him just so she could be his personal housemaid. Helping out around her mom's house was nothing compared to taking care of her father. He had been little more than a second full-time job for Kim for years before the courts had decided he shouldn't be around his children anymore.

"Dad, you know I can't do that," she said.

"Yeah, I know, Buttercup," he said. "But a man can always dream, can't he?"

Gabby tried to ignore the fact that he'd called her by the pet name he'd always used for Meg back when they all lived together. Did he even know who he was talking to?

"Look, Dad," she said. "We really need help. Mom has been sick, and—"

"You know, I wish I could," he said. "But isn't that what I pay child support for?"

Gabby jerked the phone away from her ear and stared at it. Her father may as well have slapped her. She put the handset back to her ear. "But, you don't pay child support," she said. "You haven't since you were in prison. Even then, it was just a couple of dollars a month that they took out of your prison pay." As if the four to twelve dollars a month they had gotten out of her father back then were enough to be of any help. Gabby knew her father owed her mom at least $50,000 in back child support. He got extra money from the VA for his "dependents" that he was supposed to be sending to her mom every month, but she had never seen a penny of that money.

Gabby's father just laughed at her. "Well, if I did give you money, I'd send it to the child support agency so they could apply it to my balance," he said.

"So, do that," Gabby said.

"Nah. You know, I'd love to help you, but I'm not paying for a bunch of kids that I don't ever get to see. How's that fair?"

"You helped bring us into the world," Gabby said. "Don't you think you should help take care of us?"

"I did help take care of you until your bitch-ass mother took you away from me. I'm the injured party here."

An image of Owen as a toddler flashed into Gabby's head. His arm was bent at an unnatural angle, and his face was twisted up in pain. "You think you're the injured party?" she asked in disbelief. What planet was her father living on? Had he completely lost touch with reality?

"Yes, I am," he said. "I did everything I could for you kids and your bitch-ass mom. And, she just took you all away from me for no reason at all. Now she has you calling me asking for money? Well, you can tell her to go fuck herself."

"Are you kidding me right now?" Gabby said. This was insane. Her father was completely insane. She knew he didn't have PTSD as he claimed. The worst place he'd ever been stationed in the military was Minot, North Dakota, and the "top secret missions" he claimed he'd been on so he could get on VA disability were complete fantasies. Did the VA not even check out his outrageous stories before throwing money at him? Although he might not have PTSD, Gabby had to admit, the man was absolutely, certifiably, insane. There was no other explanation.

"Look, Meg," he said. "It was nice to hear from you, but I got to go. Some of the guys are coming over later for poker, and I have to go pick up some beer."

"It's Gabby," she said. "Your oldest daughter. Remember me?"

"Yeah, yeah, sure. Bye now." *Click.*

Gabby slammed the phone down on the table.

"Don't break the phone," Meg said. "It's my only lifeline to the outside world." She picked the handset up and cradled it in her arms like a baby. "What was that all about, anyway?"

Gabby shook her head and rolled her eyes. "Your father," she said.

"You sound like Mom," Meg said. She took a seat across from Gabby. "He didn't call here, did he? He could go back to jail for that."

"No," Gabby said. "I called him."

"Why would you do that?" Meg curled her lip up in disgust.

"I just wanted to see if I could squeeze some money out of him to help out with the rent."

Meg laughed. "How did that work out for you?"

"It didn't."

"You're supposed to be the smart one," Meg said. "I thought you'd have him figured out by now."

"I was desperate," Gabby said. She got up and then shoved her chair in, banging it against the table. "I need to get to work. Someone in this family needs to be able to keep a job."

Meg huffed at her. "I will as soon as I turn fourteen and can get my worker's permit. That's only a few months away."

Gabby was taken aback. It hadn't occurred to her that her self-centered sister might have a plan of her own for helping the family. "Good for you," she said.

Meg gave her a snotty little grin. "I don't want to have to wear your ugly hand-me-downs forever," she said. She got up and went to the cupboard to dig through the piles of snack foods that threatened to spill out all over the kitchen every time they opened the cabinet doors.

Gabby glared at Meg's back. Her sister had way too much of their father in her. Gabby noticed the time on the clock that hung next to the cupboard. She needed to hurry up and get ready for work, or she would be late.

G abby, thank God you're here." On weeknights, Gabby worked the evening shift with Nina now that she was back in school. Nina's hair was coming out of the long, gray braid that hung down her back. Her plump cheeks were flushed, and her arms bowed under the weight of the heavy tray that she was carrying to a table in her section. "The new girl quit this morning, and it's been crazy busy this afternoon for some reason. Jodie refused to stay late and help out because she had to be home when her kids got home from school."

"So, you've been running the whole dining room since she left?" Gabby asked.

Nina blew a strand of loose hair out of her eyes. "Steve's trying to help," she said. "But you know how that is." Across the dining room, a customer waved to her.

"I'll just grab my apron," Gabby said.

"Hurry." Nina probably hadn't had a break since she came in for the lunch rush, and it showed.

Gabby rushed to the back and grabbed her apron from its hook on the wall next to Steve's office. She almost ran into Steve as he rushed out the door.

"Oh good, you're here," he said. "I've been trying to help Nina as much as I can, but I'm a terrible waiter."

Gabby smirked. No one could mess up taking a dinner order worse than Steve could. She wondered sometimes how he managed to keep their inventory orders straight. "I'm on my way out to help now."

"I don't know what I'm going to do," Steve said. "It's so hard to find good help. This last girl quit because it turned out waitressing was a lot harder than it looks. I mean, really? What was she expecting? I swear, Americans just don't want to work anymore."

Something clicked in Gabby's head, and she replied without giving it much thought. "I'll do it," she said. "Give me my full-time day shift back, and then you'll just need to replace my part-time hours. There are lots of teenagers around here wanting work after school."

Steve pulled back. "What? You can't. You have school."

"I'm a straight-A student," Gabby said. "I'll talk to my teachers. I'm sure they'll work with me. Just until you can find someone else."

Steve seemed to consider the offer. "It would be easier to find a high schooler to fill your evening hours than it is to find an adult willing to wait tables fulltime," he said. "And you're one of the best waitresses I've ever had. But, school. You have to stay in school, Gabby."

"I can handle school," Gabby said. "Don't worry about that. I really need the money, Steve. We got an eviction notice today. I need my full-time hours back so I can help with the rent. How am I supposed to keep going to school when I'm living on the street?"

Nina poked her head around the corner. "Gabby, can you get drinks for table twelve?"

"Coming!" Gabby wrapped her long apron strings around her back and tied them in front of her. "Please, Steve," she said. "I can be here for my old shift tomorrow. I'll just need to take my meal break a little early so I can go get Owen from school."

"Did he get suspended from the bus?"

Gabby nodded. She patted her apron pocket to make sure she had her pad and pen. Then, she stopped and looked at Steve, waiting for his answer.

"Gabby, table twelve is really thirsty!" Nina hollered at her through the hole in the wall where the orders went out from the kitchen.

"Let me think about it," Steve said. "Go get those drinks moving."

Gabby nodded and then headed out to the dining room to get to work.

CHAPTER TWELVE

Steve reworked the schedule so Gabby could work the weekends and have two days a week off to go to school. Nina didn't mind pretending to be Kim so she could call Gabby in sick at school three days a week. She was getting too old to handle the busy dining room by herself, and she really didn't care about Gabby's education one way or another. As long as it made her life easier. When Jodie found out what was going on, she just scowled at Gabby and told her she was an idiot. Gabby avoided Jodie's glowering face as much as possible for the hours when their shifts crossed.

Work carried on that way for several weeks before Nina called one morning and told Gabby that the school had said she needed a doctor's note to miss school from now on.

"What?" Gabby said. "Why? I'm keeping up with my homework, and my grades are fine. What difference does it make if I'm there every day?"

"School policy," Nina said. "I guess you can only miss a certain number of days before they start demanding a doctor's note."

"I'm off work today," Gabby said. "I'll go talk to the office when I get to school."

"I don't know why you even bother," Nina said. "You already got a good job. Waitressing maybe isn't the most glamorous work in the world, but it's honest work. What good does a high school diploma do for someone who's already working?"

College. That's what Gabby needed the diploma for. She didn't want to be a waitress for the rest of her life. She hadn't made up her mind what she did want to do, but this wasn't it. She just liked to go to school. She was good at it. She'd figure out what to do with the degree when the time came.

"I bet you could go take the GED today and pass it." Nina liked to talk, and it could be hard to get off the phone with her. "Besides, there are more college degrees in this country now than jobs that require college degrees. What's the point? My niece has a master's degree, and she's been hostessing at Chili's for four years now. She says there are too many people with her same qualifications who are all competing for the same couple of jobs that come available each year. School is a waste of time if you ask me. You young folks these days need to quit screwing around and just get to work already. You know, I was talking to—"

"I better get off here," Gabby said. "I need to get the kids to school. This is Owen's last week on bus suspension, and then I won't have to drive him anymore."

"What? Oh, okay. I'll see you at work this afternoon."

"See you then." Gabby hung up the phone. Owen was standing in the kitchen doorway with his shoes dangling from his hands. She sighed. She was so tired of tying his shoes for him, but she knew he had enough anxieties at school as it was without him obsessing over his shoes falling off his feet all day. At least he'd found both his shoes for once. "Come here," she said.

Owen grinned at her and brought his shoes to her. He sat in the chair next to Gabby and untied the knots from one shoe while she worked on the other one. He pulled one shoe and then the other one onto his feet and then put his feet up on the edge of Gabby's chair between her legs so she could tie them.

"You know, the only way you're going to learn to tie your shoes tight enough yourself is to practice," Gabby said.

Owen shrugged. "Are you going to school today?" he asked.

"I'm working," Gabby said. She tied his second shoe and then smacked his feet down off her chair so she could get up.

"I'll tell you what," Owen said. "You keep tying my shoes every morning, and I won't tell mom you're skipping school."

Ben poked Owen in the ribs as he passed them on his way to the cupboard to grab a snack to take to school with him.

"Don't touch me." Owen scowled at his little brother.

"I'll tell you what," Gabby said. "You don't tell on me for skipping, and I'll keep paying the rent so you can have a place to live."

Owen was about to talk back again, but Ben interrupted him. "Why don't you both stop it?" he asked. "We all know Owen isn't going to tell on you for skipping. And you're going to keep tying his shoes every day, even if he does. So, why argue about it?"

"How do you know I won't tell?" Owen asked.

"Yeah," Gabby said. "If I have to quit my job because of him, he's on his own with his shoes."

Ben shook his head. "You're both full of it," he said. "We always take care of each other, even when our parents don't."

"Mom takes care of us," Owen said. He was always quick to defend their mother, no matter what.

"She tries to," Ben said. "And Dad's irrelevant, but at least we have each other. Can we just go to school now? I don't want to be late."

Gabby shook her head. She wondered sometimes where Ben came from. He was way too wise for a sixth grader.

Gabby went straight to the high school office as soon as she had dropped her siblings off on the middle school side of their campus. The secretary sent her to wait outside the guidance counselor's office. She took a seat across from Joe Josephs, who had been struggling with school since the two of them were in kindergarten.

"Hey, Gabby Goat," Joe said. "Don't tell me you're in trouble, too." He'd gotten a lot taller, and his voice was deeper than it was in elementary school, but he still had that same lopsided grin and blond hair falling in his eyes that always seemed to keep their teachers from going too hard on him. Gabby hadn't had many classes with Joe since middle school when their elementary school merged with all the other schools in the district. At that point, she moved into advanced classes, and Joe squeaked by in the blow-off classes whenever he could get into them.

"You know me," Gabby said. "I've been skipping school left and right."

"Yeah, right," Joe said. He smiled at her again and shook his head.

Gabby had been a bit of a tomboy in elementary and used to play mostly with the boys. That all ended the day she turned the boys down for a game of football because she'd worn a skirt to school. That seemed to be the first time they realized she wasn't actually "one of them," and they hadn't asked her to play with them anymore after that. She'd spent most of middle school trying to fit in with the other girls without much luck and had given up altogether midway through freshman year.

Ms. Reddy stepped from her office and waved Joe in.

"Wish me luck," he whispered to Gabby.

"Good luck," she said.

Joe emerged a few minutes later with a scowl on his face. "Looks like I'm on the five-year track, Gabby Goat," he said.

"That sucks." Gabby couldn't imagine needing five years to finish high school. It was high school, for God's sake, not rocket surgery.

"Are you waiting to see me, Gabby?" Ms. Reddy asked. She stepped aside and motioned Gabby into her office.

Gabby wasn't sure where to start once she'd taken a seat across from Ms. Reddy at her desk. She stared at her tangled fingers in her lap and reminded herself to breathe.

"Is everything okay, Gabby?"

Tears pricked at the corners of Gabby's eyes, but she managed to hold them back. She cleared her throat. "Well," she said. She looked up and caught Ms. Reddy's eye for a half second before shifting her attention to the motivational poster over her shoulder. She took a deep breath. "The thing is, my mom lost her job recently, and we're having some money issues."

"I'm sorry to hear that," Ms. Reddy said.

"Yeah, well—the problem is that I've been working full-time to help out, and I can't come to school when I'm at work."

Ms. Reddy leaned forward on her elbows and steepled her fingers together.

"So, the office told us yesterday that I need a doctor's note to miss school from now on, but I can't get a doctor's note because I'm not sick. But, I'm keeping my grades up, so I don't see what the big deal is. As long as I'm learning what I need to and getting good grades, why do I need to be here every day?"

"I see," Ms. Reddy said. She folded her arms in front of her on the desk. "I'm sorry to hear about your mom's job. But, you're a teenager, and your job is to go to school. You shouldn't be working full-time during the school year. In fact, I hate to see a bright girl like you working at all when you should be focusing all of your attention on getting into a good college."

Gabby blinked her eyes hard. Had Ms. Reddy not heard a word that she had said? "But—but I have to," she said.

"Do you really have to, or do you just think you have to?" Ms. Reddy sat back in her chair. She gave Gabby a patronizing smile. "Gabby, I know you think you're practically a grownup, but you still have a lot to learn about life. I know you want to help your mom, but you should really leave these grownup worries to the grownups and concentrate on being a teenager. You need to be in school to do that."

"You don't understand," Gabby said. "We almost got evicted. We almost lost our car. Someone has to pay the rent so we can live."

"And, I'm sure your mother will figure all of that out. There are lots of resources available to help families like yours. Has your mom applied for government assistance?"

"Well yeah, but—"

"There you go," Ms. Reddy said.

"No," Gabby said. "You really don't understand. I have to work."

Ms. Reddy sighed. "No, Gabby. You don't understand. You have to go to school. It's the law. What do you think would happen if we allowed you to just come to school whenever you feel like it? Next thing you know, all the other kids would want to do the same thing. Not everyone can manage to keep their grades up without coming to class every day."

"But I'm not most kids—"

"You're right. You're not most kids. That's why I'm so surprised and disappointed to see you sitting across from me asking me to allow you to skip school several days a week."

Gabby balled up her fists in her lap. She'd always thought Ms. Reddy was cool when she was advising her on what classes she should take and helping her get into all the ones she wanted just because she had the grades to do whatever she wanted. It had never occurred to her that the guidance counselor might turn on her the second she needed real help.

Ms. Reddy stood up. "You should get to class," she said. "No more skipping. You're just going to have to tell your boss that school takes precedence."

Gabby was frozen to her seat. Of course, school should take precedence, in a perfect world. But her world was far from perfect. It wasn't about her boss. It was about keeping a roof over her head. She couldn't just let it go and allow her family to end up in the streets when there was something she could do to help out. "So—" she finally managed to get her mouth to work. "What happens if I keep missing school without a doctor's note?"

Ms. Reddy shook her head in disappointment. "You don't want to do that, Gabby," she said. "Eventually you'll be cited for truancy, and your mom could go to jail for not making you come to school. You don't want that, do you?"

This was crazy. This was not at all what Gabby had expected when she'd rehearsed the conversation in the van on her way to school that morning. She had really believed Ms. Reddy would want to help her. "This isn't fair," Gabby said. "And it doesn't make sense. My grades are fine. I need to work. I don't see why I can't do what I need to do to take care of my family."

"I'm sorry, Gabby. These are the rules. I don't make them. I just enforce them. I expect to see you here at school every day from now on unless you have a valid doctor's note."

"But, can't you bend the rules sometimes? I mean, these are special circumstances. It's not like I want to skip school. I like school."

"If I bent the rules for you, I'd have to bend the rules for everyone. You need to go to class now so you're not marked absent. I don't want you to be truant. You can't graduate if you're truant."

Going to class seemed pointless now. Gabby had to work. There was nothing Ms. Reddy could say – short of offering to pay her rent for her – that was going to change that. If Gabby was just going to end up getting her mom in trouble for missing classes for work, then what was the point? What was the point of going to all this trouble if she wasn't going to be allowed to graduate anyway? It was all so unfair. It wasn't as if she had asked for any of this. She just wanted life to go back to normal so she could focus on school and save her money to buy her own car instead of paying her family's bills. Gabby unfolded her frozen body from the chair.

"That's a good girl," Ms. Reddy said. "I know you'll make the right decisions from now on."

"I—I quit," Gabby said.

"What?"

"I quit school. I'm seventeen. I can do that now, can't I?"

"Don't be silly," Ms. Reddy said. "You're overreacting."

"No. I'm not overreacting." Gabby was sure she wasn't. She'd been living in this situation for months now, and she'd twisted her brain every which way she could think of to try to come up with a better way to deal with her family's problems. Regardless of what Ms. Reddy thought, she was doing what she had to do. It just wasn't fair that the school refused to work with her so she could continue to go to school and meet her family's needs at the same time.

Ms. Reddy put her hands on her hips and rolled her eyes. "This is ridiculous. You are the last person I would have ever expected to behave like this. You turn around and march yourself to class right now."

Gabby shook her head. "No," she said. "I quit. You won't listen to me or try to help me. I don't see what else I can do here."

"You have to get your mother's permission," Ms. Reddy said. She grinned as if she had thought of a genius way to get Gabby to do as she was told. "There's a form she has to sign giving you permission to drop out. If that form's not signed, you'll be considered truant, and then your mom can go to jail."

"Where do I get this form?" Gabby was surprised at how confident her voice sounded when she was trembling so much inside.

Ms. Reddy's jaw waggled in disbelief for a second. Then, she clipped her teeth together into a scowl and bent to open a file drawer in her desk. She flipped through a couple of folders and then pulled out a sheet of paper before slamming the drawer shut with a clang. Her fingers trembled as she extended the paper toward Gabby. "I'm giving you this sheet because I am required to provide it upon request," Ms. Reddy said.

Gabby reached for the sheet of paper, but Ms. Reddy pulled it back. "I don't expect to get this form back from you," she said. "I expect you'll think this over and realize what a gigantic mistake it would be for you to drop out."

Grabby snatched the form from Ms. Reddy's grip, tearing a tiny notch from the paper in the process.

"There's no way your mother is going to allow this," Ms. Reddy said.

"I don't see how my mom can keep me from doing anything now that I'm the one paying the bills," Gabby said.

Ms. Reddy's lips parted as though she couldn't get any more words to cross them. Gabby shook her head in disgust. She turned on her heel and stalked out of the office with her heart fluttering up a storm in her chest and her blood boiling in her veins. It wasn't fair. She shouldn't have to quit school. Tears began to stream down her face as she pushed through the school's outer doors and rushed toward the parking lot. It wasn't fair. It just wasn't fair.

Gabby crawled into bed when she got home and cried herself into a stupor that matched the one her mom lay in down the hall. She slept through lunch and woke up to her stomach growling, aching for food. She pushed herself up to the edge of the bed. The dropout form lay on her nightstand, slightly crumpled. Gabby sighed. Her head was foggy, and she didn't want to deal with this. But, she didn't know how long it would take the school to send the police after her mom once she stopped going to school. She got out of bed and went to find her.

Kim was sprawled out on the couch, staring at the television at an afternoon talk show. She startled when Gabby appeared in front of her. Gabby was certain her mom would have heard her coming down the stairs, but apparently, she was too zoned out to notice.

"Where did you come from?" Kim asked. "Have you been home all day?" She pushed herself up and reached for the remote control on the coffee table in front of her. She winced in pain at the movement.

"I need you to sign this form for me," Gabby said. "For school."

Kim took the form from her. "Are you in trouble?" she asked. She smiled at Gabby as if she had made a joke. Gabby had never been in trouble a day in her life.

Gabby sighed. "I need permission," she said. "Permission to drop out of school."

Kim laughed. "Oh, okay," she said. "Just grab me a pen, and I'll sign right off on that."

Gabby handed her the pen that she had grabbed from her nightstand and brought along with her.

Kim lay the form out on the table in front of her and bent to sign it. Her eyes passed over the form, and her hand hovered over the signature line. "Wait. What?" she said. "I thought you were kidding."

Gabby shook her head and held back her tears. She had to do this. Her mom had to let her. What would happen to them if she didn't keep working full-time?

Kim lay the pen on the table. "What is this about?" she asked. "And why on earth do you think I would ever allow you to drop out of school?"

Gabby plopped onto the couch next to her mom. She should have known Kim wasn't going to let this just happen. "I have to," she said. "I've missed too much school because of work, and they said they're going to arrest you if I miss any more."

"What now?" Kim pressed the power button on the remote control and shut the television off. "You're not making any sense. Start over from the beginning and tell me everything."

Gabby poured out the whole story, filling her mother in on every detail of her work and school life over the past few weeks as though her mother hadn't been around to witness any of it.

As she finished out the final details, it occurred to her that her mother really hadn't been there at all, at least not her mind. Her body was there, but her head seemed to have left the family some time ago.

Kim crumpled the form into a ball in her fist and held it there. "You're not dropping out of school," she said.

"What am I going to do, then?" Gabby asked. "What are we going to do? Ms. Reddy is no help at all. She hardly listened to a word I said to her."

"We'll go talk to her," Kim said. "Right now. We'll go figure this out. There has to be some way you can keep working and go to school at the same time. I don't want you to have to, but until I find another job——" She let the words hang in the air between them. What if she never found another job? "There has to be another option. I refuse to believe that you have to either quit your job or quit school."

Gabby shrugged. Maybe her mom was right. It didn't seem fair to her either. Maybe Ms. Reddy was just saying whatever she could to get Gabby to behave. Maybe there was something else that could be done if it was a parent asking instead of a student.

Kim shoved herself up from the couch and went to put her shoes on. Gabby wished she would change her clothes first, but she didn't say anything. Her mom had been gaining weight steadily since she'd lost her job and hadn't been able to fit into her jeans in some time. She refused to waste money buying clothes for herself until she had a job to wear them to, so a pair of old, stretched-out yoga pants and baggy t-shirt had become her standard uniform for all activities, from grocery shopping to sleeping.

Ms. Reddy seemed relieved to see Kim when they stepped into her office thirty minutes later. "Mrs. Gimble," she said. "I'm so happy you've come to talk to me. I hope we can get Gabby back on track today." She motioned them to the two chairs across the desk from hers.

"So, how bad is it?" Kim asked once she'd settled into her seat.

"Pardon me?"

"How many assignments has Gabby missed?"

Ms. Reddy tapped her fingers on her computer keyboard and pulled Gabby's gradebook up on the monitor. "Let's see," she said. "Some of the teachers are slow to post grades, so it's possible that not all of Gabby's missing assignments will show up in the gradebook yet."

"Well, let's start with the grades that have been posted and work our way out from there."

Ms. Reddy's cheeks turned pink. "Um—" she said. "Well, it looks like Gabby hasn't actually missed any assignments. At least none that have been posted so far."

"So, her grades have tanked, then?" Kim said. "How bad is her GPA? Is it going to keep her from getting into community college?"

"Well, no," Ms. Reddy said. "That's not the point. The point is that Gabby has missed too much school. She's about to be considered truant if she continues on her current course."

Kim tapped a finger to her chin in thought. "So, Gabby is still getting good grades?" she asked.

"Yes, but that doesn't change the fact that she's not coming to school. She needs to actually attend classes to graduate."

Kim sighed and folded her hands in her lap. "But, why?" she asked.

"Wh—what do you mean, why? That's just how it works."

"But why?" Kim asked. "I mean, I can understand why most kids need to attend school to be able to graduate. Most kids can't keep their grades up without having a teacher to actually teach them their lessons. But, Gabby is different. She's a special case. She's always had remarkable reading and comprehension skills. She's responsible and completes her work on time. She asks for help when she does need it. I don't see what the problem is."

"The problem is, we have rules here," Ms. Reddy said. "Not that—the fact that we have rules, that's not a problem, exactly. That's just the way it is. We have rules, and Gabby must follow them just like everyone else. It is simply not possible for her to continue missing school the way she has been without being cited for truancy."

"Even though her grades are perfect," Kim said.

"This isn't about her grades," Ms. Reddy said. "It's about attendance."

Gabby rolled her eyes. They weren't going to get anywhere with Ms. Reddy. She wished her mom would just sign the damned form already so they could go.

"What about the alternative school?" Kim said. "They go to school for what—three hours in the morning, right? Maybe they could be more flexible with Gabby's hours than you can."

Ms. Reddy shook her head as if that was the dumbest idea she'd heard all day. "Impossible," she said. "Gabby doesn't qualify for the alt-school. She hasn't been in any trouble."

"She's almost truant," Kim said.

"She hasn't been in any real trouble," Ms. Reddy said. "The alt-school is for the dangerous kids. The ones who have actual criminal records and are failing out of school. It's a last resort. It's not for kids like Gabby who could graduate if only they'd show up for class. I have students who are going to be here five, even six years who can't get into alt-school because they haven't been in any real trouble."

Gabby thought of Joe Josephs and wondered if he was one of the kids who would be able to graduate in four years instead of five, if only he was "bad enough" to qualify for alt-school. It didn't seem fair. She wondered how many kids simply dropped out and disappeared from the school district simply because they needed to get jobs and move on with their adult lives more than they needed to spend an extra year or two in high school.

"What are our other options?" Kim asked.

"There aren't any," Ms. Reddy said. "Gabby needs to start coming to school every day. That's all there is to it."

"There have to be other options," Kim said. "We're talking about my daughter's future here. She's a good student. You can't just wash your hands of her – or worse yet, make her life even harder than it already is – just because you refuse to be flexible."

"I can't be flexible. Like I told Gabby earlier, I don't make the rules. I just enforce them."

"But rules should be broken when they don't work. In this situation, the rules are pushing my daughter to drop out of school. Surely you don't think that's right."

"The rules aren't forcing your daughter to drop out of school. You are. Get a job, Mrs. Gimble, and take care of your family so your daughter doesn't have to."

Kim slumped back in her seat as though she had been slapped.

Gabby jumped to her feet. "You don't know my mom," she said. Her entire body shook with rage. She wanted to reach across the desk and grab Ms. Reddy by her smart hairdo and slam her head against the desk. "You don't know anything about us. My mom is trying to get another job, but it's not so easy when you don't have a college degree and connections and money like you probably had."

"Gabby, that's enough," Kim said.

Gabby growled and stormed from the office. She was so done with this school. She was never coming back here again. Never facing Ms. Reddy again. That woman had a lot of nerve treating her mother like she was some sort of loser after all she had been through and all she had sacrificed for her kids. It wasn't Gabby's mom's fault that she was the one who needed help now. Ms. Reddy had probably never had to do without anything in her whole spoiled rotten life. She seemed like the kind of woman who had always had everything handed to her.

The van vibrated with the bass from Gabby's favorite rock band as she waited for her mother to join her. She lay her head back against the passenger seat's head rest and let the music pour through her, shoving everything else away.

Gabby's eye's fluttered open at the sound of the driver's side door opening. Her mom climbed in and turned the music down before starting the van and backing out of her parking space. She pulled out of the lot and headed down the country road toward home without saying a word to Gabby.

Finally, Gabby couldn't stand the suspense any longer. "So, what happened?" she asked. "Am I officially a high school dropout now?"

Kim shook her head. "Nope," she said. "No child of mine is dropping out of high school. I won't allow it."

"Is she going to work with me then, so I can keep my job?"

Kim pursed her lips together in the beginning of a scowl. But then, she relaxed and smiled. "Oh, no. That bitch wasn't about to give an inch. She'd rather see you drop out of high school than bend even one rule to try to come up with a workaround for you."

Gabby threw her hands up in despair. "So what, then? Are you just going to let them put you in jail so I can keep skipping school?"

Kim laughed. She reached over and patted Gabby's knee. "I love you dear," she said. "But I'm not going to jail for you."

"Then what?"

"Homeschool."

"Homeschool?"

"Yep. Homeschool. I'm going to homeschool you, and you're going to get a high school diploma."

Gabby sat up in her seat and turned toward her mother. "But, how does that work?" she asked. "I mean, will it actually count? Will I be able to get into a good college with a homeschool diploma?"

"You can get into community college with a GED if it comes to that," Kim said.

Gabby sank back into her seat and crossed her arms. The fading rows of corn flickered by alongside the van. She had never wanted to consider community college. She wanted to go away to a four-year school and live in the dorms. She wanted to get away from all her responsibilities at home and just be a free college student with no one to worry about but herself. But, how could she go away to college if she was needed at home to work for her family's living? She sighed. It was a pipe dream. But, at least she could still go to college. At least she could keep working without having to become a loser high school dropout.

CHAPTER THIRTEEN

Good news, Nina," Gabby said. "I don't need you to call me in sick at school anymore." She leaned against the counter where they all tossed their purses and keys when they came in to work each day and watched Nina prepare to start her shift. The restaurant had been slow that morning, and they had a few minutes of quiet time before the lunch rush would start.

Nina tied her apron strings around her wide middle and patted her pocket to make sure she had her pen and pad. "Did you finally come to your senses and drop out?" she asked.

Jodie stepped around the corner then to grab her purse. She froze and crossed her arms instead. "Dropping out?" she asked. She tapped her toe against the tile floor. "You're dropping out of high school? What, are you pregnant?"

Gabby laughed. "No, I'm not pregnant," she said. As if. You had to have sex to get pregnant, and the only person who had ever showed any interest in her in that way was Ryan Greggs, the creepiest, too-tight jeans and cowboy boots-wearing slime ball she'd ever met. He asked at least two girls out every single class period in the hopes that he'd eventually wear one of them down. She grinned at the idea of not having to put up with his nonsense anymore. At school, they expected the girls to be nice and polite to guys like Ryan Greggs no matter how much he harassed them. As if his awkwardness excused the constant sexual harassment. If Gabby saw him outside of the school now, she could just tell him where to go and walk away.

"Then, why are you dropping out?" Jodie said. "Are you a complete fucking moron? What the fuck?" She grabbed her purse from the counter and fumbled around inside for a pack of cigarettes and a lighter.

Gabby was taken aback. Jodie's response to her dropping out of school seemed a little extreme for someone who barely tolerated her presence most days.

"I'm not dropping out," Gabby said. "I'm going to start homeschooling."

"Are there any waitresses in the house?" Steve called from the front. "Or, are we going to just have our customers serve themselves today?"

"Coming," Nina called. She headed out to the dining room.

Gabby poked her head around the corner and saw that Nina could handle the party of two that had just taken a seat in her section. She leaned back against the counter to enjoy a few more minutes of peace while she still could.

Jodie had a cigarette dangling from her mouth as if she might light it up right there in the restaurant. "Homeschool?" she said. "So what, are you going to turn into one of those loony religious freaks and start wearing prairie dresses?"

Gabby flushed. Why did Jodie have to treat her like a complete idiot? "No," she said. "I'm going to study the same subjects I did in school. I'll just do it on my own, and my mom will give me a diploma and make up high school transcripts for me to use when I apply for college."

Jodie's cigarette slipped from between her lips and twirled to the floor. "Shit," she said. She bent over to retrieve it. Then, she stood up and eyed Gabby suspiciously. "You can do that? I mean, you can just study on your own, and your mom can give you a high school diploma? And, that's legal?"

"Sure," Gabby said. "My mom and I went to the library yesterday afternoon and did a bunch of research. It's all totally legit. We have a plan all worked out, and the librarian is even going to help us get the textbooks we need."

Jodie chewed her bottom lip and narrowed her eyes at Gabby. She held her cigarette between her fingers and put it to her lips as if it were lit. Then, she seemed to realize it wasn't and dropped her hand to her side. "Do—do you think I could do that, too?" she asked.

"Do what?" Gabby asked.

"Homeschool," Jodie said. "Like you're doing. Do you think I could homeschool myself and get a diploma, too?"

"You don't have a diploma?" Gabby asked.

Jodie shook her head. "My dad kicked me out when I got pregnant," she said. "I had to quit school and go to work. I didn't know I could have homeschooled myself. I would have totally done that. Maybe I would have even gone to college, and then I wouldn't be stuck in this shit hole for the rest of my life."

"Well, I'm not homeschooling myself," Gabby said. "My mom is homeschooling me. I'm not sure if they would let you make up a diploma for yourself."

Jodie frowned, but then she lit up as an idea struck her. "Do you think your mom would homeschool me?" she asked. "I wouldn't need much help. I always did really good in school. She could just check to make sure I did my work and then sign off on the diploma."

"I don't know," Gabby said. "Why don't you just go get your GED? You don't need a diploma to get into community college."

Jodie shook her head. "I've tried. The GED classes are too much of a time commitment for me to be able to get to them without missing a bunch of work, and I can't afford to miss work. Besides, I want a high school diploma. Losers get GED's. It would be so cool if I could actually be able to say that I graduated from high school."

Gabby wasn't sure how getting a GED would make a person more of a loser than not having either a GED or diploma at all, but she wasn't about to tell Jodie that. This was the nicest Jodie had ever been to her and probably the most words they'd ever spoken to one another.

"Gabby!" Steve called. "Tables are filling up."

Jodie glanced at the cigarette in her hand. "Shit," she said. "I'd better go smoke this quick or I'm going to be a total bitch before the lunch rush even gets started. Talk to your mom, okay? Please? It would mean so much to me."

"Yeah, sure," Gabby said. "Okay."

Jodie grinned and headed for the back door to smoke her cigarette outside. Gabby shook her head as she hurried out to the dining room to get to work. It was weird for Jodie to be so nice to her. She was always a bitch—cigarettes or not. Would Jodie hold it against her if she wasn't able to help her out?

Gabby stopped by the library after work to see if the books she had requested had come in yet. She was tired but anxious to get started. Based on the plan she and her mom had worked out, she could work at her own pace and finish the school year way in advance of her classmates if she wanted to. Boy, did she want to! That would show Ms. Reddy!

Lynn, the library director, saw her coming and carried a handful of textbooks out from her office. "I thought I'd see you today," she said. She took the books to the circulation desk and began to check them out. "Most libraries don't carry textbooks, but I was able to find these on GlobalShare. I requested an extended due date on all of them, so you'll have the rest of the semester to study from them. Just make sure you get them back to us by the end of December."

"Thanks," Gabby said. "Hey, I have a question for you. A girl I work with was wondering if she could homeschool herself and get a diploma. She's an adult and doesn't have parents who could teach her. Do you think that's possible?"

Lynn frowned. "I don't know about that," she said. "Why doesn't she just go get her GED?"

"That's what I asked her, but she has her heart set on getting an actual diploma. Plus, she says the GED classes don't work with her schedule."

"I think for a diploma, she would need someone to sign off on her work," Lynn said. "I don't know. Homeschooling is really based on the honor system in a lot of ways. I mean, what's to stop a parent from giving their kid a diploma without ever teaching them anything? But at the same time—I don't know. I'll have to think about it. What if she just studied for the GED on her own?"

"How would she do that?" Gabby asked. "I mean, how do you find out what's on the test?"

"Well, let's take a look and see what we can find," Lynn said. She turned her computer monitor so she and Gabby could both see it and then pulled up an internet browser. She typed in a search term and glanced over the results. She chewed her bottom lip while clicking through to several different sites. She shook her head every time she came across an option that required signing up and paying for classes. Finally, she ran a search for GED study guides.

"It looks like there are a lot of different options for studying online," Lynn said. "Depending on how much money you want to spend. But you know, it occurs to me that the latest GED test materials are something that every library should have on hand as a matter of course. I don't know why I've never thought of this before. I'm going to put in an order for a couple of these books, and your friend can just check one out from the library. I really do think it would be in her best interest at this point to study for the GED rather than spending time on a diploma."

"I think you're right," Gabby said. "But she really has her heart set on getting an actual diploma. I hope she doesn't give up on it just because she can't do it the way she wants to."

"I'll tell you what," Lynn said. "Once the book comes in, you bring your friend by to talk to me. We can use the GED materials as a guide for her study plan, and I'll find out if I can sign off on an honorary diploma for her once she passes the official test. Then, she can have it both ways. A diploma from me may not count for getting into college, but it might give her the sense of accomplishment and recognition that she's looking for."

"I'll let her know," Gabby said. "Thanks so much for all of your help. I don't know what we would do without you."

"That's what I'm here for," Lynn said. "This is the community's tax dollars at work."

Just then, a pile of books dropped onto the counter next to Gabby. She startled at the noise and the sudden closeness of the male patron who had snuck up on her.

Gabby had known Will Clark since preschool, but she hadn't seen him around much since he dropped out of school the year before. Will grinned at her. "Did I scare you?" he asked.

Gabby rolled her eyes. The last place she expected to see Will Clark was at the library. He wasn't exactly the academic type. "You didn't scare me. You just startled me."

"Sorry," he said. He pushed his pile of books across the counter toward Lynn.

"All set?" Lynn asked.

"I think so," Will said. "This should keep me busy for a day or two."

"You're going to read all these books?" Gabby asked. She eyed the Hunter S. Thompson novel on top of the stack and tilted her head to the side to try to see what else he had, but his hand blocked her view.

Lynn took the stack of books and started to check them out for Will.

"Nah," Will said. "I'm going to put them under my pillow tonight and soak them in through my ears."

"Funny as always," Gabby said. "But, I guess that makes more sense. I never pictured you as someone who could read."

Will grinned at her. "I know, right? I mean, I'm a total loser. High school dropout and everything."

Gabby's cheeks flushed. That was exactly what she had thought of Will. He'd always been trouble in elementary school and never seemed to care that he was supposed to be there to learn. He refused to do his work and was always questioning their teachers. In middle school, he spent more time in detention and in-school suspension than he ever spent in class. Freshman year, he'd almost gotten himself arrested over a chemistry experiment gone wrong. It had been no surprise to her when she'd heard that he had dropped out.

"Maybe Will should join your homeschool," Lynn said. "He could probably teach you more than your mother or I can. This guy checks out more books than anyone else in town."

"What?" Gabby couldn't believe what she was hearing. Will Clark not only read books, but he read lots of books? More than anyone else in town?

Will shrugged. "Nah, I'm too stoopit for school," he said. "Just ask every teacher who's ever had the misfortune of having to try to teach me anything."

"You're anything but stupid," Lynn said. She pointed a finger at Will. "And you need to finish school, young man. At least get your GED. I'm ordering GED materials for one of Gabby's friend. I want you to use them, too."

"What for?" Will asked. "I don't need a formal education to get a good job. My uncle Eric made me a partner in his welding business. I bet I make more money now than any of my old teachers do, and I didn't have to take out a bunch of student loans to do it."

"Do it for your own self-edification," Lynn said. She slid his books across the counter toward him. "Heck, do it to prove all those teachers wrong."

One of Will's intense brown eyes glinted in the light from the florescent overhead bulbs at the mention of proving his old teachers were wrong about him. He picked his books up and turned to go. "I'll think about it," he said.

"You do that," Lynn called after him. "You know where to find me."

Will waved his hand in farewell without turning to look at them. He disappeared through the double doors at the front of the library.

"That's one kid who was sorely let down by the public school system," Lynn said.

"I went to school with him," Gabby said. "He was always a trouble maker. The teachers couldn't help it if he refused to follow the rules and learn."

Lynn shook her head. "It's a public system," she said. "It wasn't his responsibility to learn the way they wanted him to learn. It's their responsibility to figure out why their usual methods aren't working and find something that will work. A child doesn't fail at school. It's the school that fails the child. Until schools start to take responsibility for their role in that failure, they'll continue to leave smart kids like Will behind." She shook her head as if shaking her anger at the school system away and smiled up at Gabby. "I'll get down off my soapbox now. I'm sure you're excited to get started on your classes."

Gabby smiled. "I am," she said. "I'm especially excited to be able to work at my own pace. I feel like I've wasted so much time in class sitting around waiting for my classmates to catch on to stuff that I've already learned. It will be so nice to be able to learn a chapter and then move right on to the next one without having to sit through long, boring lectures that basically repeat everything I've just read."

"I know how you feel," Lynn said. "Some teachers don't know anything beyond what's in the textbook they're teaching from. They want you to memorize the facts, but they don't know how to analyze what the facts mean to us in real life. In my opinion, if a teacher doesn't have anything to add to what you've read, why do you need them?"

"Exactly," Gabby said. Lynn was quickly becoming one of her favorite adults ever. It was nice to have a grownup talk to her like she was a thinking human being capable of having ideas of her own.

A mom with three little boys in tow stepped up to the counter next to Gabby. Her kids started piling picture books and DVDs on the counter in front of Lynn.

"Well, hello there," Lynn said. "Did you find some good books to read today?"

Two of the boys shoved at each other as they climbed the little step stool in front of the counter so they could see Lynn better. "Hi, Miss Lynn," one of them said.

Gabby took up her stack of books. "I'll see you later," she said to Lynn. She was suddenly very tired and ready to go home and shower the restaurant odor out of her hair.

"Feel free to come here to study any time you need to," Lynn said. She was already busy checking out the other patron's materials.

"I will." Gabby left the library and headed home with her books. It was such a relief to have a plan and to know that college was still an option. Maybe things would work out somehow after all.

CHAPTER FOURTEEN

Gabby and Jodie soon fell into the habit of studying at the library in the evenings several days a week. Jodie would bring her three kids and help them pick out books and coloring pages to keep them busy while she studied. She would settle them into one of the restaurant-style booths that lined the wall along the Young Adult section of the library, and then she would slide into the next booth with Gabby. Once in a while, if the kids got too rambunctious, Lynn would offer to pop in a DVD in the meeting room if it wasn't being used.

"Thanks," Jodie said to Lynn one day when she seemed particularly frazzled after a long day of work. "I can't imagine being able to take my rowdy kids to an actual class and accomplish anything."

"I don't mind," Lynn said. "This isn't one of those big city libraries where everyone is expected to be silent at all times. I want kids to feel comfortable here so they'll keep coming back as they grow up."

"Well, it really means a lot to me," Jodie said. "I mean, I can't believe I'm actually back in school. I never thought I'd be able to do it, at least not until my kids are old enough for me to be able to leave them home alone."

Gabby was surprised at the emotion in Jodie's voice. She was learning that Jodie was not at all the person she had thought her to be. She was so good with her kids and was a completely different person with them than she had always been at work. She had even started to lighten up at the restaurant and had just that morning marveled over the fact that her customers seemed to be tipping better for some reason. Gabby hadn't wanted to tell her that it was probably because she had been much less of a bitch lately than usual. It was amazing how much gaining a sense of purpose could improve a person's personality.

Lynn headed back to her office then, and Gabby pulled out her psychology notebook to work on the questions at the end of the chapter she'd read the night before. Jodie opened the laptop she'd borrowed from the front desk to log in to her account on the GED website. They were each lost in their own studies when Will Clark suddenly slipped into the booth next to Gabby.

Gabby jumped. "Darn it, Will!" she said. "Do you have to sneak up on me like that?"

Will elbowed her arm playfully. "What are we learning today?" he asked.

"Psychology," Gabby said. She rotated her writing wrist to give it a stretch. It was sore from carrying heavy trays of food all day.

"Sht—" Jodie said. She glared across the top of the laptop at them. "I'm taking a practice test."

Will pulled two fingers across his lips as if he were closing a zipper. Then, he turned his fingers at the corner of his mouth as if he were turning a key in a lock and then tossed the invisible key away from him. Gabby shook her head and tried not to smile. She bent her head back over her work.

Will sat silently next to her while she and Jodie continued their studies. What did he want? Gabby kept glancing across the table at Jodie, who refused to be distracted by the uninvited guest at their table. A couple of times, Gabby felt Will lean into her. She thought he was trying to cop a feel, but when she glanced over at him, he seemed to be engrossed in reading her textbook over her shoulder.

Finally, Jodie finished her practice test. "Done," she said. "Now, can we help you with something?" She cocked her head to one side and raised a decidedly unamused eyebrow at Will.

"I'm thinking about joining your study group," Will said.

"Humph. I don't recall inviting you," Jodie said. "Gabby, did you invite him to join us?"

"It was Lynn's idea," Will said. "Actually, she won't stop hounding me about getting my GED every time I come in here. I reckon maybe I'll just take the test and get it over with so she'll leave me alone about it."

"So, go take the test, then," Jodie said. "Why are you bothering us about it?"

"How did you do on your practice test?" Will asked.

Jodie scowled. "Better than the last one," she said. "But not good enough yet."

"What are you getting stuck on?" Will asked.

"Stupid science. None of it makes a damn bit of sense to me," Jodie said. Her fingers wandered to the edge of her lips as if she was holding a cigarette. "And the study guide is so boring! How am I going to be a nurse someday if I can't make sense of a stupid high school science lesson?" Her eyes glistened with unshed tears.

Will reached for the giant, paperback GED study book at Jodie's elbow. "May I?" he asked.

"Knock yourself out," Jodie said. She sat back in her seat and crossed her arms in front of her. She sniffled and looked away from them as if she might break down into tears if she met their eyes.

Will flipped through the book to the science section. His eyes wandered over the pages as he turned them. "Damn, this is dry," he said. "Why do they have to take all the fun out of it?"

Jodie slapped her hands on the edge of the table and leaned in toward Will. "See?" she said. "It's so stupid. It's making me feel like a total idiot and a complete waste of time."

"You're not a waste of time," Will said. "This book is. Can I borrow a pen and paper?"

Gabby turned to a clean sheet in her notebook and slid it over in front of Will. He took her pen and began to scribble notes in the notebook. He went page-by-page through the science section of the GED book and wrote down a list of topics that it covered. Finally, he closed the book and slid it across the table to Jodie.

"Put that away for now," he said. "Forget about the book." He tore his list out of Gabby's notebook and handed it to Jodie. "Pick a subject from the list and look it up online. Find some interesting articles that talk about the subject in real life. Find out if there are any novels that touch on it. Heck, go on YouTube and find some videos about it. I guarantee there's someone out there who has found a way to make it more interesting than that stupid book does."

Jodie gave Will a wan smile. "Okay, you can join our homeschool," she said.

"I don't know," Gabby said. "Will's so smart, he could probably just take the GED test without studying. What does he need us for?" She wasn't sure how she felt about adding another person to their study sessions.

"Where's the fun in that?" Will asked.

Gabby shrugged. Was it supposed to be fun? She just wanted to finish high school so she could get to college and start her real life.

"It's like we're starting our own little high school right here in the library," Jodie said.

"High school for the do-it-yourselfer," Will said.

"DIY High!" Jodie laughed.

"That's cute," Gabby said. She looked at the clock by the circulation desk. The library would be closing soon, and she hadn't finished anywhere near as much work as she had planned to. She also needed to check out a novel to read for an English project she had in mind. "Let me out, Will," she said.

Will got up from the booth so Gabby could escape. Then, he sat back down and launched into a discussion on one of the topics he'd put on Jodie's science list. Jodie leaned in and listened in rapt attention. Who knew Will would turn out to be such an intellectual?

Gabby found the book she was looking for, and then she headed to the documentary section next to the movies. Will's earlier commentary had given her an idea about her English project. She flipped through the documentaries until she found one that looked relevant: *Joseph Campbell and the Power of Myth with Bill Moyers.* "As seen on PBS," the DVD case proclaimed. Gabby took the DVD and the book she'd picked out to the circulation desk. She wasn't sure the DVD would be any help, but it couldn't hurt anything to add a new dimension to her learning. She was already getting bored with reading her dry textbooks. She didn't miss all her teachers, but she did miss the ones who made learning about more than just what she read in her books.

Another librarian, Rose, was working the circulation desk when Gabby checked out. "Oh, this is a good one," she said. She handed the DVD back to Gabby. "Joseph Campbell is so fascinating. These interviews are more than twenty-five years old, but the concepts he discusses are timeless."

"Sounds interesting," Gabby said.

Rose handed her materials back to her. "Let me know if you need any recommendations for what to watch next. We have some really great documentaries that almost never get checked out."

"Thanks," Gabby said. She returned to the booth where Jodie was packing up her stuff.

Will had taken over Gabby's entire side of the booth. He sat with his back against the wall and his long legs stretched across the red vinyl seat. His battered leather work boots hung over the edge. "So, what are we studying next, teacher?" he asked Gabby. He swung his feet to the floor and patted the seat next to him.

Gabby slid into the booth but kept her distance from Will. "I thought you were the teacher," she said.

Will shook his head. "Nope. This is your school, your rules. I'm just here to learn."

Gabby grabbed Jodie's GED book just as she was about to pick it up and slide it into her bag. She passed the book over to Will. "Here you go," she said. "Everything you need to learn to pass the GED"

Will put his hand out to push the book away. "No thanks," he said. "I've made a mental list. I'll pick it up as I go in case I need to take the test someday. In the meantime, I think I'll go the diploma route like you are."

"My mom can't give you a diploma," Gabby said. Her mom had already completely disengaged from the entire process as soon as she'd seen that Gabby and Lynn had a plan in place. The first time Gabby had tried to "turn in" her math homework to her mom, Kim had waved her away and told her to just put it all in a folder and give it to her when she was done with the entire textbook. Gabby wasn't about to bother her mom to grade papers and hand out transcripts and diplomas to every dropout in town.

"That's fine," Will said. "I know how to use a computer. If I decide I need an actual diploma, I'll just go online and print one out."

Gabby rolled her eyes. "Good luck getting into college with that."

"I'm not going to college," Will said. "I'm already practically running my uncle's business by myself. I know everything I need to know for that. If I want to know anything else, I'll just come to the library and get a book on it."

"So, why do school with us at all, then?" Gabby asked.

"Hey, I need to go," Jodie said. "My kids have school in the morning. I'll see you at work tomorrow?"

"I'll be there," Gabby said.

"It was nice to meet you, Will," Jodie said. She threw her backpack over her shoulder and headed toward the meeting room to collect her kids.

"I don't know," Will said. "I guess I'm just bored, and studying with you sounds like a nice way to pass the time." He leaned in toward Gabby. The corner of his mouth cocked up in a shy grin. Was he hitting on her?

Gabby got up and started to collect her books and notebook and pens. "I'm not doing this for fun," she said. "Or to pass the time. I'd rather be at home watching TV or reading a book just because I want to and not because I need to do a project for English. I don't need any distractions." She swept her belongings into her backpack and zipped it up.

Will slid out of the booth beside her. "I won't distract you, I promise. I'll help. It will be fun, and we'll both be graduated from DIY High before we know it."

Gabby sighed. He wasn't going to take no for an answer, was he? "Fine," she said. "As long as you don't slow me down, you can study with us."

Will grinned. "Great," he said. "When do we meet next? What are we studying?"

"Jodie and I are meeting here after dinner Monday through Friday, so we'll be here around six or so tomorrow night. I guess you could start by picking out a novel to read and analyze for English. We're writing a five-page research paper on our novels."

"Five pages?" Will said. "Holy shit!"

Rose shushed him from the circulation desk. "There are children in here," she said.

"Sorry," Will said. He looked back to Gabby. "Five pages? Is that really necessary?"

Gabby gave Will a self-satisfied grin. "It turns out DIY High has two tracks for you to choose from," she said. "There's the GED track that Jodie is on, and then there's the AP college prep track that I'm on. You can feel free to study with Jodie if you like."

"That sounds like a challenge to me," Will said.

Gabby shrugged. "Maybe it is. Maybe it isn't."

"Challenge accepted," Will said.

The next week, Jodie showed up for class with a friend and several extra kids in tow. "This is my cousin Brittany," she said. "She's going to study for the GED with me."

Gabby met Will's eyes across the booth they'd commandeered for the evening. Then they both eyed the seven kids who were chattering around Jodie and Brittany and climbing all over the adjoining booths like a bunch of Mountain Dew-drunk monkeys.

"Uhhh—" was all Gabby could get out of her mouth. How in the world was anyone supposed to get any studying done with all these noisy kids hanging around?

"I know what you're thinking," Jodie said. "The kids might be a problem. But, we'll put them in the meeting room with a movie, and it'll be fine."

Gabby sighed. She wished she could believe it would be fine, but Jodie's kids had already started to try the librarians' patience on their own. Four more kids would be a disaster. They needed supervision to keep them from destroying the meeting room, and the librarians couldn't be expected to provide that kind of supervision on top of their other duties.

Just then, Lynn stepped around a nearby bookshelf and stopped short when she saw the group of kids that filled the space around the study booths. "Well, who do we have here?" she asked.

"This is my cousin Brittany," Jodie said. "She's going to study for the GED with me. And these extra kids are hers."

Lynn eyed the kids and frowned. "I was just coming over to tell you the meeting room is booked tonight," she said. "I was going to suggest that maybe you study at Jodie's house this time so the kids can be more—comfortable."

Jodie's face fell. "But, I don't have internet at my house," she said.

Lynn patted her arm. "The kids are welcome to go hang out in the children's section to read and color," she said. "But, they really do need to be supervised. It can get pretty wild over there with this many unsupervised children running around."

"Maybe this wasn't such a good idea after all," Brittany said. "I don't want to get in anyone's way. And she's right, my kids can turn into a bunch of monsters without someone watching them."

"Maybe our school needs to hire a child supervisor to keep the kids busy while we're in class," Will said.

"Are you going to pay for that?" Gabby asked.

Will shrugged.

"I would pay for it," Brittany said. "Or at least for my kids. I don't have a lot of money, but I'd be willing to pay someone a couple of dollars to keep my kids distracted while we study."

"But, who's going to do that?" Jodie asked. "Babysitters are expensive. Believe me, if I could afford one and also find someone who's free this time of day, I'd already be dropping my kids off with them on my way here every day."

Just then, Gabby caught sight of Meg wandering through the Young Adult section, browsing through the novels. "Meg!" she said. Everyone else's heads swiveled around in Meg's direction.

Meg scowled at her sister. "What?" she asked.

"Are you still interested in getting a job?" Gabby asked.

Meg's scowl loosened a notch. "Yeah, why?" She moved toward Gabby, glancing around at the gaggle of people who stood and eyed her in return. There weren't usually this many people in the library at any given time.

"This is my sister, Meg," Gabby said. "Meg, Jodie and Brittany are looking for someone to keep their kids occupied while we study."

Meg glanced around at the kids who had all stopped their clambering to examine their potential new babysitter.

"I know there are a lot of them," Jodie said. "But, we'll pay you. All you have to do is take them over to the kid's section and read to them or color with them. Just keep them quiet and out of everyone else's hair for an hour or two."

A slow smile played across Meg's mouth. She clamped it back with a shrewd glint in her eye. "I could maybe do that," she said. "For one dollar per kid per hour."

Jodie and Brittany looked at each other and smiled. They both seemed relieved that a solution had presented itself so easily—and so inexpensively.

"I think I can manage that," Jodie said.

"Works for me," Brittany said.

Lynn put her hands together and clapped twice. "Perfect," she said. "Meg, why don't you move the children over there and get them settled around the table by the easy readers? I just put out some new coloring pages for Halloween."

"I'm going to be a Pokémon for trick-or-treat this year." One of Brittany's little girls grabbed Meg's hand and began to fill her in on her Halloween plans as Meg herded the kids away from the study group.

"Brittany, is it?" Lynn asked. She extended a welcoming hand to the newest DIY High student.

Brittany nodded and shook Lynn's hand. "I'm Jodie's cousin," she said.

"Welcome," Lynn said. "Do you need to check out a laptop?"

"That would be great," Brittany said. "I don't have internet at home, though."

"That's fine," Lynn said. "We can probably PDF some of the study guides and worksheets for you to work on at home. Come with me. I'll get you a laptop to borrow, and then I'll show you what you need to do to get started on the GED website. I believe Jodie has our study guide checked out still."

"It's in my bag," Jodie said. "We'll be sharing it." She slid into the booth across from Will and Gabby and started to unpack her backpack.

A few days later, Joe Joseph's mom dragged him into the library to ask if he could be admitted to DIY High. "That damned high school would keep him enrolled 'til he's thirty if they could get away with it," she said. "It's ridiculous. One of my cousins has found Joe a plumbing apprenticeship that he can start right away at the end of the school year, but he needs to be done with high school first. Can you help us?"

Will grinned and winked across the table at Gabby. She sighed. DIY High was beginning to get out of hand. But, how could she deny Joe? It was pretty ridiculous for him to keep going to the high school for an extra year or two when he had a high paying job waiting for him at the end of this school year. It wasn't like he was ever going to go to college, so what was the purpose of him continuing to take classes that he obviously wasn't learning anything from?

"Sure," Gabby said. "Does he need a diploma, or will the GED work?"

Joe's mom waved her hand. "A GED will be fine. I don't understand why the high school can't have a GED program right at the school. We knew Joe wasn't going to be able to graduate on time by the end of his sophomore year. It would have made a hell of a lot more sense for him to start studying for his GED then instead of failing him in class after class to try to get him ready for a college that he's never going to go to."

Joe shuffled his feet and stared at the ground. His cheeks were bright red with embarrassment. His mom had a point, though. Joe didn't need college prep courses. He needed to get done with high school and learn a trade so he could support himself someday.

Soon, Joe had settled in with Jodie and Brittany a couple of booths away so they could focus on their GED lessons and Gabby and Will could discuss world history without the two groups distracting each other. Regardless of the distance, Gabby was distracted anyway. Occasionally, one of the GED students would call over to her to ask for help with something they were stuck on.

"Gabby!" Brittany called across the tops of the booths for the fourth time that evening.

Gabby sighed and began to turn toward Brittany to find out what she wanted.

"I'll get this one," Will said. "You keep working."

Gabby sighed and went back to the questions she was working on at the end of the chapter. But, she couldn't focus. Tears pricked her eyes at the thought of all the homework she needed to get done. Chances were, she would have to help Owen with his homework too when she got home. It wasn't fair. She hadn't signed up to be a teacher. Why did everyone always have to lean on her for help?

Will slid back into the booth. He started to grin at Gabby, but then he stilled. "Are you okay?" he asked.

Gabby nodded. She turned her head away and blinked back the tears.

"That bad, huh?" Will asked. He leaned back in his seat and gave Gabby a moment to collect herself.

Gabby took a deep breath. She was glad Will didn't push her to spill her guts or fawn over her and tell her everything was going to be okay. She hated pushy people. She hated to be told that everything was going to be okay, even when she knew deep down that it would be eventually. Probably. Somehow. She dried her eyes and turned a wan smile toward Will. "Sorry," she said.

Will shrugged. "Don't worry about it," he said. "You've got a lot going on right now, and there have been a lot of distractions today."

Gabby nodded. She took another deep breath and allowed herself to relax as she exhaled. "I just never thought that homeschooling might turn into me running a school," she said.

Will laughed. "I know, right? How did this happen?"

Gabby laughed, too. "This whole thing is so crazy," she said.

"It is, but it's good, too. Just think of how many people you're helping."

It was true. Gabby wasn't sure Will would stick around for an actual diploma, but the others seemed dedicated to finishing their GED's. Jodie had turned out to be a completely different person now that she had a plan for the future and goals that didn't revolve around waiting tables. "I guess so," she said.

"I got an idea." Will snapped his fingers and then pointed at Gabby. "Isn't the whole idea of homeschooling that you can plan your own classes instead of having some school dictate what you're learning?"

"I guess so," Gabby said. "I mean, there are core classes that have to be included, but I think I can learn whatever I want when it comes to electives."

"So, why are we sitting here studying these stupid textbooks and doing the same tired homework that we'd be doing if we were in school?" Will asked. "Why don't we make up our own elective classes? We could make up a course on managing a GED program and mentoring students. That way, you could get credit for the work you're doing mentoring your GED students and maybe take one less regular class."

"Would that really work?" Gabby asked. "I mean, is that something we could get actual high school credits for?"

"I don't see why not. We could do some research and write a final paper or something on it at the end of the course. Something that would show that we've learned from the experience."

"That does sound interesting," Gabby said. "A lot better than this stupid bio textbook, at any rate." She slammed the book shut. The truth was, she didn't feel like she was learning anything from it. She was memorizing terms and definitions that she didn't understand and would probably forget as soon as she moved on to the next chapter. What was the point?

"Exactly," Will said. "See, this is why I quit school. I mean, it's not that I think learning about biology is useless. It's just the way they teach it that sucks. They take all the fun out of it."

"To be fair, I don't think it's supposed to be fun," Gabby said. "I mean, I've had a few fun teachers. But, for the most part, it's not their job to entertain us. It's just something we all have to get through."

"But, they expect everyone to get through all the same things in all the same ways, as if we'll all be doing the same jobs when we're done. Or like we're all going to go to college instead of getting jobs right away after high school. It's stupid. Not everyone needs to go to college. A lot of us just need to become employable."

"I've always liked school," Gabby said. "But, I'm starting to see that the way it's set up just doesn't work for everyone."

"Yes!" Jodie shouted at the other table.

Brittany and Joe laughed, and Brittany gave Jodie a high five.

Gabby turned to see what the commotion was about.

Jodie blushed when she caught Gabby staring. "Sorry," she said. "I just passed the science pre-test. I think I'm ready to go take that part of the actual test."

"That's great," Gabby said. And it was. She was excited for Jodie and happy at the progress she was making. At this rate, Jodie probably wouldn't even be studying with them for much longer.

"I knew you'd get it," Will said. He gave Jodie a thumbs-up.

Jodie flushed with pride. "I can't believe I'm actually getting this done," she said. "Or that it's so easy! Everyone always made it sound like it would be so hard."

Gabby smiled, and all her previous anxieties began to melt away. She would never have thought that she would see Jodie so happy. Or so nice. The help she had given Jodie was actually improving her life. Maybe it wasn't such a bad thing that she had been roped into helping these people.

Jodie started to pack up her things. "I'm going to knock off early tonight," she said. "Let's take the kids out for ice cream to celebrate."

"Sounds good to me," Brittany said. "How about you, Joe?"

"I could eat," he said.

The three of them packed up and headed out with Jodie and Brittany's kids in tow. They invited Meg along, and she was actually smiling for once, too. She seemed to enjoy hanging out with the kids.

Gabby begged off the ice cream trip, and Will stayed behind with her. They wanted to throw together a lesson plan for their new course while they still had some momentum going.

Once again, Will seemed to already know a lot about the material they had decided to study. "You know our education system is designed to train most of us to do factory work, right?" he said. "The government wants us little people to be a bunch of conformists who don't expect anything better than a boring factory job and a regular paycheck. But where are those factory jobs now? Pht—gone! Our education system needs to catch up. It's like the schools think everyone is going to either go straight to college or straight to a factory."

"How do you know so much about all of this?" Gabby asked.

"I watch a lot of public television," Will said. "And the History Channel, stuff like that. And, I read a lot of books. The library has Smithsonian and National Geographic Magazines." He shrugged. "I don't mind learning the things I'm interested in—or the things I actually need to know for what I want to do in my life."

"I wish I knew what I wanted to do with my life," Gabby said. She closed the laptop she was borrowing from the library and began to gather her things together. The library would be closing soon, and she still had what she now thought of as her "third shift" of the day to get through once she got home if her mom wasn't up to getting her brothers through their homework, chores, and bedtime routines. Sometimes it felt like this would be her life until her brothers got old enough to take care of themselves more. Well, maybe not so much Ben, but Owen—

"Well, what are you interested in?" Will asked. "I mean, what do you like to do that you will probably always do whether you have to or not? My grandma says that's how you find out what you're supposed to do in life. That's kind of how I got into welding. I like to catch things on fire and melt stuff."

"I don't know," Gabby said. "I spend so much time working and taking care of my brothers, it doesn't seem like I have time for much else."

"We need to get you a hobby," Will said.

"Yeah, maybe," Gabby said. "Maybe I could learn to knit and make Christmas sweaters for poor kids for a living someday."

"Probably not much money in that."

"You think?" Gabby tapped her pencil against the table. Why couldn't she just go back to school and focus on being a student? "I want to go to school for a living."

Will scrunched his face up in disgust. "You mean, like be a professional student? You need rich parents to do that. And anyway, why? School is awful."

"Maybe for you," Gabby said. "But I've always loved it. Maybe not all the classes and not all the teachers, but for the most part, I actually enjoy going to school."

"What are your favorite subjects?"

"History and English."

"So, maybe you want to be a history teacher or an English professor?"

"I don't know," Gabby said. "Maybe." She hadn't really thought about being a college professor, but she'd discounted the idea of being a school teacher a long time ago. She loved her siblings, but if she was totally honest, she didn't really like kids in general. She couldn't imagine spending all her days with them for the rest of her life. But maybe teaching adults wouldn't be so bad. "It's something to think about," she said.

CHAPTER FIFTEEN

Gabby's mom was making dinner when she got home that night. It was about time she got up and cooked instead of laying around in bed waiting to be served like a queen. Gabby regretted the thought as soon as it crossed her mind. It wasn't her mom's fault she was sick. Her pain had gotten much worse lately, and most days she could barely function. Gabby had reminded her mom more than a couple of times that she needed to shower because she was starting to smell bad. The scent of desperation seemed to ooze out of her pores and was infiltrating the entire house. Even Gabby's brothers were quiet most of the time when they were at home.

Gabby deposited her books in her bedroom and then headed to the kitchen to see if she could sneak a taste of whatever her mom was cooking. She wasn't happy to find the kitchen in complete disarray once she got there. The sink was piled high with dirty pans and mixing bowls. Baking ingredients were strewn across the countertop by the sink. A pile of chocolate chips cookies sat on a plate in the middle of the table next to a couple of loaves of banana bread cooling on a rack. Owen was stirring a giant pot of chili on the stove, while Ben buttered a plate full of saltine crackers to go with the chili.

But their mom was the worst part. Kim paced the kitchen, wringing a damp towel in her hands. Beads of sweat mottled her brow. The boys grinned at Gabby as if they were enjoying spending time in the kitchen with their mom. They didn't seem to realize their mom wasn't looking so hot.

"What's going on here?" Gabby asked.

"Cooking school!" Owen said. "Mom's teaching us how to cook so we can start helping with dinner more."

"I hope she plans to teach you to clean up the mess afterward, too," Gabby said.

Owen's face dropped as he looked around and realized how big a mess they had made.

"We cooked, so you get to clean up afterward," Ben said.

Gabby put her hands on her hips and tapped her toe. "Okay, so from now on, when I cook, you two will clean up afterward."

"Nuh-uh!" Owen said.

"Yes-huh," Gabby said. "That sounds fair to me. I don't know why you two don't already help with the dishes. I work way too much to be the only person keeping house around here."

"I'm not big enough to wash dishes," Ben said.

"Would you just quit?" Kim's spat the words out like poison. Her hands trembled as she wound the towel around her fingers and squeezed it in a death grip. "Shut up. Just shut up!"

Gabby and her brothers stared at their mom. She had never told them to shut up before.

Just then, Meg stepped into the kitchen. "Mom, what the hell?" she said. "You sounded like Dad just now."

Kim's face fell. The dish towel slipped from her hands. "I—I'm sorry," she said. "I just—I can't right now." She fled the room and left her children staring after her.

"Good going," Owen said. "You made Mom cry."

"I don't care," Meg said. "She was being a bitch. Someone needed to say it."

"I'll go talk to her," Ben said. Gabby reached out and grabbed him before he could slip out of the room. Ben was an old soul, but he was only eleven. He didn't need to take responsibility for their mom's outburst.

"You stay here," Gabby said. "Straighten up in here and set the table so we can eat. I'll go talk to Mom."

"Why bother?" Meg asked. Her cheeks were red with anger. "She's in the wrong here. Let her come apologize to you. She shouldn't be talking to us that way. Lily's mom would never tell her to shut up."

Meg was right. Their mom was in the wrong. But, this wasn't like their mom. Something was off. More so than usual.

"Just let me go talk to her," Gabby said. She left the kitchen and headed upstairs to their mom's bedroom.

Kim was curled up in a ball amid a tangle of sheets and blankets. Her whole body trembled. Her skin was pale and damp with cold sweat.

Gabby put a knee on the edge of the mattress and leaned toward her mom. "Mom?" She tapped her shoulder.

Kim jumped. She rolled her head in Gabby's direction and stared at her. Her pupils were like giant holes in the middle of her eyeballs. She moaned.

"Are you okay?" Gabby asked.

Kim gasped. "No," she said. "I need my meds. It hurts so much."

"Where are they?" Gabby asked. "I'll get them for you."

Kim shook her head. Tears began to stream down her face. "I don't have any." She pounded a fist against the mattress. "Stupid fucking foot doctor," she said. "I went in today to get my refill, and he cut me off. I can't get a refill from my back doctor until tomorrow."

"What about your fibromyalgia doctor?" Gabby asked. This was the first she'd heard of her mom getting drugs from more than one doctor.

Kim's bottom lip trembled. "I'm not seeing that bitch anymore. She won't do crap for me. I may as well take Tylenol as to bother with the meds she offered me."

Gabby swallowed past the growing lump in her throat. "Did you try taking some Tylenol?" she asked. "Or ibuprofen or something? Just to get you through until tomorrow? Maybe a hot bath would help with the pain."

Kim shot up in the bed. "I need my meds," she said. "This is ridiculous. Christ, this is why people turn to heroin." She wrapped her arms around her knees and began to rock back and forth. "What the hell am I supposed to do when I hurt this bad and the doctors refuse to give me what I need?"

"Heroin? Really?" Gabby stood up. Her mom was a mess. A disaster, really. This was more than just fibromyalgia. This was something much worse.

"Oh, don't look at me like that. I'm not going to do heroin. I wouldn't even know where to get something like that."

Gabby's mom's words were like a punch to her gut. Would her mom start doing heroin if she did know where to get it?

Kim groaned again and rolled out of the bed holding her stomach. She brushed past Gabby and ran for the bathroom. Gabby followed her. She wasn't done yet. She needed to know if her mom was turning into a drug addict. She was afraid she already knew the answer to that question. Meg had been trying to tell her this for a while, but she didn't want to believe it.

Kim threw the toilet lid open with a clank and leaned over the seat while she vomited. Once she had emptied the contents of her stomach, she sank back on her behind and leaned against the open door. She struggled to catch her breath, and her entire body shook.

"Mom, I think you need to go to the hospital."

Kim waved a hand at Gabby in dismissal. "The ER won't give me anything either. I tried that already.

"That's not what I meant," Gabby said. "I think you're going through withdrawal. You need help."

"Withdrawal?" Kim shook her head. "No. I'm not addicted. I'm just in a lot of pain. I need my meds."

"I think you are addicted. You need to stop taking these pills."

Kim struggled to her feet. She pointed a finger at Gabby. She swayed with the effort of holding herself upright. "I am not an addict," she said. "I am sick. I need those pills for the pain."

Gabby straightened her back and leaned toward her mom. "If that's true, then why won't your fibro doctor give you a prescription? Why are you going to all these other doctors?"

"I have plantar fasciitis," Kim said. "It's really painful. My feet hurt all the time. And my back is all fucked up from your dad shoving me down an escalator when I was eight months pregnant with you. So, don't you stand there and judge me. I am not an addict."

"I lived with Dad long enough to know what an addict looks like," Gabby said.

Her mom's hand shot out and slapped Gabby across the cheek.

Gabby's head whipped back. She blinked, shocked that her mom had hit her. She raised her hand to her cheek and rubbed her fingertips across the tingling hot skin her mother's hard palm had left in its wake. She shook her head in slow disappointment. "Exactly," she said. She spun away from her mom and ran down the stairs, her feet pounding against each step. She needed to get out of the house for a while and away from her mom. Away from the responsibilities of parenting three kids and an adult who shouldn't be her responsibility.

"Gabby!" Kim yelled. "Gabby, wait! I'm sorry. Please!"

CHAPTER SIXTEEN

Kim was blissed out on the couch when Gabby got home from work the next day. Her eyes were glazed over, and she didn't seem to be paying attention to the divorce court show that was blaring from the television.

"Looks like you got your refill today," Gabby said. She didn't try to hide the sarcasm in her voice. She was done tiptoeing around her "sick mom."

"Not that it's any of your business," Kim said. "But I did. My back doctor was happy to write me another script. He understands how much pain I'm in."

"Just because you're in pain, that doesn't mean you're not addicted to the drugs he's giving you," Gabby said.

Kim scowled. "I have a prescription, okay? The doctor wouldn't give me one if I didn't need it. I think he knows a little bit more about it than you do."

"Whatever," Gabby said. "I need to get to study group." She left her mom lolling on the couch and knew that it would be up to her to get dinner for everyone when she returned later that night. It wasn't fair. Her mom was home all day. The least she could do was make dinner. The very least.

Will was waiting outside the library for her when she got there. He leaned against the brick building with one leg crossed over the other. He was really quite handsome. Gabby was surprised at herself for having such a thought. She used to think Will was a total loser and would never have considered him in such a way before. But he was so very smart and an all-around nice guy. Plus, he seemed like an adult already compared to the other boys their age.

Jodie and Brittany pulled up in Brittany's mini-van just then, and their kids immediately spilled out. Gabby wondered if any of them had been buckled in or if the van even had enough seatbelts for all of them.

"Hey, hey!" Brittany said. "Guess what! I took the reading section of the GED this morning and aced it!" She advanced on Gabby with one hand in the air for a high-five.

Gabby slapped Brittany's hand. "That's awesome," she said.

"Congrats," Will said. He gave Brittany a high-five as well.

"We're going out for ice cream!" One of Brittany's little girls grinned up at Gabby, showing off her missing front teeth.

Brittany's face flushed. "I hope you don't mind," she said. "We're going to take a break from studying tonight and celebrate."

"We're making it a tradition," Jodie said. "Each time one of us passes a section of the test, we're going to take our kids out to celebrate so they can see how important it is."

"That sounds like a good enough reason for skipping class to me," Gabby said.

"Actually—" Will touched Gabby's elbow with his fingertips. "The reason I waited outside for you today was because I wondered if you could come over to my house. I want to show you something."

"I bet you do," Jodie said. She grinned and winked at Gabby. Jodie had been giving her a hard time about Will at work, telling her it was only a matter of time before the boy asked her out.

Will's ears turned bright red. "Something educational," he said.

"You mean like sex ed?" Brittany whispered so her kids wouldn't hear her.

"No, not sex ed," Will said. "Sheesh, Brittany get your mind out of the gutter."

"Brittany lives in the gutter," Jodie said. She and her cousin cackled. They were having a bit too much fun at Gabby and Will's expense.

Will shook his head and rolled his eyes. He turned away from Jodie and Brittany to cut them out of the conversation. "I'm being serious," he said. "You can bring your brothers too, if you want. In fact, you should bring them. I bet they'd like it."

"Um—okay," Gabby said. She couldn't imagine what Will might have to show her and her brothers at his house that could be so interesting.

"Great," Will said. "Are your brothers at home now? We can swing by and get them."

Gabby pictured her mom sprawled out on the couch stoned out of her mind and thought it might be a good idea to get the boys out of the house for a while. "Okay, let's do it," she said.

After they had said their goodbyes, Gabby climbed into the passenger seat of Will's beat-up pickup truck. She was surprised to find the interior was immaculate despite its apparent age. The bench seat was clothed in a clean, denim seat cover, and the dashboard shined around the cracks in the vinyl. The floor mats also seemed brand new. Apparently, Will was a neat freak.

Will hopped in the driver's seat and started the truck with a roar. Gabby started at the noise.

"Diesel engine." Will grinned at her. "That's why it's so loud."

Gabby pointed Will in the direction of her apartment building. He waited in the truck while she went inside to collect her brothers. Meg had run off to Lily's house as soon as she found out she didn't need to babysit Jodie and Brittany's kids that evening. Their mom barely registered their exit as they clambered out the front door. Ben and Owen crowded into Will's truck between him and Gabby.

Gabby and her brothers soon found themselves watching in awe as Will melted chunks of metal in a special furnace in his uncle's workshop. He sounded like a teacher as he explained each step of the process, first loading the crucible with metal and then adjusting the gas and air flow to bring the furnace to maximum heat. His voice was muffled through the protective helmet he wore, but the boys hung on his every word. Gabby had to keep pulling them back so they didn't get too close to the fire.

Once the molten metal had reached the right temperature for pouring, Will lifted the vat from the furnace and moved it onto a block where he skimmed the slag from the top. He dumped the slag into a box of sand and then stirred the metal again.

"It's almost ready," he said.

"What are we going to do with it?" Owen asked.

"You'll see," Will said. "I'm trying an experiment that I saw on a YouTube video. I really hope it works."

"Even if it doesn't, just watching you melt metal like that is pretty cool," Gabby said. She had never known anyone who could do something like that. It looked dangerous. She was glad Will had provided them all with protective gear in case the melted metal splattered them.

Soon, the metal was ready. Will picked up the vat and moved toward the door. "Follow me," he said. "But stay a few feet behind me so we're not tripping on each other."

Will led them into the back yard of his grandma's old farmhouse that sat across the driveway from the workshop. The screen door at the back of the house banged shut, and an older lady with short-cropped silver hair practically hopped down the back steps.

"You finally going to take care of that damned ant hill?" the woman asked. She wiped dish soap from her hands onto her jeans and hurried to catch up with them.

Will nodded at her and grinned.

"Well, it's about time," she said. She ran ahead of Will to a gigantic ant hill at the back of the yard. The ant hill had a large, chicken wire cage around it as if to protect it.

"This is Grandma Beth," Will told Gabby.

"How do?" Grandma Beth nodded at Gabby and the boys. She hurried to remove the wire cage from the ant hill and tossed it aside.

"Careful," Will said. "Don't knock it over on me now."

"I'm not going to knock it over," Grandma Beth said. "You just be careful with that hot metal. I don't want to be held responsible if one of these kids gets hurt."

Will rolled his eyes at his grandma. They seemed to be the bickering sort. Gabby puzzled over what the two of them were doing. What could an ant hill possibly have to do with the melted metal Will had brought outside?

Will brought the vat of molten metal to the edge of the ant hill and stopped to lecture the boys on what he was doing now. "What do you boys think will happen if I pour this into the top of the ant hill?" he asked.

"Destroy it!" Owen grinned in anticipation of the destruction.

"Will the sand melt into glass from the hot metal?" Ben asked.

"Good question," Will said. "I never thought of that. I'm not sure how much of the ant hill is sand, though. I guess we'll find out, won't we?"

Owen clapped his hands in excitement. Ben's eyes gleamed. Gabby hadn't seen either of them this excited in a long time. Will located an opening in the ant hill near its top and began to pour the dripping metal into it.

"Do you know what the inside of an ant hill looks like?" He asked Owen.

"Lots of tunnels," Owen said. "Like on that bug movie we watched a while back."

Will nodded his head. A bead of sweat rolled down his cheek as he continued to pour the metal into the hill. Once the last of the metal had poured inside, he set the empty vat aside. "If I did it right," he said. "The metal should have filled all of the tunnels. Once it's hardened, we'll be able to pull it out of the dirt and see what the inside of the ant hill looked like." He took his protective leather gloves off and then shoved the plastic shield that covered his face up out of his way.

Grandma Beth shook her head. "I don't know where you get your ideas sometimes," she said. "But it does sound pretty neat."

"Grandma, this is Gabby, Owen, and Ben."

Grandma Beth shook Gabby's hand. "It's nice to meet you finally," she said. "Will can't stop talking about you and your school. I'll be relieved to see him finally graduate."

Gabby smiled. She wished she could say something similar, but Will hadn't ever really talked about his grandma. She didn't know much about his family aside from the fact that his uncle had made him a partner in his business. "It's nice to meet you," Gabby said.

Grandma Beth turned to Owen and Ben. "You boys don't like cookies, do you?"

"Yes, we do," Owen said. "We love cookies!"

"Well, come on in the house and try my special butter cookies while we wait for Will's little experiment to harden."

"Can we?" Ben asked Gabby.

Gabby nodded her head. Grandma Beth took each of the boys by a hand and led them into the house. Before she let the door slam shut behind her, she poked her head back outside.

"It's about damned time you got rid of that ant hill," she said.

Will laughed. He pulled his helmet off and set it aside. "I hope this works," he said. "Otherwise, Granny will never let me hear the end of it. She's been after me all summer to knock that ant hill down, but I wanted to see how big it would get."

Gabby followed Will to a nearby picnic table and sat on the bench next to him. She shivered. It was getting cooler outside, and she hadn't thought to grab a jacket.

Will leaned into her, sharing his body heat. "It's getting cold out," he said. "We'll be dealing with ice storms before we know it."

"Not for a few more months," Gabby said. She snuggled into Will's warmth, and he wrapped an arm around her shoulders.

"How did you get into this metal melting stuff, anyway?" Gabby asked.

"I'm a welder," Will said. "I told you, I like fire and melting things. I almost burned my grandma's house down one time playing with fire. So, my uncle took me to work with him and showed me how to channel my fascination into something productive. I've been working with him ever since."

Gabby laughed. "I always thought you were such a trouble maker," she said. "I'm glad your uncle found a way to keep you out of jail."

"I've never made trouble on purpose. I just like to experiment with fire and chemicals and stuff to see what will happen. It's how I learn."

"And what have you learned?"

"Sometimes chemicals explode," Will said.

The two of them laughed. Gabby gave Will a playful nudge to the ribs. She hadn't been this easygoing with a boy since she was a kid.

"So, that's pretty cool that your uncle made you a partner in his business, huh?"

"Yeah, it's cool," Will said. "It was actually more my grandma's doing than his. My uncle is a little—different."

"How so?"

"I think if he was growing up now, he'd probably be diagnosed as autistic. It was really grandma that got his business going. He does all the welding, but she always took care of the business side of things until Uncle Eric taught me to weld and stuff. She was happy to drag me into it so she could retire. I don't know where my uncle would be now if she hadn't taken charge like she did, though."

Gabby wondered where Will himself would be if his grandma hadn't taken charge and started a business for her son and grandson to run. He was lucky to have someone step up for him in that way and make sure he was settled into a job where he could make a living long after she was gone.

The screen door slammed shut. Gabby pulled away from Will at the loud noise. The cold settled into her shoulders again when he removed his arm.

Owen and Ben ran down the back steps toward them. "Is it done yet?" Owen asked. He could barely contain his excitement.

Will got up and headed for the ant hill. "I bet it is," he said. He put his protective gloves back on and picked up some tongs he had left in the grass nearby. "Now, the metal should be hardened at this point, but it will still be hot. So, nobody try to touch it, okay?"

Owen and Ben nodded and took a step back. Will plunged the tongs into the ant hill and grabbed the chunk of metal inside. Dirt spilled from it as he lifted it upward so they could see it. Will reached out with a gloved finger and started to knock chunks of dirt from around the intricate shapes that had once been ant hill tunnels.

"Wow," Ben said. "That is so beautiful."

Owen nodded his head in agreement. "Are all the ants dead, now?" he asked.

Will chuckled. "Yeah, buddy," he said. "I'm pretty sure they are."

"What are you going to do with it?" Gabby asked. "It looks like an expensive piece of art."

"Maybe you could sell it," Owen said.

Will shook his head. "Nah. I'm just going to add it to my collection." He gestured for them to follow him, and then he led them to a small outbuilding at the back of the yard next to a field of browning corn stalks.

Once inside the building, Will flipped a switch, and light illuminated the single small room. Gabby gasped at the rows of metal sculptures that lined the floor-to-ceiling shelving unit that covered one wall. Some were made from molten metal poured into molds like the one Will had just made, while others were constructed from scrap metal pieces welded together. A couple of low tables made from chunks of logs held the biggest pieces.

"This is real art," Ben said. He picked up a small piece from a shelf and turned it in his hand, tracing the details with his finger. "It's amazing."

"It really is." Gabby half whispered, as though she had entered a fancy museum where silence was expected. "This is—art. Will, you're an artist."

Will turned away from Gabby to try to hide his embarrassment, but she could still see the pink tops of his ears. He settled his latest creation onto a work bench and then took off his gloves. "It's nothing," he finally said. "I'm just fooling around."

"This isn't nothing," Gabby said. "It's—it's—"

"Amazing!" Owen said.

"Can you teach me how to do some of this stuff?" Ben asked. "I love art. It's my favorite subject at school."

The boys chattered with uncontainable excitement between Gabby and Will on the drive back to their apartment. They were in awe of Will and couldn't wait to help him with his next big project. They seemed to have a million questions and ideas for the sculpture he had promised to make with them. Will seemed just as eager as the younger boys. It would be so good for the boys to have such a positive male role model take an interest in them. Gabby chuckled at the idea that she now considered Will a good role model after how much of a loser she always thought he was before.

"What's so funny?" Will asked. He turned his truck onto Gabby's street and then gunned the engine.

"Nothing," she said. She winked at him and then was surprised at herself for doing so. Was she flirting? She didn't think she had it in her.

Will grinned at her, then returned his attention to the road in front of him. "Uh-oh," he said. "There's an ambulance up ahead." He took his foot off the gas pedal and allowed the truck to coast toward the flashing lights.

Gabby's blood chilled when she spotted the flashing lights of the ambulance parked in front of her apartment building.

"Is it at our house?" Owen asked. He grabbed Gabby's arm and squeezed tight.

"I think it is," Ben said. He sat forward in his seat and peered over the dashboard. "It's in front of our building."

"Maybe it's Miss Greta," Gabby said. "She is getting pretty old. I know her son has been trying to talk her into moving out of our building to go to an assisted living place."

The paramedics rolled a gurney out Gabby's front door as Will pulled the truck to the curb and put it in park. Meg followed the gurney outside. She was chewing her nails and fluttering around behind the paramedics.

"Mom!" Owen said. He practically shoved Gabby out of the truck door in his rush to get to their mother. He ran, screaming, across the yard to the ambulance where Kim was about to be loaded in the back. "Mom!"

Gabby ran after Owen and grabbed him. She was afraid of what he might see. She breathed a huge sigh of relief when her mom rolled her head toward them and blinked her eyes. Gabby and the boys ran to her side. The paramedics stepped aside to allow them to get close to her.

"Mom, what happened?" Gabby asked.

"Are you okay?" Ben said.

Kim whispered. "I'm fine," she said. "I just passed out. I'll be okay. I really don't even need to go to the hospital." She glared at the paramedics.

"You're not fine," Meg said. She stood over Kim on the opposite side of the gurney now. "You were practically dead when I found you."

"Step back, please," one of the paramedics said.

Gabby and her siblings stood back so their mom could be lifted into the ambulance. One of the paramedics slammed the door and then told Gabby which hospital they were taking her mom to before jumping in the driver's seat and speeding away. The siren and lights told Gabby this was worse than her mom simply passing out. She turned to Meg who had her arms wrapped tightly around herself and was trying not to cry.

"What happened?"

Meg shook her head. "She—she overdosed," she said. "She wouldn't wake up. There were empty pill bottles all around her. How could she do this to us?" Meg finally broke down and started sobbing, her shoulders heaving with the effort.

Gabby grabbed her sister and wrapped her arms around her, holding her close. Meg clung to her. The boys joined in, and the four of them held each other tight. They all seemed to realize that they only had each other now.

Soon, Will cleared his throat to get Gabby's attention. She looked up at him and realized that he had been standing there watching the whole time. Her cheeks flushed with embarrassment. After this, he was going to be the one to think her family was a bunch of losers.

"Why don't we go inside?" Will said.

Gabby glanced around and realized that the whole neighborhood seemed to be outside on their porches or looking through their windows watching them. She nodded her head and allowed Will to lead them all into their apartment. Once inside, Gabby flopped onto the couch, and the boys both tried to sit on her lap at the same time, though they were both too old for that. They ended up sitting on either side of her, as close as they could get, both huddling against their big sister for reassurance.

"What are we going to do now?" Meg asked. She paced the living room and continued to chew at her fingernails. "I don't want to live with a drug addict again."

"What did the EMTs say?" Will asked. "How bad did they think it was?"

"I don't know," Meg said. "But I thought she was dead." Meg snuffled between sentences. "She wouldn't wake up. I didn't know what to do." She wailed and buried her face in her hands.

Will went to Meg and patted her shoulder. "Why don't you come sit by Gabby," he said. He led Meg to her siblings and motioned for Ben to move over so Meg could sit by Gabby.

Meg curled into Gabby, and Gabby gathered her to her, holding her close. "It's going to be okay now," Gabby said over Meg's sobs.

"How?" Meg pulled away and wiped her face. "How exactly is it going to be okay? You had to quit school to support us. That is so wrong! You're not our mom. Our mom isn't even our mom anymore."

Ben and Owen both started to cry. This wasn't good. Meg was just getting everyone worked up.

"Okay, okay," Gabby said. "Shush, all of you. We need to calm down and figure out what to do right now. We can only deal with one thing at a time."

"We need to find out if Mom is okay," Ben said. "We need to go to the hospital."

Gabby wasn't sure if it was a good idea to take the boys to the hospital. "I'll go," she said. "We may be sitting there for a long time. You all stay here, and I'll let you know what I find out."

"I'm going with you," Meg said.

"Meg, no. Someone has to watch the boys."

"You didn't see her," Meg said. "You didn't find her and think she was—" she glanced at the boys and didn't finish her sentence.

"Hey," Will said. "Why don't I take Owen and Ben back to my house so we can draw up a plan for our art project?"

"I couldn't ask you to do that," Gabby said.

"It's no problem. We can go to Casey's and grab a couple of pizzas and some junk food and make a party of it."

"Sounds good to me," Owen said.

"I don't know."

"Just take them," Meg said. "Come on, Gabby. We need to go."

"Grandma will love the company," Will said. "Really, you'll be doing her a huge favor. She always complains that I grew up too fast. She misses me being their age."

"Please, Gabby?" Ben said.

Gabby was surprised and a little hurt that the boys weren't more worried about their mom. But, maybe that was a good thing. It wouldn't do them any good to sit around in a hospital waiting room all evening worrying. "Okay," she said. "I'll come back as soon as I can to get them."

Once the decision was made, they hurried off to their vehicles and went their separate ways. Gabby tried not worry about the boys as she sped into town. Owen, especially, needed his routines. Hopefully he wouldn't have a meltdown while he was at Will's. She almost considered turning around to go get him, but then she reconsidered. Owen wasn't exactly going to be sticking to his regular routine if he went with her, either.

Meg chewed at her nails in the passenger seat. She pressed her right foot to the floor as though she were pressing an invisible gas pedal that could make Gabby drive faster.

"Are you okay?" Gabby asked. She took her own foot from the real gas pedal and coasted up the exit ramp as they pulled into town. Luckily most of the evening rush hour traffic had cleared out. They would be at the hospital in just a few minutes.

Meg stopped chewing her nails and scratched her arm. "Not really," she said. "What's going to happen to us? We already got taken away from Dad. Are they going to take us away from Mom now, too?"

This thought hadn't even crossed Gabby's mind. She had been taking care of her siblings already, so it hadn't occurred to her that anything would change for them. She just wanted her mom to be okay and get some help for her problem. It was obvious now that she did have a problem—the kind of problem that a person could lose her children over. What would happen to them? Surely, they wouldn't lose their home now, after all Gabby had done to save it.

"No," Gabby said. "Mom isn't as bad as Dad was. She has a prescription for the drugs she's using. And she hasn't abused us. Our house is clean, and we have plenty of food. There's no real reason for them to take us away from her."

"You had to drop out of school and get a full-time job," Meg said. "You don't think that's abuse?"

"I didn't drop out."

"Yeah, right. As if anyone is going to believe that your homemade homeschool certificate is the same thing as a high school diploma." Meg rolled her eyes and turned away from Gabby.

Gabby clenched her fists around the steering wheel and glued her eyes to the street in front of her. She didn't want to think about what Meg had just said. She didn't want to have to consider the fact that Meg might be right. She followed the street signs to the hospital and turned into the parking lot.

Once she'd found a place to park, Gabby hopped out of the van and headed for the entrance. She didn't look behind her to see if Meg followed. She didn't want to look at Meg at all right now. She wanted—needed to just focus on one thing at a time. One thing at a time.

Meg remained silent as she followed Gabby through the hospital on the hunt for their mother. They found her in an Emergency Room cubicle behind a curtained door. She was curled up on a hospital bed with an IV line hanging from one arm. Her skin was pale and beaded with sweat, but her eyes were open. An empty pail sat on the bed next to her. Probably a puke bucket. Maybe she just needed to vomit up the extra pills and then she would be fine. Maybe Gabby would be able to take her mom home soon, and everything would be just fine.

Meg pushed past Gabby and entered the cubicle first. She didn't speak to their mother but instead plopped onto a chair at the foot of the bed and crossed her arms in front of her. Gabby went straight to her mom. She patted her shoulder.

"I'm so sorry," Kim said. Her shoulder trembled under Gabby's hand. "I took too many pills. I don't know what I was thinking. I just hurt so bad, and I wanted it to stop. I should have been more patient and waited for the first pill I took to kick in instead of taking more." She started to heave and then just barely lifted her head up fast enough to vomit into the empty pail beside her.

Gabby averted her eyes but kept her hand on her mom's shoulder. The smell of her mom's puke stung the inside of her nostrils. For a moment, she thought she might also throw up. She finally stepped away and went to the door. A nurse came around the corner toward her, and Gabby waved to her.

"My mom just threw up," she said.

"I was just on my way to check on her," the nurse said. "Are you her daughters?"

Gabby nodded. Meg's arm brushed against hers. The vomit must have been too much for her as well. They stepped aside so the nurse could enter the cubicle. Then, they stepped into the hallway so they wouldn't have to watch her clean up their mother's mess. A few minutes later, the nurse joined them in the hallway.

"You two shouldn't be here for this," she said. "Is there an adult we can call to take you home?"

Gabby was about to shake her head no when Meg finally spoke up. "Our grandma's on her way here," she said. "She lives in Missouri, but she should be here in a couple of hours."

Gabby frowned. They didn't have a grandma in Missouri. Their mom's mom had passed away when she was in high school, and their dad's mom—well, she was crazier than their dad was.

The nurse nodded. She seemed relieved that the girls had someone coming to take care of them. "You girls should go on home and wait for your grandma there," she said. "Your mom is going to be here for a couple of weeks, and you're not going to be able to see her."

"A couple of weeks?" Gabby asked.

The nurse patted Gabby's arm. "I'm sorry," she said. "Your mom is going to be moved to a detox unit here in a bit. Kids aren't allowed to visit there."

A couple of weeks. What were they going to do without their mom for a couple of weeks? Gabby wished they really did have a grandma to step in and take care of them. Meg was glowering, but she kept her mouth shut now.

"Can we tell her goodbye?" Gabby asked.

"Sure."

The nurse held the door open, but only Gabby entered. Meg just glared at her sister and refused to budge from her spot in the hall. Their mom was shivering in her bed as though it were freezing cold. Gabby hadn't seen her mom look so bad since— she tried to shove aside an unwelcome image of her mom with a swollen and battered face that her dad had given her years before when they were still together. The image wouldn't go away. The same fear that had wracked her entire body back then rushed through her again now like an electrical current. Her intestines clenched up, and suddenly she needed to use the restroom very bad.

"Mom?" Gabby said. Her mom didn't seem to notice her. "We have to go, but hopefully we'll see you again soon." She patted her mom's back once, then turned and hurried out of the room.

Gabby ran to the restroom across the hallway and shoved the door open. Once inside, she barely made it to the toilet. Her insides exploded. Her skin was cold and clammy. She held her stomach and groaned. Why did this always happen when memories from when they lived with their dad popped up? It wasn't fair. It seemed so long ago now, but sometimes the images that intruded at the worst possible times seemed more real than what she was living in the here and now.

A knock at the door brought her back. "Are you okay in there?" It was the nurse.

"I'm fine! I just need a minute." Gabby flushed with embarrassment. She wished the nurse would just go away now.

She finished up and then went to wash her hands. She wetted a paper towel with cold water and mopped the sweat from her brow. The mirror above the sink reflected her stringy hair and flushed face. Her eyes were swollen. She didn't want Will to see her looking like this. Then she laughed at herself. Why did she care what Will thought now? Her family had probably already scared him off for good. Finally, she left the restroom.

Meg leaned against the wall next to their mother's closed cubicle. "Ready?" she asked.

Gabby nodded. She pulled her keys from her pocket and headed out to the van with Meg. Neither of them spoke as they drove home to their brothers and their now parentless home.

CHAPTER SEVENTEEN

Not much changed at the Gimble house with the matriarch away in rehab. If anything, Gabby felt as though she had one less child to worry about with her mom away. At first, she tried to feel guilty for thinking such thoughts about her mother. But then, the guilt turned to anger at the position her mother had put them in. They were lucky no one had called the police yet to come put them all in foster care.

Gabby was about to push through the doors into the library when a flyer caught her eye. She couldn't believe what the flyer said. Lynn was retiring from her Library Director position. How could that be possible? Lynn wasn't old enough to retire, was she? Besides that, she had always been the library director for as long as Gabby could remember. The library just wouldn't be the same without her there.

Gabby was relieved to see Lynn at the circulation desk once she got inside. She went straight to the desk. "You're retiring?" she asked.

"Well, hello to you, too." Lynn laughed. "And yes, I am retiring."

"But why? We need you."

Lynn sniffled. Gabby thought she might cry, but she just smiled. "You'll manage without me," she said. "You are a very capable and resourceful young woman, Gabby Gimble."

Gabby tried to shake off her sadness. She was being selfish. She should be happy for Lynn. "I'm sorry," she said. "What I meant to say is, congratulations."

Lynn jumped up from her seat and came around the counter to hug Gabby. "I will miss you," she said.

Gabby hugged her back. "You are my favorite librarian of all times."

Lynn laughed. She held Gabby away at arm's length. "You've grown up so much since the first time you came in here with your sister and brothers to get your library cards. I hope you know how proud I am of you."

Now it was Gabby's turn to hold back the tears. Her mom had been so excited when they moved to a small town with a library that her kids could treat as a second home. They had all spent many hours there over the years and relied on the library for most of their entertainment. And Lynn had been there for them all along. Gabby nodded her head as one tear snuck out from the corner of her eye. She wiped it away. "So, who's going to take your place?" she asked.

"I'm not sure," Lynn said. "None of my library assistants are interested in the promotion, so we are taking applications. You should send your mom in to apply. I think she'd be good at it."

Gabby took a step back. Apparently, Lynn hadn't heard what was going on with her mom. "Um—sure. I'll let her know about it."

Lynn hurried back around the counter and grabbed a sheet of paper from the desk. She handed it across the counter to Gabby. "Take her an application," she said. "She has until the end of the month to get it in, and then the library board will meet on the third to decide who they want to call in for interviews."

Gabby took the application from Lynn. She didn't know if her mom would even be in any condition to apply for a job by the end of the month, but it couldn't hurt to take her the application. It would be nice if she got a job as soon as she got home from the hospital. Maybe then things could finally go back to normal.

"Thanks."

"I hope you'll all come to my retirement party too," Lynn said. "I'm moving down south to be closer to my grandkids, so I probably won't see you much once I've retired."

"We will," Gabby said. "If I'm not working, I will definitely come to your party."

Lynn grinned. Then, she glanced over Gabby's shoulder. "Looks like the rest of your gang is here," she said. "Have a good study session."

The students of DIY High had all arrived at the library at the same time. Will held the door for everyone else to enter, and most of them headed toward the study booths. Will winked at Gabby as he passed. Her cheeks flushed with pleasure, and she smiled at him.

Jodie went straight to Gabby and grabbed her arm. "What was that?" she whispered.

"What?"

"Are you two an item now?"

"What? Of course, not—well, maybe." Gabby's cheeks were practically on fire now. "I don't know."

"You could do worse," Jodie said. "Will seems like a good guy."

"You think?"

"I do. That Joe, on the other hand—I mean, not that he's a bad guy, but—he's kind of stupid, isn't he?"

Gabby shushed her. "He'll hear you," she said.

Jodie shrugged. "Even if he does, he probably wouldn't understand what I'm saying anyway."

"Be nice."

"I don't mean anything by it. I'm just getting a little frustrated with trying to help him learn the GED materials. He doesn't need a GED. He needs someone to teach him how to do some very useful task that requires no thought and just put him to work. He's actually a really hard worker. I just can't shake the feeling that he's wasting his time studying when he needs to go learn to do something useful so his parents don't have to support him for the rest of their lives."

"But he can't get a job or get into that apprenticeship program his mom has lined up for him without the GED. That's just how it is."

"I know," Jodie said. "But that doesn't mean it's not stupid. Even if we can manage to get him through the test, he's going to forget everything he memorized as soon as he's done. What a stupid waste of time and money."

Gabby shrugged and headed toward the study booths. She got an idea as they made their way over to the rest of the group. "Hey, Will," she said. "Would you mind studying with Joe a bit tonight? He needs help, but Jodie and Brittany are both going to be busy taking practice tests."

Will's face fell for a second, but then he perked back up. "Sure," he said. "What are you going to be working on?"

"College application essays," Gabby said. She made a face to show him how unpleasant she thought the task would be.

"Oooo, college applications!" Brittany said. "That sounds fun. Where are you applying to? Not community, I take it. You don't need to write essays to get in there."

"Just State and a couple of other places. Nothing too far away." Gabby shrugged. She didn't want to tell them that she was applying to an Ivy League school. It wasn't like she was going to get in anyway. She was applying later than she should have because she hadn't realized she needed to apply in the fall for the best chance of getting in. She was probably wasting her time anyway. She would probably end up at community with the rest of them. It wasn't like she could afford an Ivy League school. And, who was going to take care of her siblings so she could go to school out of state? No, she was mostly just applying to see if she could get in. She just wanted to know if she was good enough, even if there was no possible way she could afford to actually go.

The group divided up to go to their study spots for the evening, and Gabby went to use a library computer. She had thought the essays would be easy, but once she sat down to write them, the words just wouldn't come. She didn't have all the extracurricular activities and volunteer work the other applicants would probably have. She did spend all her free time taking care of a poor family, but since it was her own family, she doubted any college would appreciate her noting it as an extracurricular.

Gabby sighed and fell back in her seat. This was never going to happen. She was wasting her time.

"Gabby?"

She glanced up to see one of Owen's old teachers standing over her.

"You're Owen's sister, right?"

Gabby nodded. She remembered Meg and Lily joking that he liked her that time she had picked them up from school. Surely, he didn't?

"I'm Mr. Stein," he said. "Owen was in my class last year."

"I remember," Gabby said. What did he want? Surely, he didn't go out of his way to talk to all of his students' siblings like this.

"Hey, listen," Mr. Stein said. "I heard about what you're doing with your school here at the library, and I think it's great. I was wondering if there is anything I could do to help out. Maybe I could tutor some of the students or something?"

"Um—yeah, sure." Maybe Gabby could get Mr. Stein to take over with Joe. "That would be great," she said.

Mr. Stein grinned. "Thanks," he said. "This means a lot to me. To be honest, I dropped out of high school myself. I probably never would have amounted to anything if someone hadn't stepped up and helped me get my GED a few years later. By that time, I was ready to take school seriously. I went to community college for two years, then went on to State to study to be a teacher. Graduated at the top of my class, too."

"Wow," Gabby said. "That's great." It had never occurred to her that someone could drop out of high school and still have a chance of being a teacher someday.

"So, what are you working on?" Mr. Stein asked.

Gabby sighed. "I'm trying to write a college application essay."

"Not going well?"

Gabby shook her head. "I just don't know what to write about. I don't have any cool missionary experiences. I've never studied abroad. I've just never done anything at all."

Mr. Stein chuckled. He rubbed his chin. "What about this?" he asked. He gestured toward the study group across the library. "DIY High. You did this. That's something. That's a big something, if you ask me. From what I hear, you're helping a lot of people."

"I wouldn't say 'a lot,'" Gabby said. "Just four."

"Four, plus the family members who will be impacted when those students are able to get better jobs. Who knows who else you might help in the community beyond that. By helping these four people, you may have created a ripple effect that will reach farther than you ever imagined possible."

Gabby thought about Jodie, who wanted to be a nurse. Jodie would be helping a lot of people someday. Brittany didn't seem to have any plans for college since she enjoyed being a stay-at-home mom and farming with her husband. But, she had mentioned that her kids had started playing school at home a lot. Not to mention the fact that her oldest was reading a lot better since Meg had been working with her when she watched the kids during study time. She had been teaching the younger kids their ABC's and had them counting and naming colors everywhere they went. And Meg. She was still a grouch at home, but she was a totally different person when she was babysitting. Plus, she had stopped complaining so much now that she had her own money to spend. Maybe Gabby was helping a lot more people than she had previously thought.

"I guess you have a point," she said. Now, she wished Mr. Stein would go away so she could type up her ideas before she lost track of them. "Well, I should get back to this. If you want to go check in with the others, I think Joe could use some help. He's really struggling. Jodie is doing her best with him, but she has her own studying to do."

"I'll do that," Mr. Stein said. "Good luck on your essay."

"Thanks."

The following Friday, Brittany and Joe didn't show up for study group.

"They went to the community college this morning to take the science section of the GED test," Jodie said. "Brittany's husband took a break from farming so he could take her out for dinner tonight to celebrate."

"She passed?" Gabby asked. "Good for her."

"Yeah, but Joe didn't," Jodie said. "He's pretty depressed about it. We might have to talk him into coming back to study with us. It sounds like he's about ready to give up."

"That sucks," Will said.

"Do you know where Joe lives?" Mr. Stein asked. "Maybe I'll go talk to him tomorrow. I think he just needs a bit more help and maybe some extra accommodations when he takes the test. He seems to do a lot better when I read the questions to him out loud rather than making him read them to himself. We might be able to get them to allow him to take the tests verbally."

"I can get his address for you," Will said. "I know where he lives, but I'm not sure of the house number. I'll text it to you later."

The four of them decided to play a trivia game that Mr. Stein brought that he thought would be a fun way of testing their knowledge on the topics that they should all be learning at the high school level. He and Jodie teamed up against Will and Gabby. Soon, Jodie was calling Mr. Stein by his first name, Ian. Then Will picked up on it as well, but it seemed odd to Gabby to call a teacher by his first name, even if he had never been her teacher.

After a while, they were having so much fun, Lynn came by to ask them to quiet down. "Don't make me kick you out of here," she warned them. She winked at Gabby to let her know she wasn't too serious.

"Sorry, Lynn," Will said. "Who knew learning could be so much fun?"

"Too bad I can't get away with playing games with my students all day every day," Mr. Stein said. "I would probably be able to hand out a lot more good grades if I could."

"We're just wrapping up this game," Jodie said. "Then I think I'll be ready to call it a night. I'm all studied out for the week."

"I don't know about you, but I'm pretty hungry." Mr. Stein said. "Jodie, do you want to go to the diner at the truck stop for a slice of pie before you call it a night?"

Jodie stuck her tongue out in distaste. "You realize I work at the diner, right?" she said.

"I could go for pie," Will said. "How about the Palms Café? Their pie is really good, too. Then you wouldn't have to feel like you're going to work."

Gabby elbowed Will. Didn't he see that Mr. Stein was trying to ask Jodie out? He probably hadn't intended to ask Gabby and Will along too.

"That does sound good," Jodie said. "But my kids—"

"Meg will watch your kids. I'll go ask her now." Gabby hopped up from the table. Meg was going to babysit Jodie's kids if she had to twist her arm to make her do it.

Luckily, Meg didn't need any arm twisting once Gabby explained what was going on. She seemed happy to live vicariously through Jodie dating her teacher crush. Meg even offered to watch the kids at Jodie's house, give them their baths, and put them to bed so Jodie could stay out as long as she liked.

Gabby rode with Will while Jodie and Mr. Stein dropped Meg and the kids off at Jodie's house. Gabby glared at Will once they had climbed into his truck and slammed their doors shut.

"What?" he asked. "You've been giving me that look for at least ten minutes now."

"You realize Mr. Stein was trying to ask Jodie out on a date, right?"

Will backed his truck away from the library and then shifted it into drive. "Well yeah," he said. "I saw what was up. Jodie's the one who was clueless. You'd think no one ever tried to hit on her before. Why do you ask?"

"They don't need us to tag along on their date."

"There would be no date if I hadn't stepped in and encouraged Jodie to come. Now it's a double date."

"Oh, is it?" Gabby's breath caught in her throat. She'd never been on a date before.

"If you want it to be," Will said. He winked at her, then turned his attention back to the road as he turned the truck onto Route 66 to head toward the next town south of them.

"I think—yes. Yes, let's make it a double date."

Gabby and Will smiled at each other, then immediately looked away. Out Gabby's window, a freight train chugged down the railroad tracks that ran alongside the highway. Snippets of graffiti on the train cars flashed by in the spill of the truck's headlights. Will stepped on the gas and outpaced the train in just a few seconds. A few minutes later, they were pulling into the small town where the café was.

Downtown, Will parked the truck in front of a giant Paul Bunyan statue that held an equally giant hot dog.

"So, what's the deal with Paul Bunyan and the hot dog, anyway?" Gabby asked. They got out of the truck and stood on the sidewalk looking up at the statue.

"No clue," Will said. "It's just always been here."

They had a few minutes before Jodie and Mr. Stein would catch up to them, so they loitered at Paul Bunyan's feet.

"Lean against the leg there and let me take a touristy picture of you," Will said.

Gabby wrinkled her nose at him but did as he asked. She crossed her arms and leaned against the statue's leg while Will snapped a couple of pictures with his phone.

"Give me some attitude, baby," he said. He made his voice high and nasally like some stereotypical high-fashion photographer.

Gabby turned around and wrapped her arms around the statue's leg.

"Yeah, baby. That is hot!" Will said. He was bouncing about and snapping pictures of Gabby hamming it up on Paul Bunyan's leg when Mr. Stein's car pulled up to the curb.

Jodie rolled her window down and hung her head out, gaping at them. "What in the world are you two idiots doing?" she asked. She laughed, then pulled her head back inside and rolled her window up.

Mr. Stein rushed around to open the door for her. He bent his knees in an awkward curtsey as Jodie exited the practical black sedan. "M'lady," he said.

Jodie giggled. "Good sir," she said. She stepped out of the car and headed toward Will. "Give me your phone and let me take a picture of the two of you."

Will handed his phone over and then went to pose with Gabby. The two of them took a spot on either side of Paul Bunyan's leg and wrapped their arms around it. Jodie rolled her eyes but snapped a couple of photos anyway. Then, she made them stand together for a serious shot. Will put his arm around Gabby's shoulders, and she grinned at the camera. For a few moments, she was able to forget about her problems and just have some fun.

It wasn't until they were sitting at a table inside waiting for their pie that Gabby remembered she should probably head home soon so her brothers wouldn't be alone too long. Even though their mother was often out of it when she was home, her presence alone was enough to make the boys feel safe. Since their mom left in the ambulance, they were both on edge. How could Gabby run off and have a good time without them, knowing how their mom's absence was affecting them?

Jodie and Mr. Stein took their time with their pie and coffee, but Gabby started to scarf hers down. They didn't seem to notice Gabby at all, but Will soon nudged her.

"Are you in a hurry to get home?" he asked.

"Is it that obvious?"

Will shrugged. "I just think pie this good deserves to be savored. Plus, I'm afraid you're going to choke yourself eating so fast."

"I'm sorry," Gabby said. She set her fork down. "It is really good pie. I just don't want to be out too late. Owen will start to worry that I got run over by a train or something, and then next thing you know, he'll be dialing 911 to ask the police to look for me."

"Poor Owen," Mr. Stein said. His attention was temporarily pulled away from Jodie, with whom he seemed to be enthralled. "He does have some major anxiety issues. Reminds me a lot of myself at his age."

"Really?" Jodie asked. "What does a kid that age have to be so anxious about?"

"I don't know about Owen, but my dad made me pretty anxious. He was extremely controlling, and I always had to walk on eggshells to keep from making him angry. It got to the point that I was anxious about everything. I was constantly worried that some little thing would go wrong, and then I'd get in trouble for it. My father seemed to get off on thinking up creative ways to punish me for the dumbest things."

That did sound like Owen – and their father – but Gabby wasn't about to open up to these people about it. She preferred to forget that her dad existed most of the time. As far as she was concerned, he was irrelevant. Especially after her last phone call to him.

"You poor thing," Jodie said. "I swear, some of the stories I hear people tell about their dads, sometimes I'm glad my kids' father decided to run off to Texas. They're way better off with no father at all than they would be with a P.O.S. like him hanging around making their lives miserable."

Mr. Stein took Jodie's hand in his and patted it. The two of them seemed to disappear into each other's eyes like two clichés in some tired old romance novel. Gabby and Will shared a glance and snickered at each other.

"Eat your pie," Will said. "Just slow down a little bit and taste it. Your brothers will be okay without you long enough for you to enjoy yourself that much."

"I guess you're right," Gabby said. She took a bite of her pie and made the effort to chew it slowly and really taste it. The plump cherries burst in her mouth as she bit into them. Even the crust tasted good. She cocked her head to one side and smiled at Will. He winked at her and dug into his blueberry pie.

Before long, the two of them had finished and were ready to go. They said their goodbyes and left Jodie at the restaurant with Mr. Stein.

On the way home, Gabby made Will swing through the McDonald's drive thru so she could get a couple of apple pies for the boys to assuage her guilt at going out for pie without them while they sat at home worrying about her. Will shook his head at her as he handed the pies across to her after they had been handed to him through the drive thru window.

"What?" Gabby said. She held the small bag of pies on her lap.

Will shifted the truck into drive and pulled forward out of the drive thru lane. "Nothing," he said. "Your brothers are lucky to have you."

Gabby stared out the window at the houses they passed on the way to her apartment building. A block before they reached her home, they passed a recently restored Victorian home whose owners often left their front curtains open. Anyone passing could watch the mother of the family playing cards at the dining room table with her five children. Gabby couldn't remember the last time her mom had played a game with them. "I just wish they didn't need me so much," she said as they drove past.

"Life isn't always perfect," Will said. "It's not fair, but we do what we have to. There's no point wishing away what is."

"I guess."

"I'm quoting my grandma, you know. I bet that didn't make you feel any better than it ever makes me feel when she says it to me."

Gabby laughed. "Not really. But I guess your grandma has a point. If I sit around wishing for things to be different, I'll probably just depress myself. It's better to just keep moving forward. My brothers will grow up eventually."

Will pulled his truck up to the curb in front of Gabby's house. He cut the engine and turned to her. "Don't let your own life get away from you while you're taking care of them," he said. "You have a right to go out and do teenage stuff sometimes even if you are basically their mom for now."

"I know." But did she know that? Gabby hardly ever did anything for herself anymore outside of her schooling. She wanted to go away to college if she could get into a good school, but there was no way that could ever happen as long as her brothers needed her at home. It wasn't fair.

Will put his arm across the back of the seat between them and took a strand of Gabby's hair between his fingers. He twirled the lock of hair in his fingers and leaned closer. Gabby's body seemed to move toward him without any direction from her brain.

"Do you mind if I kiss you?" Will asked.

"Yes. I mean, I don't mind. Yes, kiss me."

Will smiled and leaned closer to press his lips to Gabby's. One of her hands slipped around the back of his neck and lingered over the strong muscles under his smooth skin. His hand caressed her arm, and her skin tingled at his touch. Will pulled away before Gabby was ready for the kiss to end. She leaned toward him as he pulled away. He was looking over her shoulder toward the apartment building.

"We have an audience," he said.

Gabby turned to look out the window. Owen and Ben were leaning across the back of the couch in their living room, staring out the window at them. Owen scowled, while Ben grinned at them.

"I guess I'd better go," Gabby said.

CHAPTER EIGHTEEN

G abby was nervous as she pulled the van up to the curb in front of the hospital to pick her mom up. Kim had called her less than an hour before to tell her that she had been released and needed a ride home. Luckily Gabby wasn't working that day, or her mom would have been left sitting there for a long time.

Kim sat on a bench just outside the front entrance. She had lost a bit of weight since Gabby saw her last. She was still a little overweight, but now she looked—normal. No, normal wasn't the right word. Healthy, that was it. She looked healthy for the first time ever in Gabby's memory.

Gabby brought the van to a stop in the circular drive, right in front of the bench where her mom sat. Kim hopped up and ran to the van. She threw the door open and then jumped into the passenger seat. She flung herself across the center console to hug Gabby without bothering to close her door first.

"Oh, my sweet Gabby. I missed you so much!"

Gabby stiffened under her mom's embrace. She didn't lean toward the passenger side to make it easier for her mom to hug her. Kim had to pull away to keep from falling into the open area between their seats. She reached for her door handle and slammed the door shut. "Let's go home," she said. "I need to see to rest of my babies as soon as possible. This is the longest I've ever been away from you kids." Her eyes gleamed with unshed tears, but they appeared to be happy tears.

Gabby put the van in gear and pulled out of the hospital's parking lot. She stared straight ahead at the road, afraid to look at her mom. Soon, they were on the interstate, headed for home.

"I know you're mad at me," Kim said finally. "And I don't blame you, Gabby. Really, I don't. I messed up big time. I know it's going to take some time for you to forgive me, and a lot of work on my part. But, I want you to know that I am so, so sorry for what I've put you kids through the last couple of years."

Kim was right. Gabby wasn't ready to forgive her. But, it was nice to hear her acknowledge what she had done and how it had affected her kids. What a huge difference from her father, who always seemed able to find someone other than himself to blame all of his problems on. "I know, Mom," Gabby said.

Kim sighed. "Detox really sucked," she said. "It needed to happen, though. And I'm glad I did it. But I never want to have to go through that ever again."

Gabby had heard it all before from her dad. It was hard to believe it would be any different with her mom. An addict was an addict. You couldn't believe a word they said, especially when they talked about getting clean. She wasn't going to get her hopes up.

"They wanted me to go to rehab. Four months! Can you believe that? How am I supposed to go to rehab for four months when I have kids at home waiting for me to come take care of them? These two weeks must have been awful enough for you, huh?"

Gabby shrugged. As worried as she had been when her mom first left in the ambulance, it had turned out that nothing much changed with her mom gone. She had only realized just how much she had become mom to her siblings and just how little their real mother had been there for them in the past two years. Her mom may as well have gone on to rehab for another four months if that's what she needed to get better. Gabby and her siblings would be fine without her.

"Well, don't you worry," Kim said. "I do have a plan. I met with a counselor while I was on the detox unit, and I'm going to keep going to counseling. I'm going to get a job, too. Even if it's just a little part-time job at McDonald's or even volunteering out at the nature center. Anything to get me out of the house on a regular basis so I'm not tempted to fall back into my old habits. My therapist thinks it would be a good idea for us to move to a new place, too, but I don't know how we could possibly afford that. Apparently, it's common practice to encourage people in rehab to move into a fresh environment to get away from the environmental triggers that prompt their drug use." Kim fluttered her hands about and laughed nervously. "Listen to me," she said. "I'm babbling. I'm sorry, Gabby." Her hands flew up, and she buried her head in them and started to cry. "I'm so, so sorry. I've been the worst mother ever." Her shoulders bobbed up and down as the sobs wracked her body.

Gabby flicked her turn signal on and took the next exit, even though their hometown was still a few miles further down the road. She drove toward the nature center where they used to spend so much time when she was younger. Before her mom had gotten sick. Her dad hated nature and had never visited the nature center, as far as Gabby knew. It was the one place where her mom could take the kids where they could all let loose and just be themselves.

Kim lifted her head from her hands and looked out the window as the car slowed. "What are you doing?" she asked.

"Let's run by the nature center for a bit first," Gabby said. "You need to pull yourself together before you go home to the kids."

Gabby turned the van off the highway and then took the narrow, winding country road that ran through the woods and ended at the nature center. She stopped the van in the gravel parking lot and cut the engine. The two of them sat for a minute and stared out the windows away from each other. The van's engine ticked as it cooled.

Finally, Gabby took a deep breath and shoved the driver's side door open. She turned to her mom. "Let's take a walk," she said.

Kim opened her door and got out of the van. She followed Gabby to a path that started at the edge of the parking lot. At first, her feet dragged against the ground behind Gabby. But then, she started to pick them up and move with purpose.

Gabby led the way across a ditch and followed the path where it ran between an overgrown meadow on one side and woods on the other. The air was crisp with the scent of dried prairie grasses. Soon, the path cut into the thin shade of the woods that had lost all its leaves. The brown carpet of rotting leaves that covered the ground alongside the path was crisp from the cold. Up ahead, a familiar wooden bench beckoned. Gabby sat on one end of the bench and pulled her jacket tight across her chest, huddling into its warmth. Her mom sat at the other end of the bench and took a deep breath, inhaling the woods deep into her lungs.

"I needed this," Kim said. "I can't believe how long it's been since I've been out in the woods. We used to come out here all the time, remember?"

"I remember," Gabby said. "This was our favorite spot."

Kim sighed. "I don't blame you if you don't believe that I'm going to straighten up and get my act together," she said. "I know exactly what you're feeling right now. I felt the same way watching your dad sink into his addictions. But you know, the thing about your dad was, he was a horrible person whether he was drunk, high, or sober. He never cared about anyone but himself. But, you kids—well, you and your sister and brothers are my whole life."

Gabby shrugged. She didn't want to admit to her mom that she wasn't ready to trust her yet. Maybe she would never trust her again. She just didn't know.

"I need a job," Kim said. "I need to get back to work as soon as possible."

"What about your fibromyalgia?" Gabby realized that her mom seemed to be in less pain than she was before. Kim had no problem following her out into the woods. Before she went to the hospital, Kim would have balked at even trying to walk that far from the parking lot. She was always in too much pain to do much of anything except watch her kids from the sidelines of their lives.

Kim laughed. "Get this," she said. "All those pills I was taking for the pain apparently just made it worse. They're not meant to be taken long-term for chronic pain. The doctors told me that the most recent clinical trials have found that opioids are not only not effective for chronic pain, but they make chronic pain worse. I probably should have never been taking them to begin with."

"So, what are you going to do for the pain now?"

"There are things I can do to manage it. Like exercising and watching my diet. You know, my two favorite things in the world."

Gabby smiled despite herself. She and her mom had always shared an extreme disliking for dieting and working out. They both liked to eat. "We should start coming out here regularly again," she said. "Remember how you used to chase us through the woods? I didn't mind that kind of exercise."

"That's a great idea." Kim moved closer to Gabby on the bench and took her hand. "What about you, kiddo? How's school going?"

Gabby smiled. "Good," she said. "I really like it, and we're up to five people in our study group now. Plus, one of Owen's teachers from last year is coming to help with tutoring."

"So, you're learning and keeping up with your lessons like you would if you were going to school?"

"Yeah," Gabby said. "I'm learning a lot, and not just from my school lessons. I'm also learning—I guess you could say I'm learning life lessons, too. Not just the stuff that's in my textbooks but also stuff about living and surviving in the real world."

Kim breathed a sigh of relief. "That's good to hear," she said. "I've been sitting in the hospital worrying about this. I'm supposed to be homeschooling you, and I haven't done much of anything. But I'm going to get involved now. I'm going to start spending time at the library with you, and I can help with the tutoring as well."

"That reminds me," Gabby said. "You know Lynn, the library director?"

Kim nodded. They all knew Lynn.

"Well, she's retiring."

"No way! I can't imagine the library without Lynn there. It just won't be the same."

"I know," Gabby said. "But that's not all. Lynn asked me the other day if you would be interested in applying for her job. She wants you to come in before the end of the month and fill out an application."

Kim frowned. "But wouldn't I need a library science degree or something? I think librarians typically have to go to graduate school for library science."

"Maybe not, since it's a small-town library. I don't think Lynn has anything like that. She didn't mention it anyway."

"Hmm—I'll have to go check it out, I guess. I would love to work at the library. Books are my favorite."

"I know," Gabby said. Now that she thought about it, a job at the library would be perfect for her mom. Before she'd gotten sick, she used to take them all to the library at least once a week and would come home with stacks of books for herself in addition to the books the kids checked out. She just hoped her mom wouldn't slide back into her old habits and get fired again. If that happened, none of the kids would feel comfortable going to the library anymore.

"What do you say we head home, now?" Kim patted Gabby's leg. "I miss your sister and brothers."

Gabby smiled. "They've missed you too." She got up and offered her mom a hand up from the bench. The two of them headed back to the parking lot, arm in arm.

The boys clambered for their mom's attention when she got home. They had been waiting at the laundry room window, watching for her, and they ran out the back door to the parking lot as soon as they saw the van turn in. They flew into her arms before she could even exit the van and hugged her.

"I missed you so much!" Owen said. He took one of his mom's hands, and Ben took the other. They led her toward the house with Gabby close behind them.

"Owen, your feet are going to freeze!" Kim scowled at his bares toes peeping out from the end of his slides. "You should at least have socks on in this cold, if you're going to refuse to wear your sneakers."

"We're going right back inside," Owen said. He let her hand go and ran ahead to open the door for her.

Once they were inside, Kim walked through to the living room. "Meg!" she called. "Where's your sister?" she asked the boys.

Owen shrugged. "Are you thirsty, Mom? Can I get you something to drink?"

"I'm fine, thank you," Kim said. "Where's Meg?"

"Probably hiding in her room," Ben said.

"Well, go get her. I want to see all my kids. I've missed you guys!"

The boys ran upstairs to find their sister while Kim took her coat off and hung it behind the front door. She went to the couch and flopped onto it, putting her feet up on the coffee table. "It's so good to be home," she said. She sniffed the air and wrinkled her nose. Then, she turned her face into the cushions to smell them once before jerking her head away from the couch. "Whew!" she said. "This couch smells terrible. Did it smell this bad before I left?"

Gabby shrugged.

A few minutes later, the boys came pounding down the staircase. "She's not here," Owen said.

"Did you check the bathroom?" Gabby asked. She had just settled on the couch next to her mom. It did kind of stink. Like old sweat and desperation.

"We checked everywhere," Ben said. "She's not here."

"What the hell?" Gabby said. "She was supposed to watch you two until I got back."

"We don't need watching," Ben said. "We're here by ourselves all the time."

Gabby scowled at him.

"Well, we are."

"Why wouldn't Meg stay here to see me?" Kim asked.

Gabby bit her lip. She knew Meg was angry with their mom, probably angrier than any of the rest of them had been. She didn't want to hurt her mom's feelings, but she knew there was a good chance Meg wasn't there because she simply couldn't look at their mother right now. "She probably ran to Lily's for something and lost track of the time. I'll call over there and let her know you're home."

Gabby went to the kitchen to get the phone. She called Lily's house, only to find that Lily hadn't seen Meg all day. Lily gave her a few other numbers to call, but Meg wasn't at any of their other friends' houses either. Where could she be?

Kim stepped into the kitchen entryway and leaned against the door frame. "No luck?" she asked.

"I'm sure she'll be home soon," Gabby said. The two of them shared an uncertain glance.

Then, Kim clapped her hands together. "What do you want for dinner?" she asked. "I'm starving after eating hospital food for the past two weeks."

Owen and Ben crowded past their mom to get into the kitchen. "Tacos," Owen said.

"Pizza," Ben said.

"No, tacos!" Owen said. "Please, Mom? Can we have tacos?"

"But I want pizza!"

"I know," Kim said. "How about taco pizza?"

"What's that?" Owen asked.

"You'll see," Kim said. "Let's see what ingredients we have, and I'll show you boys how to make it."

"What about Meg?" Gabby asked.

Kim shrugged. "She'll come home soon, I'm sure. She can't have gone too far."

Gabby hoped her mom was right.

I t was almost ten that evening when Meg finally stomped in the front door and tossed her coat on the chair next to the door. Her curfew was at nine, so Gabby had a feeling Meg had purposely stayed out that late just to test their mom.

"There she is," Kim said. She sat up from the couch where she had been trying to relax in front of the television. "Come give your mom a hug, Meg. I missed you."

"Sorry I'm late, Gabby." Meg made a point of ignoring their mom. "I was watching a movie with Jodie's family and lost track of the time."

"Why did you leave to begin with?" Gabby asked. "You were supposed to be here waiting with the boys when I brought Mom home."

Meg shrugged. "They're old enough to be home alone for a little while." She yawned. "Look, I'm really tired, and we have school tomorrow. I'm going to bed." She headed for the stairs.

Gabby jumped to her feet and was about to follow Meg, but their mom grabbed her by the pant leg and held her back. "Don't you think you should at least say hi to Mom?" Gabby said.

Meg was halfway up the stairs by this point. "Good night, Gabby." Her feet disappeared upstairs.

"It's okay," Kim said. "She's mad at me. I get it. She has good reason to be mad. Let it be for now."

Gabby sighed. "I'd better head to bed, too. I have to work in the morning."

"And I need to go job hunting in the morning," Kim said. She stood up and stretched, her hands reaching for the ceiling. "You go ahead. I'll lock up and shut everything off down here."

"Good night." Gabby stood in front of her mom and shifted her feet.

Kim smiled at her and opened her arms for a hug. Gabby stepped closer and let her mom pull her in close. For the first time in a long time, Kim felt like Mom and not some stranger who had inhabited her mom's body. She no longer smelled like stale sweat. Her sweatshirt smelled fresh, like laundry detergent, and the scent of strawberries wafted from her hair. Gabby relished the moment of just being a kid again, in her mother's arms and allowed all her worries to melt away.

"I love you, baby girl," Kim said. "Sleep tight."

Gabby peeled herself away from her mom's warmth and smiled at her. "Don't let the bedbugs bite," she said.

Kim winked and tweaked Gabby's nose. The two parted, and Gabby headed upstairs.

After she had brushed her teeth, Gabby climbed into her bed and snuggled under her blankets. Her mom used to crochet a lot, a long time ago, so one thing the kids always had plenty of was blankets.

"Meg?" she whispered.

"Ugh—what?"

"Give Mom a chance, okay?"

"Yeah, no," Meg said. "When she proves she's worth it, then I'll give her a chance."

Gabby sighed. "She was good mom before—"

"And then she wasn't a good mom. So now, she has to prove that she is again. She's the adult here, not me."

There was no point arguing with Meg when she'd made her mind up. "Good night," Gabby said.

CHAPTER NINETEEN

The smell of garlic met Gabby at the front door when she got home from work the next day. "Spaghetti?" she called into the kitchen. She kicked her shoes off by the door and followed the scent into the kitchen.

"Chicken parm!" her mom replied. She held out a spoonful of sauce for Gabby to taste.

The sauce was piping hot. Gabby licked the edge of the spoon. "Mmm—we haven't had chicken parm in ages."

Kim's cheeks were rosy from standing over the hot stove. "I know," she said. "I am so hungry all the time now since I got off those stupid pills. Can you call your brothers to come set the table, please?"

Gabby wiped a slash of chocolate frosting from the edge of the freshly iced cake that set on the countertop by the refrigerator. She licked the frosting off and mumbled a yes at her mom on her way out of the kitchen.

The boys were sitting in the middle of an elaborate racetrack they had built on a gigantic piece of cardboard on their bedroom floor. They zipped their matchbox cars around the course, jumping them over the homemade ramps.

Gabby stood in their bedroom door and watched them play for a minute before interrupting them. Her brothers amazed her sometimes. Owen usually came up with the ideas for their cardboard creations, but Ben was quick to jump on board and help execute his plans. Owen was the engineer, and Ben added creative flair. Gabby cleared her throat to get their attention. "Mom wants you two to go set the table and wash up for dinner."

"Ah, man," Ben said.

"We're right in the middle of a race," Owen said.

Meg ambled past Gabby on her way out of their room. "I can do it," she said. "Let them play a while longer."

"Really?"

Meg shrugged and rolled her eyes. It wasn't huge, but it was progress.

Gabby went to her room to change out of her work uniform. Once she was dressed, she smiled as she examined herself in the full-length mirror that hung on the back of the bedroom door. For the first time, she found herself checking herself out and wondering what someone — Will — would think of how she looked. She combed her hair to one side. Would it look better parted on the other side? She combed it the other way. Nah. Maybe it was best to just leave it alone. Will seemed to like her just fine the way he saw her every day at study group.

"Dinner's ready!" Meg called up the stairs.

"Dinner!" The boys called to Gabby as they scrambled from their bedroom and pounded down the stairs.

Gabby's stomach grumbled in anticipation. She dropped her brush on the dresser and headed downstairs to join them.

In the living room, Kim was slipping her feet into a pair of dress shoes. She had removed her apron, and Gabby was surprised to see that her mom was dressed up in slacks and a nice blouse.

"You're not eating with us?"

"I'll eat when I get back." Kim pulled her jacket from its hook behind the door and stuck her arms into it. "I have a job interview at the library in ten minutes."

"Already? That was fast!"

"I got my application in just in time."

"That's awesome!"

"Well, don't get your hopes up too high." Kim frowned. "I mean, it's exciting, but I don't know if I'll be able to take the job."

"Why not?" Meg stood in the kitchen doorway with a scowl on her face. "Don't you think at this point that you should just take whatever you can get?"

Kim sighed. "The problem is, it's only part-time. Being such a small town, the library is only open five hours a day. And the pay isn't that great, either. Nothing like what you could get at a library in a bigger town. Of course, at a big library, I wouldn't qualify to be a director anyway with only an unfinished English degree—"

"So what?" Meg said. "Take the job. You have to."

"The thing is," Kim said. "I'm worried that it will pay just enough for us to lose all of our foodstamps and other welfare benefits, but not enough for us to live on—"

"So, we'll go back to eating ramen like we did when you worked full-time," Meg said. She was in the living room now, standing with her hands on her hips. "Big deal. Worse things have happened to us."

Gabby laughed. "Meg, you're the one who always complained the most about having to eat Ramen. What if Lily finds out?"

"I don't care what Lily thinks," Meg said. "It's not our fault the world is stupid."

Kim laughed and dragged Meg into an awkward hug. "I love you, kid," she said. She took Meg's face in her hands and looked her in the eyes. "If they offer me this job, I'm taking it," she said. "No matter what. I promise. Whatever happens, we'll figure it out. As long as you keep up that attitude, there's no way we'll fail."

Meg blushed and looked away from her mom, but she couldn't completely hide the smile that threatened to take over her face.

Kim let her daughter go and looked around. "Now, where did I put that folder with my resume and stuff in it?"

"It's in here—Oops." Owen shuffled out of the kitchen with the folder in his hands. A large glop of spaghetti was soaking into the manila folder.

"Oh, Owen." Gabby grabbed the folder from him and was about to run it back to the kitchen to clean it off.

"That's okay," Kim said. She took the folder from Gabby and pulled a couple of papers from it. "I don't need the folder. But, I do need to get out of here, or I'll be late. Wish me luck."

Ben threw himself around her waist before she could get all the way out the door. "Good luck, Mom!"

Gabby's mom got the job at the library and started just a few days later. She continued to worry about how it would affect her welfare benefits for weeks and started economizing as she used to back when she was working full-time. She took her foodstamps card away from Gabby and began to plan their meals and bought only what they needed. She wanted to make the money she had on the card last as long as possible in case it would be their last. The junk food in the pantry dwindled away, and soda became a thing of the past. When they wanted a snack now, they made popcorn. If they needed to satisfy a sweet tooth, they baked cookies from scratch.

Kim was sitting on the couch one evening opening their mail when Gabby came in from study group. Gabby sat next to her on the couch and put her feet up. She snuggled into her mom. She was feeling more and more like a kid instead of a grownup the longer her mom was home. She had stopped worrying about what they would have for dinner because her mom was keeping on top of things. Even when Kim had to be at the library until close, she now took the time to assign one of the other kids to make dinner instead of letting it all fall on Gabby. Even Ben and Owen were learning to cook a few simple dinners so they could take their turns, too. Gabby no longer had to worry about getting anyone up and ready to go in the morning except herself. The only downside was that she no longer had unfettered access to the van and couldn't use the family's foodstamps to supply her own junk food stash. Gabby really needed her own car already.

Kim held an envelope in front of Gabby. "I've been afraid to open this one," she said.

Gabby eyed the return address. The envelope had come from the human services office that managed their welfare benefits. She sat up and turned to watch her mom open the envelope. What were they going to do if they were cut off? Kim's paychecks were enough to cover their rent, utilities, and van payments, but not much else.

Kim pulled a stack of paperwork from the envelope. She drew a deep breath and paused for a second before unfolding them. Her eyes moved back and forth across the page as she read the words that were machine printed on them.

"What does it say?" Gabby asked.

Kim clasped the papers to her chest and exhaled. "Thank God," she said.

"What?"

"I'm just under the cutoff for insurance, so we can all keep using our medical cards."

"That's a relief. What does it say about the foodstamps?"

"I need a pen," Kim said.

"What? Why? Are we losing our foodstamps?"

"Patience, grasshopper." Kim lifted the lid of their coffee table and sifted through the junk that had collected inside the compartment underneath until she found a pen. She closed the lid, set the papers on top, and began scribbling numbers and calculations on them.

Gabby watched her mom add and subtract several numbers that she recognized as the amounts of their rent and van payments. Otherwise, none of it made any sense to her.

Finally, Kim clicked the pen shut and set it down on the table. "This is ludicrous," she said.

"It'll be okay, Mom. I can still help out with the rent and stuff if I need to."

Kim laughed. "You don't need to," she said. "If my calculations are correct, we are actually going to be better off financially with me just working part-time than we were when I was working full-time."

"How is that possible?" How could that be right? Why would they be better off if her mom was only working part-time?

Kim shook her head in disbelief. "I can't believe I'm going to be bringing home more money with part-time income combined with welfare benefits than I was ever able to bring home when I worked full-time and didn't qualify for anything. Why does anyone bother working full-time at all unless they can get into management where they can actually earn a living wage?"

"I still don't get it," Gabby said.

"Meg's right. The world is a stupid place. Our welfare system is set up to punish people when they try to escape it. At this point, I guess I may as well settle in and accept it since it doesn't look like it's ever going to change."

"So, you get to keep working part-time?"

"I guess so. In fact, I might need to tell the board not to give me any raises until I get a couple of my kids moved out."

"That is stupid."

"Yeah, it is. This is the United States. Anyone who works a full-time job here ought to be able to earn enough money to support a family. But, that's hardly possible anymore. It sucks."

"It may suck, but it's good news for you, isn't it?"

"I guess," Kim said. "I like my job so far, so I'm happy to be able to keep doing it. And, I can be here for you kids more than I was when I worked in town full-time. I just—I don't know, it just doesn't feel right to me. I wasn't brought up to live off welfare and handouts. But, there doesn't seem to be much choice these days."

"At least we don't have to go to the food pantry again." Gabby grimaced at the memory of all the rotten food they had gotten that time they had been reduced to shopping at the food pantry. She didn't think she would ever be able to get that smell out of her nose.

"Thank God for that," Kim said.

I t was strange having her mom at the library so much now. Gabby especially hated that her mom had caught on to the fact that she and Will were dating. It wasn't that her mom didn't approve, but she had started keeping an eye on the two of them and would occasionally walk by the table and clear her throat if she thought they were sitting too close together. Gabby was beginning to think maybe they should start studying somewhere else so they could have some privacy.

One day when Will was working late, Gabby's mom slid into the booth next to her where she was chatting with Jodie and Brittany. Mr. Stein—Ian—was working with Joe at a computer across the library, and Brittany was using the opportunity to dish about Ian and Jodie's relationship.

"I think someone's getting a ring soon," Brittany was saying as Kim joined them.

"Who?" Kim asked. She glared at Gabby. "It's not you, is it?"

"Mom! I'm seventeen!"

"No, not her," Brittany said. She leaned across the table and whispered. "I think Ian is getting really serious about Jodie."

Jodie elbowed her cousin. "Oh, stop," she said. "I'm not getting my hopes up for anything at this point. How do you know I even want a ring?"

Brittany laughed. "Please. I've seen how you look at him."

Gabby smiled. She had noticed it, too. Did she look at Will that way, too? She hoped not. She had no interest in getting married anytime soon—if ever. She had no idea what she wanted to do with her life, but marriage wasn't yet part of the plan. There would be plenty of time to worry about that after college.

"Can we please change the subject?" Jodie asked. "Don't we have something we should be studying?"

"Actually, I have some news," Kim said.

"What?" Gabby didn't know what kind of news her mom could have. Surely, she hadn't met someone new, too. Not that her mom didn't deserve to have someone in her life, but she had enough to worry about right now without adding a new relationship to the mix.

"I had a doctor appointment this morning," Kim said. "They scheduled me with the nurse practitioner instead of the doctor. She took one look at me and said, "You look really tired.""

Gabby's mom had looked tired for as long as she could remember. So much so that she didn't even think about it as being out of the ordinary. She just thought that was her mom's natural state.

"Well, you have plenty of reason to look tired," Jodie said. "I don't think she meant anything by it."

"I told her I have fibromyalgia. Of course, I look tired."

The other ladies nodded their heads.

"Anyway, she shook her head at me and said, "I'm going to put in an order to check your vitamin and iron levels anyway." So then, I go and have a bunch of blood drawn—and guess what?"

"What?" Gabby asked. Her mom could be painfully slow at telling a story sometimes.

"I have severe vitamin D and B-12 deficiencies that totally explain all of the symptoms I've been having the past few years," Kim said. "It turns out I might not even have fibromyalgia. Can you believe it?"

"You're shitting me," Jodie said. "After all this?"

"I believe it." Brittany nodded her head knowingly. "A while back, I went to the doctor because I kept getting these sharp pains in my abdomen. She ordered an ultrasound and found a couple of cysts on one of my ovaries. So, then my regular doctor sends me to see a gynecologist to figure out what we should do next. Because, you know, God forbid a non-specialist doctor make a decision about what to do about a specific body part. Anyway, the gyno tells me we're just going to wait and see if they go away on their own. But in the meantime, I had some blood in my urine, so she's going to send me to see a urologist. The urologist immediately scheduled me for a test to look at my bladder with a camera."

"Ouch," Kim said. "That doesn't sound like fun."

"It wasn't," Brittany said. "They shave your girly bits, numb you up, and then they slide the camera right up through your urethra."

Gabby cringed. This was a lot more info than she ever wanted to know about Brittany's private parts. Just then, she spotted Will heading toward them from the library entrance.

"Anyway," Brittany said. "When he was done, he told me he didn't see anything abnormal. And then he says, "It's possible you have a cyst on your ovary. You should schedule an appointment with a gynecologist to get that looked at.""

"He didn't," Kim said. She shook her head and laughed.

"Oh, he did," Brittany said. "And the whole time, I'm sitting there thinking, "Dude, did you even look at my chart before you decided you needed to go fishing up my pee hole?""

Will stopped about a foot away from the table and gave Brittany an odd look. "Uh—I can come back later if this is a bad time," he said.

Brittany, Jodie, and Kim burst into laughter. Gabby's cheeks warmed with embarrassment. It was bad enough she'd had to hear that conversation, but having Will overhear it, too? Ugh!

Jodie slapped her palm against the table top. "Come join us, boy," she said. "Man up and listen to us discuss our lady problems."

The older ladies cackled. Kim got up to head back to the circulation desk. She winked at Will as she left. Maybe she would warm up to him yet.

CHAPTER TWENTY

Gabby awoke to the sound of knocking. She yawned and stretched her arms above her head. Her hand bumped against something hard that shouldn't be there. Her eyes fluttered open. "What the—?" The coffee table that belonged downstairs in the living room sat over her, its four legs straddling her body over her covers.

"April Fools!" Meg yelled.

The boys giggled. All three of Gabby's siblings had gathered to watch her wake up with the coffee table perched over her on the bed.

"Oh, it's going to be that kind of April Fool's Day, is it?" Gabby asked.

The others laughed. "You can't top this one," Owen said.

"Want to bet?"

Owen and Ben's eyes opened wide, and they both turned to run from the room. Gabby didn't know what she was going to do to them, but it was going to have to be big after this.

"You want to get this thing off me?" she asked.

Meg laughed, but she did as she was asked. Once she had set the table on the floor next to Gabby's bed, she took a seat on it. "Good morning, high school graduate," she said.

Gabby smiled. It was still hard to believe that she had finally finished high school. She had taken the GED test the day before, alongside Will, just to make applying to community college easier. The diploma her mom had given her was supposed to be legitimate, but you never knew. Some places might not accept it, and it was better to be safe than sorry. Plus, she and Will had managed to finish school several weeks ahead of their old classmates who were still trudging off to the school bus, day after day.

"I'm hungry," Gabby said. "Is there breakfast?"

"Mom just got up, but she said she'd make brunch."

"So I should stay in bed a little while longer so I don't have to help?" Gabby was also enjoying not having to help so much around the house, too. Her mom still expected everyone to help out, but it was only a normal amount of work, now. It was hard sometimes to remember that she no longer had to parent her siblings, but Gabby was getting used to being able to slack off sometimes like a normal teenager.

"Girls!" Kim hollered up the stairs to them.

Gabby and Meg groaned. They were going to have to help with brunch, weren't they?

"Coming!" Meg yelled.

Gabby got out of the bed and followed Meg downstairs.

"Hey, can one of you run to the post office and pick up the mail?" Kim asked when the girls got to the kitchen. "I forgot to grab it after work last night, and I'm expecting a check."

"I'll go." Gabby and Meg both volunteered at the same time. Neither of them wanted to help with the cooking.

"Why don't you both go?" Kim asked. "It's beautiful outside. Go on. I can manager this. Hurry up, though. We'll be ready to eat soon."

Gabby and Meg ran upstairs to throw some clothes on, and then Gabby retrieved their mailbox key from its hook by the front door. The two chattered along the way to the post office, which sat on the square downtown next to the library. Meg had warmed up a lot over the past several months, and the two of them got along so much better now that they could just be sisters rather than Gabby acting as Meg's mother.

When they got to the post office, Meg examined the flyers on the bulletin board while Gabby grabbed the mail from their post office box. Then, they headed back outside into the warm spring sunshine.

"I might need your help with my April Fool's prank that I'm planning for the boys," Meg said as they strolled toward home.

"What are you doing to them?" Gabby asked.

"I'm still working out the details."

Gabby laughed. If Meg had a good plan, she could just piggyback off her to get back at the boys for the coffee table incident. Then she could devote her brainpower to coming up with something really good to do to Meg. Gabby flipped through the mail as they walked. Junk mail. Junk mail. Coupons. Bill—. When she got to the last letter-sized envelope, her feet slowed, and then she stopped in the middle of the sidewalk. The familiar red and white Brown University logo – with its book-embellished shield under a sun whose crown of rays impaled the clouds above it – glared at her from the return address section of the envelope.

"What's wrong?" Meg asked. She had gotten several feet ahead of Gabby before she realized that Gabby had stopped walking. She returned to where her older sister stood rooted to the sidewalk. "Is it a bill? Something big that we weren't expecting?"

Gabby couldn't speak. The envelope shook in her trembling hand.

"Gabby, what?" Meg said. She snatched the envelope and stared at it. Then, she glanced up at Gabby. "Wait, what? Brown University? What is this?" Meg's face lit up like a daffodil, opening its face to the sun. "Did you apply to Brown?"

Gabby shrugged. "I'm sure I didn't get in. There's no way. It's an Ivy League school."

"Why did you apply, then?"

"I don't know. I wanted to apply to one Ivy League school to see what would happen. It was a stupid waste of money. The application fee alone was $75. There's no way we could afford for me to go there. I don't know why I did it. Just toss it."

"No way!" Meg shoved one metallic fingernail under the envelope flap and started to rip it open.

"What are you doing?" Gabby tried to grab the envelope away from her, but Meg spun away and started walking fast toward home.

"I have to know," Meg said. "And if you got in, you have to go. Seriously, Gabby! If you can go to school out of state and get out of this giant, boring cornfield that we live in, you have to go!" She pulled a sheet of paper from the envelope and flipped it open with a sharp flick of her wrist. Then, she bent her head to read it. She started to laugh.

"What does it say?" Gabby ran alongside Meg who was walking as fast as her long legs would take her.

"I thought you didn't want to know." Meg held her arm out straight to hold the letter as far away from Gabby as possible.

"Give it here!" Gabby leapt in front of Meg and made her stop walking. She was about to give her a shove when Meg laughed again and handed the letter over without any further resistance. Gabby took the letter in two hands and began to read it out loud—

Dear Gabriella,

Congratulations! I am delighted to inform you that you have been admitted to the 252nd class to enter The College of Brown University—

"I got in?" Gabby said. She looked into Meg's sparkling brown eyes. Meg nodded at her and grinned. "I got in!" Gabby started to jump up and down with excitement, and Meg joined her.

"I'm going to get my own room!" Meg said. "And, I'm coming to visit you over spring break. You have to take me to a frat party! OMG, my big sister is going away to college! Let's go tell mom!"

Gabby stopped jumping and took a deep breath. She grabbed Meg's arm to keep her from flying home to tell their mom about the letter. "Wait," she said. "You can't tell her. This has to be our secret."

"Why? She'll have to find out eventually. I mean, I'm pretty sure she'll notice you're gone once you've left for college."

"Meg, come on. You know we can't afford this. Community college is going to be expensive enough. There's no way I can go to an Ivy League school. It will just make Mom feel bad to know that I got in but can't go because she doesn't make enough money to pay for it."

"But, what about your FAFSA? You said your expected family – whatever it was called – was zero. Mom said you'd probably get enough grants to cover everything."

"That was for community college. This is a lot more expensive. There's no way—"

"So, apply for scholarships. Get a job at school. Whatever. You have to go!"

Gabby shook her head. She crumpled the acceptance letter in her fist and shoved it in her pocket. Then, she started to head for home. "Come on. Mom will wonder what's taking us so long."

Meg fell into step beside Gabby, but she wasn't ready to let it go. She started to speak several times, but just mumbled a word or two before stopping. "You're so stupid," she finally said.

"I'm smart enough to get into Brown." Gabby stuck her tongue out at Meg. Even though she wouldn't be able to go away to college, it still felt like a huge win to get into an Ivy League school. She just hoped she wouldn't spend the rest of her life imagining what kind of life she could have had if only they'd been able to afford it.

As they made their way up the front walk, Meg ran ahead of Gabby and slipped in the front door of their apartment. She slammed the door shut behind her. The deadbolt slid to with a loud thud. Had she just locked Gabby out of the house? Gabby turned the doorknob and pushed, but it wouldn't budge. That little—

Meg knocked on the window next to the door. "I'm telling Mom!" Her voice was muffled through the glass. Then, she let the curtain fall and disappeared.

"No!" Gabby ran around to the back of the apartment building. Luckily the back door was open.

Inside, their mom was flipping blueberry pancakes in a sizzling griddle pan on the stovetop. Meg leaned against the countertop next to her. Kim handed Meg the spatula and turned to Gabby.

"You got into Brown? I thought the plan was to start at community and then transfer to state."

Gabby shrugged. "I just wanted to know if I could get in," she said. "Community college is still the plan."

Kim scowled. "Oh, no it's not," she said. "You're going to Brown."

"But there's no way we can afford that. It's way out on the East Coast. How will I even get there?"

"We'll figure it out. Meg, you're burning the pancakes." She took the spatula back from her and started to move the pancakes to a plate in front of Meg. "Butter these," she said.

"Mom, it's not possible," Gabby said. "Don't worry about it. I'm happy to go to community college. You always said it's just as good as going anywhere else." Why were they even discussing this? As far as Gabby was concerned, there wasn't anything to discuss. It simply wasn't possible. She pulled a stack of plates from the cupboard and went to set the table. Besides, she didn't want to get her hopes up about something that could never happen.

Kim poured another batch of pancake batter onto the griddle, one sizzling dollop at a time. "It is just as good for most people," she said. "But, you got into an Ivy League school. That's like a whole different universe. You can't pass up this opportunity."

Gabby dropped the last plate on the table with a clatter. "I'm going to go tell the boys that brunch is almost ready. Maybe I can get Owen to wear something other than his boxer shorts to the table." As far as she was concerned the Brown conversation was over. But, Meg kept talking after Gabby had left the room. She lowered her voice, but Gabby still heard her before she headed up the stairs.

"You have to make her go, Mom," Meg said.

Gabby took the crumpled letter from her pocket that afternoon and flattened it out, sticking it between the pages of a big, heavy book to press the wrinkles out. She would put it in her scrapbook later. It was a big deal. She had gotten into an Ivy League school. That in itself was enough. People like her didn't go to schools like that. There was no way she would fit in at a place like that anyway. Community college was definitely more her speed. It was for her kind of people. Brown was not.

Her mom and Meg didn't bring up Brown for the rest of the weekend. Not that there was much of an opportunity for them talk about it. Gabby worked Sunday and had the day off Monday, so she didn't see them much until Monday afternoon when she went to meet up with what was left of her old study group at the library. Jodie had graduated the GED program and had moved up to self-study with Gabby and Will since she started her nursing program at the community college at the beginning of the semester. Brittany was taking her time prepping for her final test. She didn't seem to be in a hurry to stop meeting her friends at the library several afternoons a week. Gabby suspected Brittany enjoyed having the excuse to get a babysitter and partake in adult conversation. Joe was the only one left who still needed help as he worked toward passing his final test, and the rest of them had become almost as invested in seeing him finish as he and his mom were.

Gabby slid into the booth next to Will. He squeezed her knee and then checked over her shoulder to make sure her mom wasn't watching before leaning in to give her a quick kiss on the lips.

"You two are so cute," Brittany said. She sat at the next booth with Joe and Ian.

Gabby rolled her eyes. Her hand found Will's under the table, and they laced their fingers together. She was going to miss study group now that she was done with high school, but she was also looking forward to spending more one-on-one time with Will without everyone else there.

Gabby's mom sidled up to their table and cleared her throat. "Guess what, everyone" she said. All eyes turned to her in expectation.

"What's up, Ms. Gimble?" Will said.

Kim took a deep breath and grinned at her daughter. "Gabby got accepted to Brown University."

Gabby's stomach clenched. How could her mom do this? She thought they were done discussing it.

"Where's that?" Brittany asked.

"That's amazing," Ian said.

"I didn't know you applied to Brown," Will said. "I thought you were just going to go to community and live at home." His fingers slipped out of Gabby's grasp, and then he settled both of his hands on the table top.

"It's in Rhode Island," Kim said. "Can you believe it? East Coast. Ivy League. My daughter!" She beamed at the students of DIY High. "Who says you can't homeschool yourself and still go to a good college?"

"I'm not going," Gabby whispered to Will. "There's no way we can afford something like that. Don't worry, Will. I'm not going anywhere."

Will relaxed and smiled at Gabby. She frowned, surprised at his response. So what if she did go away to college? Would it bother him that much?

"You are too going," Kim said. "Can you believe this girl? She got into Brown, and she thinks I'm going to let her stay here and go to community college? Not on your life!"

"Why don't you want to go?" Jodie asked.

Gabby shrugged. "It's not that I don't want to, necessarily. But, there's no way we could afford something like that. It's a pipe dream. I don't know why I even applied to begin with."

"You might be surprised," Ian said. "You're coming from a single parent family with four kids. I bet you'll get enough financial aid to pay for most—if not all—of your tuition. Don't just assume you can't go without looking into it."

"But it's so expensive," Gabby said. "I can't possibly get that much financial aid."

"Just do it," Ian said. "It won't hurt anything to find out. You can always turn them down if it turns out they can't give you enough assistance to get you through."

"Yes, do it," Jodie said. "You have to at least try."

"Do it!" Brittany and Joe practically sang the words in chorus.

Gabby turned to Will. "What do you think?" she asked him.

Will bit his bottom lip. He didn't look happy. "It's up to you," he said.

"It is up to you," Kim said. She scowled at Will. "I know you want to go. If money were no object, I know you would jump at this opportunity. But I'm the parent here, and I am telling you to stop worrying about it because I have already made the decision that you are going. One way or another."

"We'll hold a fundraiser if we have to," Jodie said. "We can sell candy bars or something. Whatever it takes."

"You would do that for me?" Gabby asked. She tried to contain her excitement. She didn't want to get her hopes up. But, what if? What if she really could go to an Ivy League school? Imagine what she could do with her life if she did.

"Of course we would," Brittany said. "Look what you've done for all of us."

"She's right, you know," Kim said. "Look what you've done for everyone. Your family. Your DIY High students. You've made a lot of sacrifices and helped a lot of people. It's time you got your reward."

Friday night, Will invited Gabby to go into town for ice cream at Carl's. The popular ice cream stand was featuring blackberry ice cream that week, and Will knew it was Gabby's favorite. He had been quiet all week, and Gabby was afraid to ask what was bothering him. Was he going to break up with her if she went away to college? She was afraid that's what was going to happen. She'd tear up, and her stomach would squeeze into a frozen, little ball at the thought of losing him. But then, a slash of heat would cut through the cold, and she'd be filled with anger at the idea that he would try to stop her from pursuing such an amazing opportunity.

These conflicting emotions tore Gabby apart as they stood at the ice cream stand's open window and waited for their desserts. Once the attendant had handed their ice cream out to them, they went to Will's truck and sat inside listening to the radio and licking their ice cream cones in silence, both of them deep in thought.

Will crunched through his ice cream cone as though he hadn't eaten all week. When he was done, he crumpled his napkins and shoved them into the paper fast food bag that he was currently using as a garbage receptacle in his vehicle. He turned sideways with his arm rested across the back of the truck's bench seat. His fingers found a strand of Gabby's hair and began to wind it around one knuckle. "I'm going to miss you so much when you go to school," he said.

Finally. They were going to talk about it. Gabby was afraid to discuss it, but also glad to get it out of the way. If they were going to break up, they might as well yank the bandage off and get it over with.

"I'll miss you too," Gabby said. She bit into a giant blackberry in her ice cream. She was afraid to look at Will. Tears threatened to spill from her eyes. She commanded them to stay away.

Will scooted closer to Gabby. He pulled her toward him and kissed her above her ear. "I'm really proud of you though," he said.

Gabby turned to face him. "Really?"

"Of course. You are an amazing woman."

Gabby smiled. She didn't really think of herself as a woman yet. She had felt like an adult while she was supporting her family, but a woman? For some reason, she had just never considered herself in that light. "So, you're going to be okay with me going away for school?"

"Absolutely. Of course, I don't want you to go. But, what kind of person would I be if I tried to stop you?"

"So, we're not breaking up?"

Will chuckled. "No way," he said. "I mean, unless you want to?"

Gabby breathed a huge sigh of relief. "Never," she said. "I promise, I'll come home every chance I get."

"That reminds me." Will leaned across Gabby's lap and felt around under her seat. Finally, he pulled out a rectangular box covered in sparkly wrapping paper. "I got you a little something to remind you of home while you're gone."

Gabby handed what was left of her ice cream to Will as she grabbed the present out of his hand. She ripped the paper from it. Inside was a new smartphone. She'd never had her own phone before. There had just never been the money for it. Meg would be so jealous!

"I love it," Gabby said. She threw her arms around Will.

"There are a couple of months' worth of phone cards in there too," he said. "So you won't have to worry about paying for minutes for a while."

"Thank you," Gabby said. She let Will go and pulled back so she could look at him. Hopefully they would be able to hold it together through a four-year long-distance relationship. She didn't know if she would ever be lucky enough to find another one like him.

"Now remember," Will said. "This isn't just for you to call me. I want you to be able to keep in touch with your family, too."

"I know." Gabby tore the box open and pulled the phone out. She opened the manual and flipped through it like she had a clue what she was looking at. She didn't have any idea where to start.

Will traded Gabby's ice cream for the smartphone and turned the device on to see if it had enough battery life to activate it. He plugged it into his car charger and then set it on the dashboard to charge. "So, why did you choose Brown, anyway?" he asked. "I bet you could have just as easily gotten into Harvard or Yale."

Gabby licked her ice cream. "It's really stupid," she said. "I decided on a whim that I wanted to apply at an Ivy League school. But, I didn't really know what an Ivy League school was or which schools even fell into that category. So, I Googled it."

"Rhode Island is really far away. Brown had better be a good school."

Gabby laughed. "I know, right? I feel so silly about the whole thing. I know all the rich kids I'm going to school with have probably visited a lot of different schools, and here I am Googling around to try to figure out where to apply on a whim. I have no clue what I'm doing, really. And no one to help me figure it out."

"You'll do great." Will took Gabby's new phone from the dashboard and started to fiddle around with it. "What do you know about the school? Why did you pick this one?"

Gabby finished the last of her ice cream and wiped her fingers on a napkin. "I think what I liked best about it is that it has an open curriculum. They have almost no required courses at all, so I can pretty much take whatever I want. It kind of reminded me of DIY High."

Will grunted. "Maybe I should go there."

Gabby gasped. The idea had never occurred to her, but how awesome would it be if Will could go away to school with her? "You should apply," she said. "It's too late for this year, but maybe you could start next year, and—"

"Nah," Will said. "You know school isn't my thing. I'm doing DIY College now."

Gabby tried to hide her disappointment. To be fair, school really wasn't Will's thing. He was probably the smartest person she had ever known, but he liked to learn on his own terms. Still, it would be nice if there was an easy solution to leaving him behind.

"Besides," Will said. "I have my business here. I'm living the life I want to live. I would just be racking up student loan debt for nothing."

"Yeah, I guess. There's no point going to college if you really don't need to. Especially for someone like you. You're probably already way more educated than a lot of college graduates."

"I'm glad you decided to go," Will said. "I'm proud of you."

"Thanks." Gabby kissed his cheek. "Really, thanks for supporting me. I thought you were going to break up with me."

Will pulled Gabby into his arms and held her tight. "This is going to be hard," he said. "I don't want you to go, but what kind of man would I be if I tried to stop you?"

Exactly. Yes, Gabby would miss Will. She would miss her family, too. But this would be the first time in her life that she could remember that she would be on her own with no one to worry about or take care of but herself. The idea thrilled her more than any other prospect she had ever imagined in her entire life.

CHAPTER TWENTY ONE

abby shivered and pulled her sweater tighter across her chest. She and Meg liked to joke that the window unit in their bedroom was mentally unstable. It only had two settings: off and on. When it was on, their bedroom turned into an ice box within minutes. When it was off, the sweltering August heat seeped in through the thin walls and the old rags they had stuffed into the cracks around the air conditioner. Her dorm room at Brown was supposed to have central air. She couldn't wait to get there.

"Sheets!" Meg said. "You still need bed sheets." She stood over Gabby with a pen and a checklist that she held on one of the boys' old hardback children's books. She was being unusually helpful with packing her older sister up for school. Gabby suspected Meg had plans to take over her half of their bedroom the minute Gabby drove away in Will's truck for the long drive to Rhode Island.

"I have sheets," Gabby said. "They're here somewhere." She dug through the pile of goods that hadn't been stuffed into boxes yet. She still couldn't believe how generous her friends and their families had been. They had thrown a surprise bridal shower-style going away party where everyone had bought gifts from the registry she and her mom had set up at Wal-Mart.

Gabby had assumed the registry was just to help her and her mom keep track of what she still needed and to make sure they didn't both end up buying the same things. It hadn't occurred to her that her mom was planning a party for her.

Gabby had received enough student financial aid to cover her tuition, dorm room, and a meal plan, but not much else. The money Gabby had been saving for her own car was now going to pay for her textbooks. She was going to have to get a part-time job as soon as she got to school, and she had thought she was going to have to do without a lot of the things that most students would probably think were necessities. But, her friends had really pulled through for her. Steve had even given her a hundred dollar gas card to help pay for gas to get to school, though he wasn't happy to lose one of his best waitresses.

Owen stuck his head through the bedroom door. "Mom is ready to go," he said.

"Tell her we'll meet her there in a few minutes," Meg said. "We're almost done here."

"You better hurry," Owen said.

"We're almost done!" Gabby said.

Owen stuck his tongue out at Gabby and scampered off.

"Towels?" Meg asked.

"Right here." Gabby picked up a small stack of brand new, plush towels and washcloths and dropped them into the box on top of her extra-long college-sized bedsheets.

Meg continued through the rest of the check sheet and marked off the items as Gabby packed them in the boxes. "That's it," she finally said. She dropped the checklist on the dresser.

This was all getting to be way too real. The boxes were packed and ready to go. Tomorrow, Gabby would load them into the back of Will's truck, and he would drive her to Rhode Island. She would be starting a whole new life there. Once Will settled her in her dorm room and left for home, Gabby would be on her own. She thought of what her life was like only the year before and couldn't believe it. If only she had known how things would go. Maybe her mom was right. The Universe was taking care of them. Everything was going to be okay after all.

Meg slipped her feet into her sandals. "We'd better get going," she said. "We don't want to miss Mom's speech."

"It's not really a speech. She's just saying a few words before the cake is served."

Meg offered Gabby a hand and pulled her up off the floor. Then, she went to flip the air conditioner off to save the electricity while they were out.

Gabby peeled her sweater off. The heat was already pressing into their room. She wasn't looking forward to walking to the library. She followed Meg outside anyway, and the two of them made their way downtown for the centennial celebration that their mother had been planning since she started her new job.

They had only gotten about a block away when Will pulled up next to them in his truck. "Need a ride?" he asked.

"Yes!" Meg ran to pull the passenger door open before the truck had come to a complete stop. "It's so hot today!"

She paused to let Gabby climb in next to Will before jumping inside. Then, she fiddled with the air conditioner vents so they would point directly at her. Gabby rolled her eyes at Meg. By the time she had the vents where she wanted them, they were at the library.

The three of them exited Will's truck and headed inside. Gabby had never seen so many people at the library before. Patrons milled around with plastic cups of her mom's pink sherbet punch and chatted in front of the displays of old photo albums and other mementos that had been brought across the square from the the village museum.

Gabby spotted Jodie and Ian back by the DVDs with Brittany and her husband. She took Will's hand and led him in their direction. Meg followed at their heels. She and Jodie had become close over the months since Kim had returned from detox. Meg spent many evenings babysitting at Jodie's house while she was at night school or out on dates with Ian.

"OMG," Meg said. "Jodie, what is that on your finger?"

Jodie turned at the sound of Meg's voice and laughed. She wiggled the fingers of her left hand in her direction. A tasteful diamond glinted from its new home on her ring finger. Meg's jaw dropped open for a second, and then she squealed and ran to hug Jodie.

"You're getting married?" Gabby asked. She could hardly believe this was the same crabby Jodie that she had worked with at the diner just a couple of years before.

"Congrats, man." Will slapped Ian on the back and then shook his hand.

Brittany beamed at the future husband and wife. "It's about time Jodie found someone who's good enough for her," she said. Her husband nodded and smiled. He wasn't much of a talker. Gabby didn't know him very well, but he seemed to be a good guy.

Gabby hugged Jodie. "That's so exciting," she said. "Have you set a date yet?"

"Next summer," Jodie said. "We want you to be there. I mean, come on—we probably would have never met if not for you and DIY High."

"Can I have everyone's attention, please?" Gabby's mom stood on the little step-stool in front of the circulation desk and clapped her hands. The party-goers wandered toward her and formed a half-circle in front of her.

"Thank you all for coming this evening to celebrate one hundred years of the library," Kim said. "This small-town library has had a long and interesting history and will be heading in some exciting new directions in its second hundred years." She went on to highlight some of the notable people and events from the library's past. Then, she asked for patrons to share some of their favorite memories before moving on to discuss the library's future.

An elderly man talked for a few minutes about going to the library back in the day when it was across the square. Then, a woman talked about how hard everyone had worked to raise the money to build the new library in its current location. Several patrons talked about programs they had attended at the library, and then Meg told everyone about how excited she was the day she got her very first library card.

"My favorite memory was definitely meeting and getting to know my future wife here," Ian said. He winked at Jodie, and she gave his shoulder a playful punch.

"That's probably my favorite memory, too," Jodie said. "That and finishing up my GED here with Gabby and Will's help. I would probably have waited tables for the rest of my life if it wasn't for them."

Kim nodded and smiled at Gabby. "Speaking of Gabby and Will," she said. "One thing I learned from their experience is that there are some major educational gaps that the public school system isn't addressing. Not only is Jodie going to nursing school now because of DIY High, but Brittany and Joe both completed their GED's here at the library as well."

Joe's mom piped up from the back of the crowd. "Thanks for that," she said. "Joe couldn't be here today because he's busy at his apprenticeship, but I know he is thankful for all the help he got here. Especially from Mr. Stein. I thought Joe was never going to finish school before DIY High. Now, he's already making more money at his apprenticeship than I make doing hair!"

Will squeezed Gabby's fingers, and then he joined the conversation. "I really fought against finishing school," he said. "But, I'm glad I went and got my GED. I probably won't ever need it for anything since I already have my own business, but there's just something about having that piece of paper." He glanced down at Gabby and smiled at her. She had never realized that it meant so much to him.

"I don't know that I'll ever need that piece of paper for anything either," Brittany said. "But, I don't feel like such a huge hypocrite when I'm nagging my kids about school anymore. Plus, sharpening up on my math and science has really helped me to help them with their homework."

"And let's not forget about Gabby," Kim said. "The girl who started it all—If ya'll don't mind me bragging on my daughter for a minute?"

"I'd brag too, if I were you." Gabby hadn't noticed Steve was there. She waved at him. Of course, Steve was there. It was like she was stuck in a cheesy Hallmark holiday movie. All the main characters from the movie had to make an appearance in the final scene.

Kim took a deep breath. She smiled down at Gabby. "I am so proud of this young woman," she said. "She basically schooled herself for her last year of high school. She helped these other young people continue their educations. And now, she's heading off to Brown University first thing tomorrow morning. Can we get a round of applause for Gabby?"

The room erupted in an explosion of clapping. Gabby's chest and face grew warm. She hadn't expected her mom to throw so much attention her way. This celebration was supposed to be about the library. It was going to be so weird to leave her cheesy small town for a faraway land where no one would know her name or her story.

After the room had quieted again, Kim continued her speech. "DIY High has really inspired a lot of people," she said. "I would hate to see it come to an end just because its founder is leaving us for the Ivy League. We have all learned a lot from this educational experiment, and I plan to continue to make the library a center of learning for our community for the foreseeable future. We are adding a great number of educational programs for kids of all ages, from birth through retirement. The library is also in the process of becoming an official GED testing center, thanks in large part to a new grant that is going to help pay for computers and GED testing materials to be used for free by our patrons. Starting this fall semester, we will also host regular classes for homeschool students who are pursuing high school diplomas in the same manner that Gabby completed hers. Several of these courses will be dual credit courses offered through the local community college, so the students may begin to earn college credits while finishing their diplomas."

Gabby couldn't believe how much her mom had accomplished in the short time since she had taken over the library directorship. No wonder she was so busy all the time!

"Of course, I can't take credit for all these new programs," Kim said. "Our former director, Lynn Davis—Lynn, where are you?"

"Over here!" Lynn waved to everyone from her seat at one of the booths where Gabby and her friends had finished their high school education.

"I am so happy you could join us for this celebration today," Kim said. "As you all know, Lynn always had so much passion for our little small-town library. She never slowed down for one second, even as she was on her way to retirement. Lynn is responsible for laying the groundwork for what is to come, and I hope that I will be able to fill her footsteps as we take the library into the future. Thank you all once more for being here this evening. Please join us now in the meeting room for cake and punch."

The crowd clapped for Kim as she stepped down from her makeshift platform.

Lynn stood up from her booth and raised her cup in the air. "Excuse me." She cleared her throat, and the people nearest her elbowed those at their sides and shushed them. Soon, the entire room had quieted again and trained their eyes on Lynn. "Can I say a few words before we move on?" she asked.

"Of course," Kim said.

Lynn smiled. "I am happy to be able to be here this evening. As many of you have probably guessed, I've been keeping myself quite busy in my retirement."

Everyone chuckled. Gabby wondered what Lynn was doing to keep busy now that she no longer had the library to devote all her time to.

"At any rate," Lynn continued. "I just want to say how pleased I am to see the library under the directorship of someone who has as much passion for it as I always did. I can see that you are in good hands, now. Can we please have a round of applause for Kim?"

The crowd obeyed and clapped for Gabby's mom. Gabby was so proud of her mom as well. She knew it had been hard for her to get off her pills and stay off them. Kim had told her just the day before that she had to recommit herself to sobriety every morning before she got out of bed. Keeping herself busy at the library was doing as much for her as she was doing for it.

"Just one more thing, and then I'll let you go eat cake," Lynn said. "As library director, I spent a lot of time thinking about new programs and services that we could offer to our patrons. As you know, we are entirely taxpayer funded. So, I wanted to make sure that our taxpayers were getting their money's worth from us. DIY High wasn't anything that anyone had planned. It started with a seed of necessity and took root here at the library. I am excited to see it bloom here now and know that it will continue to serve our community's educational needs for years to come. With that being said, I would like to propose a toast." Lynn held her plastic cup of pink punch in the air. "Let's hear it for DIY High."

"Here, here!" Brittany said. She held her cup in the air. "To DIY High."

The crowd joined her in the toast, and even Gabby cheered, her voice ringing among those of her friends and neighbors. "To DIY High!"

The End

Taste of Soda

When Mom and
Dad split,
we got food stamps
to feed our
newly-formed
family of three.

Then our
weekly trip
to the grocery store
filled the trunk of
Mom's car
with bags and
bags and
bags
of food,
white plastic handles
waving to us,
each begging
to be carried in first.

We always groaned
at the work ahead.

Now Mom works
all the time.
We never see her.

When we complain,
she says she didn't
go back to school to
sit home watching
daytime TV.

Without food stamps,
we go to the grocery store
twice a month,
come home with
only two bags and
a gallon of milk.

With food stamps,
we ate steak,
chicken,
bakery bread,
decorated cakes.

We always got
candy and soda
at the checkout.

Now it's Ramen,
butter bread,
and, "Only use half the
pound of ground beef
when you make
Hamburger Helper."

Mom says she's
working to put
food on the table,
but it seems to me
she put more
food on the table when
she didn't work.

I forget what soda
tastes like.

ACKNOWLEDGMENTS

I would like to thank my writing workshop friends, specifically Becky Healy, Lance Savage, and author Susan Kirby for their invaluable feedback that helped me revise my first draft into what would later become this novel, *DIY High*. Thanks are also due to the Mt. Hope-Funks Grove Public Library in McLean, IL, where our workshop group took advantage of the free meeting room one Saturday a month and where I also borrowed (and am still borrowing) the countless books that I read constantly when I am not writing or working for pay.

ABOUT THE AUTHOR

Amanda L. Webster grew up in Effingham County, Illinois where she spent much of her childhood writing stories and running through the woods enacting those same stories in her head. She is a veteran of the United States Air Force and has a master's degree in creative writing from Mount Mary University in Milwaukee, Wisconsin. Mandy works full-time at a state university and also works part-time at a small-town library and teaches writing courses at two local community colleges. She was recently elected to a trustee position on the village board of the small town where she now lives in central Illinois with her two sons and two cats. She occasionally has free time, and that is when she writes.

Follow the author on Instagram: @mandy_raine
and Facebook: www.facebook.com/AmandaLWebsterAuthor/.
Hashtag #diyhigh.

CPSIA information can be obtained
at www.ICGtesting.com
Printed in the USA
LVHW111958230120
644585LV00007B/1034

9 781093 976335